P9-CQN-470

Red's Hot Honky-Tonk Bar

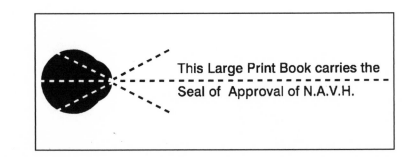

This Large Print Book carries the
Seal of Approval of N.A.V.H.

RED'S HOT
HONKY-TONK BAR

PAMELA MORSI

WHEELER PUBLISHING
A part of Gale, Cengage Learning

GALE
CENGAGE Learning™

Detroit • New York • San Francisco • New Haven, Conn • Waterville, Maine • London

GALE
CENGAGE Learning·

LIBRARY OF CONGRESS CATALOGING-IN-PUBLICATION DATA

Morsi, Pamela.
  Red's Hot Honky-Tonk Bar / by Pamela Morsi.
    p. cm.
  ISBN-13: 978-1-4104-2063-3 (alk. paper)
  ISBN-10: 1-4104-2063-9 (alk. paper)
    1. Women merchants—Fiction. 2. Bars (Drinking establishments)—Fiction. 3. Children of military personnel—Fiction. 4. Custody of children—Fiction. 5. Grandparent and child—Fiction. 6. Large type books. I. Title.
PS3563.O88135R43 2010
813'.54—dc22   2009034637

Published in 2010 by arrangement with Harlequin Books S.A.

Printed in the United States of America
1 2 3 4 5 6 14 13 12 11 10

For the citizens of Alamo Heights,
Texas,
who work jobs, raise kids, pay taxes
and vote.

Please know that anytime I'm writing
about you,
there is a smile on my face.

1

The sidewalk was full of smokers and spitters. The light from the open doorway was muted, but the sound from inside was not. It was a typical Thursday night of cold beer and live music at Red's Hot Honky-Tonk. The bar, frequented by only a certain segment of San Antonio locals, was a rough-looking spot in an old two-story mill house on the corner of Eight and B. Patrons had once joked that the area was so unloved by city hall, they hadn't bothered to name the streets.

Inside, as most nights, Red Cullens herself was at the cash register, totaling up the tabs. Backlit from the lights on the bar, she was an attractive woman. Petite, some would have described her. Only five foot three inches, she stood on a box as she worked to give her a better view of the crowd. It also gave them a better view of her.

Her figure, encased in tight blue jeans and

a soft, clingy blouse short enough to expose her bare midriff, was very good. However, what caught the eye of men, in this place and out of it, was her hair. Thick and full, it hung down past her waist. If she held her head just right she could sit on it. And it was red. Really red. She was no carrottop or strawberry blonde. Loop, one of the regulars, called it barn red, and that was certainly closer to the truth than terms like auburn, copper or ginger.

Her hair had taken over her identity. It obscured her name, her age, her past. And to Red's way of thinking, that was just fine.

A man stepped up to the counter in front of her as he pulled his wallet out of his back pocket.

"You taking off, J.B.?" she asked him.

"Yep, better get home before my wife decides to kill me," he answered.

Red shook her head. "I don't think you have to worry about that happening," she told him. "After putting up with you for thirty years, she's surely got the life insurance paid up and pinned her hopes on natural causes."

He laughed aloud at that. Red smiled broadly, revealing a slight overbite and a gap in her front teeth.

"Just to be stubborn," he told her, "I'm

planning to live forever."

He paid his bill and made his way out the front.

Red took change out of the drawer, extracting the man's tip, and dropped it into the appropriate waitress's jar on the shelf beneath the register.

The place was busy. All of the booths and most of the tables were full, and a half-dozen guys loitered around the pool table. The stage area outside had seating for forty, though tonight there was barely standing room. The band was playing here more and more often and they were developing a nice local following.

Somebody held open the front door so that Leo and Nata from the Mexican restaurant down on Jones Street could bring a couple of trays inside. The two men were dressed in their flashy yellow-and-green outfits and wearing snowy-white aprons. Passing Red, they began unloading the plates at the far end of the bar. Gracelia, the waitress who was sweet on Nata, hurried to help set them out.

As those two seemed to have it covered, Leo wandered back up the length of the bar to Red.

"What have we got tonight?" she asked him.

"Albondigas," he answered. "Those are your favorite, right? And jalapeño relleno."

"Mmm," Red commented. "You tell Mrs. Ramirez that she's going to make me as fat as her sister if she keeps this up."

Leo laughed. "I will tell her," he assured Red.

Mrs. Ramirez was famously feuding with her sibling, whom she called *la gorda* — fatso.

"How much do I owe you?" Red asked. Leo handed her the ticket and she paid it.

The honky-tonk didn't serve food beyond chips and salsa. Red had a deal with Mrs. Ramirez. She wouldn't compete with her restaurant, but at the end of the night, if Mrs. Ramirez had something that Red's customers might like, she'd bring it down. The late-night tapas were more and more a success. The regulars had begun to expect them and they sold out fast.

Knowing most of the inside customers would hang around for food and the outside customers wouldn't leave until the set was finished, Red signaled to Karl, the bartender, that she was leaving her post.

He quickly poured her a brown liquid in a highball glass. Anyone just looking would think she was having a double bourbon. In truth, it was iced tea in disguise. Red had

10

given up drinking years ago.

She took a sip and smiled appreciatively, adding to the drink deception.

Karl waved her on with one muscular, heavily tattooed arm. Red walked out from behind the counter and began weaving her way through the customers. She knew the names of many and the faces of even more. And they all knew her. Nine years of running the bar made her a local. The red hair made her easy to recognize. And the stories of her standing up to punks and knocking heads of mean drunks had made her a legend.

Red dutifully shared a word here and there, to let her customers know she appreciated them and that they were part of the good time available at Red's Hot Honky-Tonk. She patted shoulders, gave hugs and kissed cheeks as she went through.

"Hector, how are those kids doing?

"Casey, did you get that truck running?

"I guess you're feeling better tonight, Señor Puentes?"

A nearby customer gave her a hug.

"My God, Elena, what are you wearing?" Red asked, surveying her pin-striped business suit.

The woman, a curvaceous dark-haired beauty in her thirties, laughed. "I came straight from work," she said. "This is what the well-dressed office slave is wearing these days."

Red shook her head and tutted in disbelieving disapproval. "Have you got on panty hose? I didn't even know they still made them. I'll tell you, it makes me grateful I don't live in real America."

"You don't live in real America?" Elena asked.

"Nope," Red answered. "Honky-tonk bars are a whole 'nother planet."

"Down at city hall, they're still talking about redeveloping this part of the river," Elena reminded her. "I can see this place now as Red's Hot Panty-Hose Bar."

Red sucked in her cheeks, emulating haughtiness. "Perhaps we can begin competing with the Bright Shawl for lovely tea outings with the bejeweled matrons who do lunch."

Elena laughed so hard she snorted.

Red grinned. "I don't think that the Brides of the Cavaliers are quite ready for me."

There was laughing agreement from everybody within hearing. The Cavaliers were one of the most prestigious and discriminating social organizations in town.

With a backward wave she moved on to a

booth near the pool table.

"Hey, Alfred, nice to see you. Remember me to your mama."

She spoke to one of the men at the table whose face she could recall, but not his name. He'd rested his beer on the corner of the pool table.

"Better set that glass on the wall shelf," she told him. "With all the louts in this place, somebody's bound to knock it over and spoil the game."

The guy gave her a nod and moved his mug to a safer location.

Approaching the back door, she heard the music get louder and by necessity her words did, too.

"I don't think I know you folks. Is this your first time here?" she asked. "If you want to move closer to the stage, at the next break, just ask your waitress if she can set you up out there."

A buxom blonde stopped her near the doorway to get a hug. "Haven't seen you around here for a while," Red pointed out.

"I've been dieting," the woman answered. "So I've been staying away from the beer. I hear that you're still robbing the cradle?"

Red grinned and then feigned offense. "Robbery? You know I don't steal, Jenny. I'm just *borrowing* from the cradle."

13

Jenny laughed. "He's the fiddle player, right?"

Red nodded.

"Cute."

"I know. And I'm warning you off."

Jenny laughed. "You don't have to worry about me. I can't afford to take on a handsome poor boy. I need an old man who can pay my bills."

"And I thank heaven for that," she answered. "One less blonde for me to worry about."

Red stepped through the exit onto the bricked patio at the back of the building. Most of these folks were not her nightly regulars. They were at the place for the music. The beer and the crowd were just incidental. She made no attempt to greet anyone here. The lights were all dimmed, except for those on the stage, which showcased four pickers in Western gear and Stetson hats. She gave only a quick glance in their direction before skirting the edge of the bricks to a set of stairs that hugged the side of the building. A gate across the entry was not welcoming.

No Admittance
Private Property
Protected by Smith & Wesson

The warning on the gate was for others. Red unhitched the latch and went inside, going up about four steps before seating herself. She liked the band's sound. It wasn't true honky-tonk style. It was softer, smoother somehow, but with plenty of edge in just the right places. The lyrics were more pop psychology than pop-a-top. That was Brian's doing. A well-read college dropout, he wrote of the angst of Texas affluence. But it was the music that Red loved. And the music was mostly Cam. Her Cam. Long and lean, with dark eyes and an easy grin. He was smart. Smart about music, smart about people. Smart about what made her happy. Campbell Smith Early. Red shook her head in disbelief. What was she thinking, shaking the sheets with a guy who was barely thirty and had three last names?

Mentally she shrugged. It was a great deal, but it would never last. For Red, things with men never lasted. But he was good to her and the beginning part was always fun. So she was just going to lie back and enjoy it.

2

The phone was ringing. Ringing wasn't truly an apt description. The small, personal-communication device was pinging out the familiar refrain of "It Wasn't God Who Made Honky-Tonk Angels" in tinny musiclike tones.

From beneath a tangle of bedsheets, Red unhappily opened one eye. She had blackout shades on the windows, but one of them was caught up unevenly on the edge of the windowsill, allowing a broad shaft of early-morning sunshine to penetrate the room.

She pulled her pillow over her head, muffling the sound and hiding the sight. When the phone finally went to voice mail, she relaxed into the mattress. She was almost back to sleep when it started up again.

Now thoroughly annoyed, she threw back the covers and rotated to a sitting position. This elicited a slight moan from her lips. Cam, still beside her, didn't awaken, making only an *ugh* sound of protest. She retrieved the phone from the bedside table and, squinting, tried to make out the numbers on the front of it. The area code was not one she recognized.

"Telemarketer," she muttered like a curse.

She flopped back down on the bed, slinging one arm across her eyes. She was exhausted, but she knew she wouldn't sleep. Deliberately, she turned away from the window. On that side, her view was all Cam. He looked even younger than usual, almost boyish, with his face relaxed and his hair askew. Red edged up closer. She really liked him. No, she *really* liked him. Walking around in the world, he made her feel admired and desired. In bed, he made her feel . . . wonderful. She allowed a sigh to seep through her like warm molasses.

Then she caught herself, physically pulling away from him. It was crazy to let her guard down like that. And what was he still doing in her bed? She didn't let guys sleep over. Once they were done, it was time to get out. Men were a lot like stray dogs. You think you're just throwing them some scraps. But it doesn't take much for them to start making themselves at home.

Red got to her feet and walked to the foot of the bed. She ripped the covers off him.

"Sun's up, cowboy," she announced. "Time to hit the trail."

"Damn," was his inarticulate response.

Red continued to the bathroom. Without turning on the light she sat on the toilet, elbows on knees, her face in her hands, her hair falling around her like a curtain.

The phone went off again.

"Do you want me to get that?" Cam called out.

"No."

When she'd finished and flushed, she flipped on the light switch above the sink. She pulled her hair back and tied it in one giant loose knot to keep it out of the way as she washed her hands and face.

Afterward, she stood for a moment in front of the mirror, assessing her body for imperfections. The nightlife had left her skin perfectly pale. Her breasts weren't very large, but they were still high and pretty, she thought. She turned slightly to survey her backside. Her butt wasn't as good as it once was, but it was still better than most, she assured herself. And the armadillo tattoo that had been inked into her right buttock a quarter century earlier still looked perfect.

Not bad for forty-six, she thought to herself. Not bad at all.

Naked, she walked back into the bedroom. Cam was sitting on the edge of the bed. He glanced up and when he caught sight of her, he smiled.

"Come on back here," he said, patting the mattress beside him. "We don't have to get up yet."

Red appreciated the gesture, but she didn't take him up on it.

"I'm going downstairs to make coffee," she said. "You can be first in the shower."

She didn't bother with underwear as she pulled on a pair of ratty jeans and a T-shirt. She grabbed her keys and her phone and stepped out the door of her apartment. She went down the stairs to the back patio, which was strangely serene in the midmorning light. Shaded by the building, it edged up against the San Antonio River — the *real* San Antonio River, not the beautifully controlled and manicured park of the River Walk with its wide pedestrian walkways and its quaint overhead footbridges. This was no Venice of south Texas, but the narrow springfed waterway that had made the area habitable for thousands of years.

Red unlocked the back door of the bar and propped it open. The distinctive smell of beer and cigarettes could never be obliterated, but she still liked to air the place out.

Inside, she went behind the bar and got a pot of coffee dripping. She checked the floor safe and found it undisturbed. She had been robbed several times over the years. It always made her angry and scared, but intellectually she knew that it was a typical hazard of her business and not worth getting killed for, which was why the floor safe was still downstairs and everyone knew it.

The bar area was clean and neat, a place for everything and everything in its place. That was Karl more than Red, but she appreciated it. She ran her hand along the eighty-year-old mahogany top, already knowing that it would be completely free of sticky spots or water stains.

She found her ancient coffee mug in the back of the shelf. It was once bright white, now more eggshell, so well-worn that a whole network of tiny lines were visible in the finish. Many, many long years ago, a small hand had painted the name RED in block letters on the side. It was almost faded into complete obscurity, but she knew it was still there.

As soon as the coffee was ready, she filled her cup and took it out to the patio. The end of August was still terribly hot, but the morning shade was surprisingly nice. She put her coffee on a table and then sat down, propping her bare feet in a chair nearby.

Red pulled her big knot of hair away from her neck and back and held it atop her head. She'd grown so accustomed to the posture that it had become comfortable. She gazed out at the river flowing by, south toward downtown. Much narrower in this wild stretch, little more than fifteen feet across, the water ran faster as it made an easterly meander behind the property. Beyond the far bank were vacant lots that were heavily wooded, giving a pastoral feel that was only belied by the traffic noise of the nearby freeway interchange.

In moments like these, Red could sometimes be caught letting her guard down, remembering long-ago times in a distant farmhouse near the town of Piney Woods. She almost allowed herself that memory, then she jerked herself back into the present with a start. She didn't want to look back. She refused to remember.

Instead, she sipped her coffee and speculated on the future, dismissing all rumors of change for the area. She foresaw the years ahead as not much different than here and now. She'd continue keeping her customers coming in. The younger bands would bring in younger patrons, and once they got accustomed to the place, they would gradually take their parents' places in the booths and at the bar. Her absentee landlord had surprised her last year with a new lease at a higher price. She had put him off, refusing to sign anything and paying month to month. She was determined to extract some repairs for the higher price. The place looked okay at night, but in daytime, the building seemed neglected and almost sad. She really wanted to paint the exterior. How much could that cost him? Maybe they'd find a compromise. If he just bought the paint, she could get Cam to do the labor. It was her experience that musicians were always excellent and experienced house-painters. Of course, she didn't know how long Cam would be around. But if she got the paint, a man couldn't leave in the middle of a paint job, could he? Especially not a guy who played the fiddle.

Red was still pondering this question when her cell went off again. She straightened her legs in order to pull the phone out of her jeans pocket. It was the same strange number that had called before. With a sigh, she decided that they'd never stop calling until she told them she wasn't interested.

"Hello," she said.

"God, I thought you were never going to pick up," a familiar voice on the other end of the line blurted out. "Hey, Red, it's me."

Immediately she sat up straight in her chair. "Bridge?" Just saying the name aloud gave her a strange buoyant feeling. "Are you back in town?"

"No, I'm calling from Kabul," she answered. "I don't expect to be back until Christmas. I told you that."

"Yeah, yeah, you did," Red agreed. "I just . . . I guess I just didn't expect to hear from you. Are you all right?"

"Yeah, I'm fine," she replied. "But Mike's mother isn't. That's why I called. She had a stroke last night."

"Oh gosh, I'm so sorry. Is she going to be okay?"

"She's pretty bad off," Bridge said. "But she's hanging in there. The report I got is that, assuming they get her stabilized, they'll move her to a rehab facility for several weeks. They say you can't tell at first who is really going to benefit from therapy and who isn't. She's pretty strong and only sixty-six, but, of course, her diabetes is a big complication."

"Is Mike with her?"

"Mike's in Korea, remember that?" She sounded half-annoyed that Red might not be keeping up.

"Oh yeah, of course I remember."

"He's working on getting a week of compassionate leave, but it may be a few days before he gets a hop to San Antonio."

"Well, do you want me to go by and see her?" Red asked. "I'm not exactly a friend, but I could sure put the fear of God in the nurses if it's needed."

"That would be nice, Red," Bridge answered. "But what I really need for you to do is take the kids."

"Take the kids?" She repeated the words as if their meaning was unclear. "Take them where?"

"Mike's mom can't really move or speak. She may fully recover, but it'll be a long time before she can even care for herself, much less my two kids."

"Who has them now?"

"They're in the Family Services office at Fort Sam. I talked to Olivia about an hour ago. She and Daniel are pretty scared, but you know they're like me, tough inside and out. Family Services can't offer much in the way of temporary care for kids that age. They're waiting for my backup custody to pick them up. That's you."

That reality hung out there in an instant of complete dumbfounded silence.

"It can't be me," Red insisted. "I don't know anything about kids."

"What's to know? They practically raise themselves."

"No, they don't," Red responded with certainty. "They're just babies. There's no way that I can take them in."

"They are not babies," Bridge argued. "Olivia is nine and Daniel is six. And you agreed."

"You said I wouldn't have to do anything *but* agree."

There was a heavy sigh at the other end of the line. "Well, I'm sorry about that. There are things beyond my control."

Those words momentarily gave Red pause.

"That's a rare admission for you," Red pointed out.

"I suppose we all live and learn," Bridge said. "Anyway, you have to do it."

"Can't you just come home?"

"The army doesn't work that way."

"Have you tried? I'm sure if they knew that the kids are on their own, they'd want to help."

"Of course they'd want to help," Bridge said. "But they can't help. Everybody's got problems. Before we deploy, families work out their own plan. This is our family plan."

Red felt a desperate, sinking sense of unpleasant inevitability.

"I'm not any good with kids," she pleaded. "You, of all people, should know that."

"I do know it, and if there was anyone else I could hand them off to, I would," Bridge said. "There isn't anybody else."

"Can't you send them to Korea to stay with Mike?"

"That's possible," she said. "But it's not going to be easy. I'm army. Mike's air force. That's two different branches of the military. It's not just that they don't speak the same language, they each try to pretend that the other doesn't exist."

"But you can get them transferred to him."

"Maybe, *if* he agrees, though I doubt he'll be all that willing to give up his hard-won bachelor life. Even if he is, it'll require a judge's order to alter the custody agreement. And all the paperwork changing them from army dependents to air force dependents, that takes time," Bridge said. "Somebody has to pick them up today. *You* have to pick them up. Today."

Red glanced around her beloved patio bar with new eyes. "This is no place to raise kids," she insisted.

"Mother!" Bridge said sharply. She never

26

used the term except for the shock value of it. "I haven't the time or inclination to argue. I've already been on this phone longer than I should be. These are your grandchildren. You are now responsible for them. They're depending upon you. And you will not, under any circumstances, let any of us down. Do you understand?"

3

It was extremely curious that the one person in the world that Red should never have to take orders from — her daughter — was the only person who could consistently compel her to do anything.

Bridge's forceful admonition, undoubtedly delivered in exactly the same tone that she utilized with the men and women under her command, had so spurred Red that she'd immediately hurried to do her duty.

Without a word to Cam, who was still in the shower, she locked up the bar and jumped into her seventeen-year-old primer-gray Honda CRX. The car made a definite whiny sound as she started it up, but the engine did turn over and within fifteen minutes she was at the guard gate of the nearby army base.

As soon as they stopped her, Red knew she should have thought this out more thoroughly.

"Are you aware that your inspection sticker is out of date?" a soldier, still so young he had peach fuzz on his cheeks, asked her.

"Yeah, I . . . uh . . . well, I just hadn't gotten around to that," she admitted.

He nodded gravely and made a slight sniffing sound.

"Have you been drinking this morning, ma'am?" he asked.

"Oh no," Red insisted. "It's my clothes. I work in a bar and everything I own has that sort of beer smell to it."

"Please step out of the vehicle."

His words weren't merely a suggestion.

Red regretted her hasty departure from home now. Running around town without underwear was a definite no-no. Even if she was completely covered with jeans and T-shirt, she felt indecent, which made her behave guiltily, which, reasonably, made the gate guards suspicious of her.

"What's your purpose here today?" he asked her.

"I'm picking up my grandchildren."

Red didn't see any perceptible rise of the young soldier's eyebrow, but she felt it.

"My daughter is overseas and . . ."

Her explanation was much longer and more detailed than she wanted it to be. Red just couldn't stop expounding, clarifying, justifying. She heard herself talking, but she couldn't shut herself up. She was out of place. Intent on a task unsuited to her. It was as if she needed to convince both of them that she belonged here.

The soldier directed her to an office. Inside, phone calls were made and her business there was verified. After only a few minutes she was given a paper pass that she carried back to the guard.

"Get that sticker up-to-date before you come in next time," the young man told her.

Red hoped that, if she was lucky, she'd never have to come back here again.

After wandering through her directions and missing the turn twice, she finally parked in front of the Family Assistance Center. Flipping down the visor mirror, she gazed at herself in dismay. She combed through her wild hair with her fingers and pinched her cheeks to give them a little color. Then, taking a deep breath and placing what she hoped was a confident smile on her face, she walked inside.

The office was a square in pale neutral colors. Light poured in from the windows through utilitarian blinds. A large African-American woman was seated behind a desk, chatting on the phone. Red saw the children as soon as she walked through the door. They were sitting together in a secluded area visible from the main room, but separated from it. It was full of colorful furniture and toys that were being completely ignored. Daniel was stretched out on the chairs, his dark, curly head in the lap of his big sister. Olivia looked up and Red saw recognition in the young girl's eyes, but she offered no greeting.

Red smiled at her and waved.

When there was no response from the children, Red turned to the woman at the desk. She mouthed, "Hi," and then waited patiently until she'd hung up the phone.

"May I help you?"

"I'm Staff Sergeant Lujan's mother. I'm here to pick up her children."

The boy raised his head when he head her words. He eyed Red suspiciously and then said something to his sister.

"Uh-huh," the woman responded, and began sorting through the papers on her desk. "We tried to get you last night, but nobody answered and the children weren't sure of your address."

"I work nights," Red explained simply. Her attention was still on the two youngsters whispering together across the room.

"I need to see your driver's license."

Red managed to fish it out of her purse again. At least this time it wasn't stuck to anything. She was nervous, jittery. She bit her lip to keep herself from going on an explaining jag like she had at the gate. She would only answer questions that were asked. And she would only give as much information as was needed. That's the way Bridge would have handled it.

Red's comment to her daughter that she didn't know anything about kids was more true than any outsider might imagine. Red had been a single, teenage mother, alone, scared and basically clueless. It seemed, in retrospect, that Bridge had raised herself. Everything she was, everything she'd achieved, she had managed all on her own. Her daughter's childhood was a mysterious blur. Looking back, it seemed as if Bridge had always been a grown-up, responsible, dependable, unflappable. One minute Red was in a charity bed at Santa Rosa Hospital, being ordered to push. And the next, Bridge was marching out the front door in her military uniform.

"Just sign these papers and they are all yours," the woman said.

Red felt only the very slightest hesitation before she sat in the seat offered and began plowing through the mountain of paperwork she'd been handed. The army, it seemed, wanted to know everything about her and the placement of the children.

Red tapped her pen nervously over some of the questions and even had to ask for help.

"I don't know what school the children will attend," she admitted. "I mean, I'm sure my neighborhood must have a school, I guess I just never noticed it."

"You can write 'summer recess' in that blank now. You'll have to come back with enrollment evidence later anyway."

Red went back to the paperwork, but not before she caught sight of Olivia's eyes. Her expression was condemning. Red could almost hear her thoughts. *She hasn't even thought about where we'll go to school.*

Red determinedly reminded herself that by then they'd be somebody else's problem.

She signed the final page and pushed the paperwork across the desk. The woman thanked her and waved the kids over.

"Come on now," she called out to them. "Your grandma's come here to get you. Better run give her a big hello kiss."

Big hello kisses were obviously not paramount in the minds of the two children who gathered up their suitcases and backpacks as if the weight of the world was on their young shoulders.

"I need to go to the library," were Olivia's first words to Red.

Daniel didn't say anything. He just looked at her as if she were a strange alien creature, and a frightening one at that.

"Okay, maybe later," Red answered. "Let's go to my place and get you settled in first."

It was hard to imagine how she could ever get these two settled into her apartment.

Red grabbed up Daniel's book bag, which was almost as big as he was. He reacted as if she was trying to steal it and said something to his sister in Spanish.

"She's just going to help you carry it," Olivia answered the boy.

He didn't seem happy about that, but as Red led them out the door, he reluctantly followed his sister.

She opened the back hatch of the CRX and began stowing the gear inside. Daniel was talking again, in Spanish, and this time his sister was answering in the same language.

"Doesn't he speak English?" Red asked.

"Of course he does," Olivia answered. "Right now, he just doesn't want to."

Oh great! Red thought as she managed to keep from sighing or rolling her eyes.

When all the baggage was loaded, she

urged the kids to the passenger door.

"I guess Daniel should go up in the back, since he's smaller," Red said.

Olivia peered inside the car and then gazed at Red in astonishment. "There isn't anyplace to sit back there," she pointed out.

Red shrugged. "The car's a two-seater, but your brother can scoot in there cross-legged and he'll be fine."

"He needs a real place to sit and to be buckled in," Olivia said.

She sounded so much like her mother, Red thought, such a little stickler for the rules.

"Don't worry. It's okay."

"It's not okay, it's illegal," Olivia pointed out. "And it's unsafe. Nobody will let you drive us that way."

"It will be fine," Red assured her.

"I don't think so," Olivia said. "He needs to be sitting in a seat, with a seat belt."

"We don't have a seat with a seat belt, so we'll make do with what we have."

The little girl's sigh was one of long-suffering before she complied.

Red's plan to make do lasted all the way to the gate. The same grave-spoken young soldier who'd unhappily let her in was now unwilling to let her out.

"I chose to overlook an out-of-date inspection sticker," he reminded her. "But I cannot allow you out on a public street with a child who is not properly or legally restrained."

Red argued for several minutes. She'd drive slowly. She'd take only backstreets. She wasn't going far. None of it made any difference.

Red moved the car into the small waiting lot and she and the children sat down on a bench.

"I told you so," Olivia said quietly, almost under her breath.

Red didn't even acknowledge hearing that. Instead, she snapped open her phone. She couldn't think of who to call at first. It was Friday morning and everyone she knew was at work. Finally she called the only person she was sure would answer.

"Hey, Red," Cam said as he picked up. "Where'd you run off to so quickly?"

His voice was languid and silky smooth.

"I need you to do me a favor," she said, very matter-of-fact. "And I don't want to play Twenty Questions about it, I just want you to do it."

"Okay. What do you need?" he asked. His tone had changed completely from sweet-nothing whispers to all business.

"Bring your van and meet me at the

Walters Avenue gate at Fort Sam Houston as soon as you can."

There was a hesitation on the other end of the line. She was sure there were a thousand things that he wanted to ask, but she'd told him not to, and he didn't.

"It may take me fifteen or twenty minutes," he told her. "I'll go as fast as I can."

"Thanks."

She hung up.

Red glanced over at the children. They were sitting close together at the far end of the bench, as if trying to put as much distance as possible between themselves and this stranger who was, not very willingly or successfully, trying to take them home.

They had their father's looks. Both had tan skin and brown eyes. Olivia's long dark hair was thick and straight and pulled away from her face with a purple plastic headband. Daniel's was curly and badly in need of a cut. The too-long curls gave his head an oversize appearance. They both had on shorts and flip-flops. Olivia's shirt was decorated with tiny purple bows. Daniel's advertised a pirate movie that he would not be old enough to see for a very long time. They were young and scared and very alone. Red could almost remember that feeling, and it generated an empathy for them that was genuine enough to be uncomfortable.

Daniel was still talking to his sister in a language Red didn't understand. But she'd lived in San Antonio long enough that some of it sounded familiar. She immediately picked up on the word *abuela* — grandmother — and she wanted to reassure them.

"I don't know what the regulations are at the hospital where your *abuela* is," she said. "Sometimes they don't let people under twelve visit the patients. But I can sure check on that and we can try to go see her."

Olivia gave her a puzzled look before muttering thanks.

"That's what you were talking about, right?" Red asked. "I'm sure I heard Daniel say *abuela*."

"Oh yeah," Olivia said. "But he wasn't talking about our other grandmother, he was talking about you."

"Oh."

"He doesn't remember you, but I told him who you are," Olivia said. "That you're our mom's mother and that we never see you because you're very busy and you work nights and sleep all day. But you're still our grandmother."

"Oh, right," Red agreed.

"At first he didn't believe me because he

said that you don't look like a grand-mother," Olivia told her.

Red smiled, pleased.

"Daniel says grandmothers are supposed to look sweet and like you want to hug them," Olivia went on. "But you look like a stranger, the kind that Mom would tell us to run away from."

Red's jaw dropped at the young girl's frankness.

"I told him, you're our grandmother whether you look like it or not."

Red nodded. "So now he's calling me abuela, too."

Olivia raised an almost disdainful eyebrow. "Not exactly," she said. "Abuela is our abuela. Daniel is calling you Abuela Mala."

"Abuela Mala?"

Olivia nodded again. "Yeah, Bad Grandma."

4

How does a woman introduce her boy-toy to her grandchildren?

It wasn't the only question on Red's mind, but it was not as critical as most of the others, so she chose to deal with it first.

She could be casual. *Hey, these are my grandkids!* Completely ignoring the fact that she'd never before mentioned their existence.

She could tug at his heartstrings. Poor kids, their mom is in combat and they have nobody to depend on but me.

Or she could just say nothing and let him draw his own conclusions.

As far as Daniel and Olivia were concerned, she was pretty sure that she shouldn't suggest that they call him Gramps.

Olivia was pacing, her arms folded across her chest. Every few minutes, she would stop to give Red a disgusted glance that was reminiscent of her mother.

Daniel sat on the far end of the bench, his knees drawn up and bent forward from the waist as if trying to make himself as small as possible. His gaze was most often focused upon his sister, but occasionally he looked in Red's direction with enough trepidation to suggest that any moment he expected her to cackle insanely before jumping on her broomstick to fly away.

What was she going to do with these kids?

The questions stirred a panic inside her. She calmed it with the reasonable answer that she couldn't do anything. She'd hold them, keep them safe, until Mike got here and then they were his problem.

"I need to go to the library!" Olivia's announcement was voiced as a command.

"Yeah, I know, you said that already," Red replied. "I'll get you there as soon as I can. Just hold your horses. Even in Texas, late library books are not a hanging offense."

Olivia gave her a disgusted look accompanied by an audible sniff before resuming her pacing.

The waiting time was interminable. Finally, Cam's well-used slate-gray minivan pulled in to the lot beside the guard gate. It was a welcome sight. He stepped out of the driver's-side door, handsome as always. His long, muscular legs were clad in faded blue denim and his ancient T-shirt, which advertised the *Bent Bucket's National Drop-in Tour,* clung attractively to his chest. Except for the length of plaited ponytail that hung down his back, his blond hair was mostly covered by a straw hat, so weathered and misshapen its cowboy origins were almost indiscernible.

"Hey, babe!" he called out to her. When he got closer, he apologized. "I got here as fast as I could. It's not as hot today as it has been, but I bet taking in a few rays on this bench wasn't what you had in mind this morning."

Red shrugged. "I think I'm now qualified for a job watching paint dry."

He grinned at her and then glanced around. If he noticed the kids, he didn't make any comment.

"Okay, what am I loading up?" he asked.

She hesitated. It was only an instant, but it was long enough to feel that moment of regret that her next words might well bring an end to a very sweet and satisfying relationship.

"These kids," she told him.

Cam's eyebrows lifted in surprise and he glanced toward the children for the first time. When he looked back at Red, his expression was skeptical.

"I don't know which is less likely with you," he said. "Are we kidnapping or babysitting?"

"These are my grandchildren," Red answered evenly.

She watched his face for signs of shock, horror, disgust. Whatever he felt, she couldn't detect it.

"Well, all right!" Cam said, walking past her. "My name's Cam. I'm a friend of your grandmother's. I've brought an amazing American-made multitransport vehicle to chauffeur you to exciting new destinations within the city. Cool, huh?"

With oversize body language and over-the-top verbiage he caught the children off guard. They forgot that they were scared and bored and annoyed. Olivia's expression softened almost to amused and Daniel rose from his curled-up position on the bench to study the new arrival curiously. Cam greeted them individually with a high five.

"What kind of name is Cam?" Olivia asked.

He shrugged. "It's my name," he answered. "A little weird, I guess. But not so bad as it could be. It's short for Campbell. Not camera, if you were wondering about that. Or camouflage. Or chameleon. It

43

would be tough if my name was short for camel or something like that."

The two kids shared a quick, this-guy-is-kind-of-fun glance.

"I'm Olivia and that's Daniel. He's not speaking English today."

Cam nodded. "Sometimes I don't want to speak it, either," he said to the boy. "So, are you talking at all today?"

"Solamente español," he answered.

"Okay," Cam answered, and then continued painstakingly. *"Mi español no esta buena, pero hablo con mis manos."*

"You can talk with your hands?" Olivia asked. "Like sign language?"

"Not exactly sign language," Cam said. He held up both hands facing each other and flapped the fingers against the thumbs like mouths. "Hey, what are we gonna do? Daniel doesn't want to speak English and we don't speak much Spanish. . . . We can talk to each other in front of him and he can overhear us. . . . That could work. But what if he wants to say something? He could whisper it to us and we could say it a loud for him. . . . Yeah, that could work. . . . Well, let's get Daniel's opinion on that. . . . Could that work for you? What do you think?"

Both children were laughing.

Daniel stepped up close to Cam and

whispered to one of the hands. "I think this guy is crazy."

"Very astute, Daniel," Cam told him. "You're pretty smart, huh? Why don't we get into the van and get your dear granny out of the sunshine before she turns into one giant freckle?"

The kids giggled again as they hurried to the van. Cam got them inside and admonished them to buckle-up before turning his attention back to Red.

"Well done," she said to him.

Cam shrugged, feigning modesty. "What can I say, kids like me."

"Because they sense you're one of them."

He clutched his heart with a groan of pain. "I'm wounded!"

Red shook her head, refusing to be amused.

"Just drive my car home," she said, exchanging keys with him.

"I get to drive the CRX? Your baby? Oh wait, I guess I've uncovered the secret that it's not your *only* baby," Cam said.

"Oh, kiss my a—"

A quick glance toward the kids stopped Red in midsyllable.

"Your armadillo?" Cam finished for her. His mention of her tattoo would not be something that the children could pick up on. "Thank you, maybe some other time."

His smile was sardonic and although his tone was still light, Red knew him well enough to recognize foreboding. But she'd already accepted the inevitable. No hot young guy would want to be hooked up with a granny.

"See you at the bar," she answered and headed for the driver's side of the minivan. Deliberately she didn't look back. She'd learned long ago that was the best way to move forward.

Red seated herself behind the steering wheel and fitted the key into the ignition. Before turning the engine over, she glanced at her two passengers. Daniel was buckled in, but had pulled his knees to his chest and was hiding his face behind them. Olivia was glaring at Red, but surprisingly, she detected the vulnerability behind the mask.

"Look, kids," Red said to them. "This is not going to be perfect, but I think if we all do our best to get along, we'll make it through this."

Neither child seemed buoyed by her pep talk. Red sighed and started up the engine. She didn't say another word during the entire trip, but the ride couldn't have been accurately described as quiet. Daniel began whispering to his sister in Spanish. She

46

answered him similarly. Red had no idea what the discussion was about, but she could recognize the tone. Daniel's whispers were urgent. Olivia's replies were initially dismissive, followed by placating and eventually angry. By the time Red pulled in to her parking space behind the bar, the two weren't talking to each other at all.

"What's this place?" Olivia asked.

"This is where I live."

"You live in a bar?" The little girl's voice was incredulous. "Does Mom know this?"

"Of course she does," Red replied. "I live in the upstairs apartment. It's small, but we'll try to think of it as cozy, okay?"

Cozy was not what it seemed a few minutes later when the three of them were standing inside. It looked like what it was. An efficiency apartment with a couch, TV and kitchenette. Its tiny bedroom looked like a cave with the blackout curtains. And a double bed really didn't provide sleeping arrangements for three.

"You kids can have the bedroom," she told them. "I'll sleep out here on the couch."

"What about our stuff?" Olivia asked. "Where are we going to put our stuff?"

"What stuff?"

Olivia looked at her in disbelief. "Do you think this is all we have?" she asked, indicating her backpack. "All our clothes and toys and books, it's all at Abuela's house."

"It'll be fine over there," Red said. "Nothing is going to happen to it."

"We're going to need it," Olivia explained. "School starts in two weeks. We're going to need all of it."

Red didn't answer that. But she wasn't worried. By then she would most certainly have handed them over to their father. They wouldn't be here for long. But even a night or two was problematic.

She looked around the rooms she'd called home for nine years and the evidence was as glaring as the truth it represented. She had created a place for herself that ensured that she live her life alone. Even with only two small children, the rooms had become claustrophobically close. Red needed some breathing space.

"Didn't you say you needed to go to the library?" she asked Olivia.

"Uh-huh."

"Then get your stuff and let's go. I'll meet you in the van."

In three steps Red was out of the apartment, but she couldn't quite escape her current predicament. Halfway down the stairs, Cam lounged across her path. His hat was tipped back and his eyes were focused on her. She slowed her steps.

Clearly it was break-up time. She didn't want to do it.

It's like ripping off a bandage, she reminded herself. *The quicker it's done, the sooner it's over with.* Still, she hesitated.

"I don't really have time for this right now," she told him.

He raised an eyebrow. "Time for what?"

"Time to . . . to talk things over," she dissembled.

He nodded. "You mean things like why you told me you don't have any children?"

"I don't have any 'children,'" Red hedged. "My daughter is a grown-up woman, obviously."

"Obviously."

Cam continued to look at her directly. His gaze was unavoidable. "Okay, so I lied."

"Right," he said. "You lied. Why'd you do that?"

"Because . . . because I didn't think it was any of your business," she said.

Olivia and Daniel slammed the door of the apartment and hurried down the stairs behind her.

"I've got to take Olivia to the library," she said, grateful for the reprieve.

"Okay," Cam answered. "I'll come with you."

That wasn't what Red had in mind, but there wasn't any graceful way to stop it, so she let it go. At least they wouldn't be able to have their talk while the kids were in the car.

In that she was thwarted as well. When they got to the van, Cam had a better idea.

"Why don't we walk," he said. "Hey, kids, you want to walk? It's a great day for a walk."

Both Olivia and Daniel seemed enthusiastic. Red was not.

"It's too far, through a rough part of town, and it's a hundred degrees out here," she complained.

"It's eight, maybe ten blocks. That's nothing to kids," he assured her. "And the area's not rough, just empty. In daylight, it's mostly parking lots." He damped his index finger on his tongue and held it up in the air. "I'd say it's only ninety-three, maybe ninety-four. Perfect San Antonio weather."

Red wanted to argue, but the kids were already rushing out to the sidewalk.

"Don't get so far ahead that I can't see you," Red called out. "And wait at the corner."

If Olivia thought those were baby rules, at least she didn't say so.

Red and Cam followed at a good pace as

they made their way southward on Avenue B past the autobody shop, a plumbing warehouse and a couple of vacant lots. She was surprised when he took her hand.

"What?" he asked at her startled expression. "Do you think this will embarrass the kids? Or will it embarrass you?"

She didn't answer that, she just changed the subject.

"I know we need to talk about . . . about all this and where our relationship goes from here and all that," Red said. "But can we just skip it? Now you know how old I am. That I have a grown daughter with kids of her own. You can either opt out or don't, but I'd just as soon not talk about it."

Cam made a slightly affirmative sound and kept moving ahead, thoughtfully.

"Did you think that I didn't know how old you are?" he asked.

"Well, of course I knew that you knew that I'm older than you," she answered. "But having grandkids? I'm pretty sure that guys like you don't date women with grandkids."

"Is that why you didn't mention it?"

"That's *a* reason. There are several others, just as good," she answered.

"One of those being that it's none of my business," Cam said, quoting her earlier comment.

Red didn't answer that, but merely shrugged.

Up ahead, Olivia and Daniel had stopped at the corner, dutifully waiting for them.

"So, where's their mother?" Cam asked.

"Afghanistan," Red answered. "When she's deployed they usually stay with their other grandmother, but she had a stroke last night."

"Wow, tough break."

"Yeah."

He turned to give her a slight grin. "I meant for them, not for you."

"I meant them, too!" Red insisted.

"What about their dad?"

"He and my daughter are divorced," she answered. "But he'll be here in San Antonio in a day or two and take them off my hands."

They caught up to the kids and turned the corner to cross the narrow river bridge. Daniel leaned against the railing, content to watch the flow of the water. Both sides of the river were marked with bright orange flags and areas taped off. The boy seemed inordinately interested in the marking. Olivia urged him on down the street, her eagerness to get to the library apparent.

"So your daughter's name is . . . ?"

"Bridge. Bridge Lujan."

"Bridge is short for Bridget?"

"No," Red answered. "Just Bridge. It was . . . it was just something I thought up when she was born. She was like my bridge from my old life to my new one."

Cam eyed her curiously as if expecting her to say more.

She was hesitant to say too much. "You know how teenagers are," she explained, forcing a chuckle that wasn't completely sincere. "I was very dramatic and my world was full of meaning."

Red continued quickly, unwilling to give him a chance to delve any further in those things she didn't want to remember.

"Bridge is an operating-room specialist," she said. "She supervises other soldiers and they make sure that the surgical areas are safe and sterile. Most of the time she works here, at BAMC, the army hospital. But this is her second deployment to the Middle East."

"Are you worried about her?"

"Well, certainly. I am human, you know," Red told him. "But Bridge can really take care of herself. She always has."

At St. Mary's Street they turned south again, past the U-PiK-It grocery that was crammed into a vintage 1920s gasoline station. There were more buildings on the streets to see now. Small hotels, a television station, the photography building of the Southwest School of Art. Daniel was curious about all of them and dawdled. Olivia kept up a steady pace all the way to Navarro Street.

"Was she raised by her dad?"

"Huh?"

"Your daughter. Did your ex get custody?"

"What are you talking about?"

"You don't seem to know the kids very well," he said. "I thought maybe your daughter grew up with your ex-husband."

Red opened her mouth to answer, but then took a moment to reply more carefully.

"My daughter grew up with me," she said. "But Bridge and the kids, they have their own life. And I have mine."

"Did you and your daughter have some kind of falling-out?"

"Oh no, nothing like that," Red insisted. "We just don't have much in common."

Cam chuckled. "Oh yeah, right. Nothing except two kids who need you."

Red shook her head and waved away his interpretation as they continued down the street.

"Look, I know you're pissed off that I lied to you about Bridge and the kids, but I wasn't hiding anything. It's just that a time to discuss the subject didn't come up."

"It didn't come up because you deliberately didn't bring it up," Cam said.

"And when would have been a good time?" Red asked. "In the middle of 'oh baby, oh baby, yes, yes,' I should just throw in, 'by the way, I have a daughter and two grandchildren.'"

"So in the last five months that we've been together there wasn't any time when we weren't in the middle of having sex?" he asked.

"Darling, that's a good thing," Red answered, trying to make a joke of it. Cam wasn't amused.

"Don't pretend that we're just sex buddies," he said.

Red feigned incredulity. "Don't pretend we're anything else," she countered.

Cam's mouth thinned into one unhappy line and he kept his glance straight ahead.

Red forced a carefree jaunt to her step. She'd hurt him. She knew it. But it was for the best and now it was done. She'd pushed him away. And the emptiness she felt inside, that would pass. It always did. He'd find someone else. Someone younger who could give him a couple of kids to raise. That woman would make him give up music for a real job and keep him home at night.

That's what he needed, anyway. And Red, well, she'd keep the kids until Mike got there and then she'd move on. There was always another cowboy willing to give her a ride.

Ahead at the end of the block was the San Antonio Central Library. Built in the early 1990s in the unique architectural style described as Mexican Modernist, it would have been striking enough just in its design. But the building had also been painted enchilada red, a true splash of color in a neighborhood of muted gray. Many locals had initially been taken aback, but time had mellowed the paint and venerated the walls and angles to the point where most in the city would say, *That's what a library is supposed to look like.*

Cam and Red waited with the children at the crosswalk and then followed them through the Garden of Spheres and along the colonnade, not speaking.

Red wished she could have saved the breakup for the walk home. She didn't want to be with him now. She didn't want to see him after it was over. And she didn't understand why he didn't just take off. That's what she would have done, walk away. It would save everybody these uncomfortable, uneasy moments afterward. Cam should know that. Apparently he didn't. He stayed at her side.

The kids ran inside the building on their own. The two adults had to rush to keep up with them.

"Where are we going?" Red asked.

"Third floor," Olivia answered. "That's the kid area. Have you never been in the library before?"

Red didn't answer that. Instead, she followed her grandchildren to the elevator and up to the Juvenile Books section. There, the two split off in opposite directions. Daniel was on his knees on a brightly colored mat looking though the contents of a low-rise bookshelf. Olivia crossed the room to seat herself in front of a computer and immediately began typing something in.

Red stood, ill at ease, with Cam at her side.

"You don't have to stay," she said finally. "We can find our way back."

He turned and with a raised eyebrow glanced at her. "I thought you said it was a dangerous neighborhood."

"I was wrong about that," she answered. "It seemed fine when we walked through it."

"Still, I wouldn't want you and the kids to be alone," he said.

"I actually prefer it that way," she said, turning to glare at him with challenge. "I found out a long time ago that there are just very few things that I actually need a man for. Moving a heavy refrigerator is one. Another is . . . well, stamina in the bedroom, that I have to admit you are very good at. But herding a couple of kids, that's what women do. Men should just go on about their business."

He nodded slightly and there was a smile on his face, but it had nothing to do with humor.

"So let me get this straight," he said. "You don't have anything heavy to move and it's probably a bad idea for me to lead you behind the bookshelves for a quick screw. Therefore I can just leave."

"Yes."

He shook his head. "Well, you're underestimating my abilities. Who's going to translate all those English-language picture books for little Mr. Unilingual?"

"I can read to Daniel."

"I doubt if he would let you," Cam said, flapping his fingers against his thumbs as he'd done for the children earlier. "Talk to the hands."

To: buildabetterbridge@citymail.com
August 23 11:03 a.m.
From: Livy156@ABrats.org
Subject: Don't Worry

THIS RED PERSON IS WEIRD! Sorry. Know that was rude. And becuz shes your parent I have to be nice to her. Just wanna let ya know that D & me are OK. Her place is a bar, Mom. She says you knew that. True? Did you live there? Ewww. Totally gross.

D calls her Abuela Mala. TOO FUNNY! TOO TRUE! She doesnt know anything. She hasnt said nothing about food. I know Daniel is hungry and I am starfing. I looked in her fridge and there is nothing but a jar of mayo. How is she going to feed us on a jar of mayo? She doesn't know we have to buckle-up and she thinks that we dont need our stuff. I made her come here to the library. I dont think shes ever been here before. Maybe she cant read. How is she going to help us with our homework. If we have homework. She doesnt know any-thing about school. Not even where one is.

Daniel is only speaking Spanish so he wont have to talk to her. I wish I thought of that.

But she does have a cute boyfriend. I think I

hate her. I dont like to hate people. But she is weird and she is strange looking. Her skin is as white as like a vampire or something. And the hair, yuk.

Daniel is afraid of her. He is trying to disappear again. When Abuela got sick and the ambulance and everything it really scared him. I told him it's not like Buttercup. A cat can get sick and die but Abuela is in a hospital and they will make her better. He says he believes me, but he thinks that maybe he was bad or broke a rule so God took away Abuela and gave him Abuela Mala as a punishment. HE IS SUCH A BABY!

I wish you were here. But I know that you have to be there to help make sure that the soldiers that get hurt get better. A soldier has to do her duty. So I will try to do mine too. But I miss you. So does Daniel.

But don't worry about us. Everything is fine.

Livy

5

Cam stayed at the library, mostly talking to Daniel and Olivia, then walked home with the kids, pointing out the sites in the neighborhood and answering questions. Red trailed behind them, feeling very much not a part of the action.

She watched Cam with the kids with an amazement that bordered on envy. He was so comfortable with them and they seemed to relax, as if this were just a normal day and an adventurous outing.

It's because he's practically a child himself, she thought unkindly. But she refrained from saying anything to anyone, aware that her sour mood would not be welcome.

When they crossed the bridge Daniel tried to quiz Cam about the *naranjanos.*

"I don't know that word," Cam admitted.

"He means all the orange construction markers," Olivia explained.

"Oh, that's the expansion of the river,"

Cam told them. "Have you been on the boats down on the River Walk?"

Both children nodded eagerly.

"Mom took us and our *abuela* for a special dinner at Casa Real. Then we rode the water taxi over to Rivercenter Mall," Olivia recalled.

"I love to do that," Cam admitted. "And now they're going to dig the river out and make it deeper and wider along here. That way, the boats can come. All the way up the river to the art museum and even as far as that big building, way up in the distance."

They all looked north as Cam pointed to the shiny mansard roof tower of the old Pearl Brewery.

"So we could take a boat all the way to her bar?" Olivia asked.

Cam nodded. "You'll be able to float right up to your grandma's back door," he said.

"Wow," the two youngsters responded in awed unison.

Red couldn't keep her mouth shut after that.

"That's twenty years away, if it happens at all," she told them. "You'll both be as grown-up as Cam by then."

Cam gave her a strange, puzzled look, but it was Olivia who spoke.

"We'll still get to do it," she said a bit

more sharply than little girls are normally allowed. "Even if we're as old as you."

Daniel seconded her statement with an unpleasant glare.

That interaction generally set the tone for the next couple of days. Red did what she could to keep the kids fed and entertained. The two seemed only barely able to tolerate her existence.

They had their Game Boys and a color TV in the apartment, but their schedule was all wrong for Red. They were up with the sun, running loose outside. She had no choice but to supervise them. So she groggily sat in a chair, trying to keep her eyes open.

And Saturday night, in the middle of the second set, Red glanced up from the cash register to see Olivia in her pink pony pajamas walking through the bar.

"You're not supposed to be down here," Red scolded. "It's against the law to have minors in a business serving alcohol. I could lose my liquor license."

"It's noisy, and I can't sleep," Olivia complained. "Daniel can't, either. You need to send all these people home!"

Red had Karl take over. She eased her granddaughter back through the crowd and upstairs, then sat in the dark with the two restless children for nearly an hour as the sounds below penetrated the walls of the little apartment.

This was just not going to work. How was she supposed to handle this? She had a business to run and a life to live. She was no good with kids. People like her should never have kids! And they should definitely never be put in charge of other people's kids.

The two dark-haired children finally slept. Red tiptoed out of the apartment and down the stairs.

The band had finished for the night and the crowd had thinned. The noise was all laughter and tinkling glasses. Up on the stage, the guys were packing up their equipment. Brian was surrounded by his usual pack of pretty college girls, barely dressed and incessantly giggling. Tonight, however, one young brunette had ventured away from the group and was talking with Cam.

Or rather she was talking *to* Cam. The young woman seemed to be bubbling over with enthusiasm as she chattered.

Red stepped back into the stairway shadows. She didn't want to be seen watching him, but she found it very difficult to look away. She couldn't hear what they were saying, but the body language spoke volumes. The pretty girl held her hands behind her back as if she intended to offer herself to him. As she laughed, she leaned toward Cam — which served the double duty of getting her closer to him and allowing him an easy look down the front of her blouse.

Jealousy shot through Red's veins like a fire igniting a combustible substance.

How dare that little twit try her way-too-practiced moves on Cam!

Then, like a rush of cold water, Red remembered that she'd let him go. No, she hadn't just let him go, she'd pushed him away. She'd said she wanted him to find someone else.

Well, okay, she thought, *but I shouldn't have to watch it!*

Immediately she walked to the bottom of the stairs and shut the gate behind her as noisily as possible. Without even a glance in their direction, she went straight through the back door and into the bar. *At least let him have the good sense to take his love life elsewhere,* she thought.

She stood on her box behind the cash register for the rest of the evening, talking, joking, ringing up tabs and making change. The night felt overlong. She was tired and the stragglers stayed late. She let the waitresses leave and finally it was only her and Karl.

He cleaned the bar while she totaled up. Then he did a quick walkthrough to make sure everything was secure.

"That's it," he told her. "You want to lock up behind me?"

"Sure," she said, stepping down from her perch. "Thanks, Karl. You'd better get home and start sleeping or you'll miss your whole Sunday off."

The big man chuckled. "Hey, this is my weekend. I'm not going home to sleep, I'm going out to party."

"That proves that you're younger than me," Red told him. "Now, get out of here."

They both laughed as she double locked the front door and pulled the iron crossbar down into place. She went back to her tallies, but the peace and quiet of the place was not as serene as it should be. Without the noise and laughter and music, Red's Hot Honky-Tonk was just a sad old building that reeked of stale beer. Owning her own place had been a dream so improbable that the accomplishment of it seemed magical. But the night-to-night reality of the bar was no fairy tale. It was standing on your feet and smiling about it for ten hours. It was a lot of ordinary nights, but many that included mean drunks, crazed kids or enraged spouses. After she paid her rent, utilities and her staff, she had to come up with cash to compensate the bands. And she had to compete for the better ones with larger, more lucrative venues as far away as Austin.

Still, Red was unwilling to whine about her success. Of the things she'd done to support herself and her child, there were many that she hoped would never be made known. Running a honky-tonk was something that she did proudly.

As soon as she finished her counting and totaled up the bank deposit for Monday, she squatted behind the bar and got the floor safe open. She was putting the money inside when she heard something out on the patio.

She startled slightly and called out, "Who's there?" Immediately she thought of Olivia in the pink pony pajamas, unable to sleep again.

"Sweetie, is that you?" she asked.

"Yes, it is," Cam answered. "Though you haven't called me 'sweetie' any time that I can remember."

Red finished her task without responding. When the safe was locked, she rose to her feet. He was leaning against the other side of the bar. In the dim light she could see that he wasn't smiling.

"I didn't know you were here," she told him. "Karl did a walk through and said that everybody had cleared out."

Cam shrugged. "I'm sure he didn't consider me just one of the customers."

"Well, he should have because I said everything that I want to say to you this afternoon."

Cam nodded. "I heard you," he assured her. "You made it plain. I'm not your confidant. You don't want to share your life with me. You don't even think I need to know basic facts about you, like do you have a family. That's all crystal clear."

His words were matter-of-fact, but Red could still hear the tinge of anger in them.

"But you also said we were sex buddies," he pointed out. "So, it's Saturday night. I'm here for sex."

Red wiped her hands unnecessarily on a bar towel. She was stalling. She didn't want to have a big breakup, but she couldn't imagine what other course of action to take. He already knew too much. He was already aware of her weaknesses. She never let men get the upper hand and she wouldn't now. Calmly and determinedly, she walked around the bar to confront him. Hands on her hips, she was deliberately snide.

"Look, cowboy, you got a piece on Thursday night," she said crudely. "I'm over forty. I don't need it as often as the young girls do. What happened to your little coed gone wild? Wouldn't she put out?"

It was deliberate baiting.

Cam smiled, but without humor. "Oh, I did her already," he answered. "It was completely unsatisfying. You know those young girls. They just think once they let you shove it in, they've got nothing to do but pant and wiggle until it's over."

In a shocked and jealous rage, Red reacted before she thought, reaching out to slap him.

Expecting the move, Cam caught her arm before her hand connected with his face. In one smooth, strong motion he turned her and drew her against him, her back to his chest, his hands grasping her wrists to protect them both from her angry flailing.

"How dare you come to me after another woman," Red screeched at him.

He held her fast and tenderly pressed his face against her neck as he whispered the truth in her ear.

"I haven't been with another woman since the day I met you," he said. "I don't want to be with another woman. I only want you."

Red realized then that he had tricked her. He'd made her react, acknowledge the possessiveness that she felt.

"I don't care who you sleep with!" she declared, but it was too late.

He continued to hold her against him, but there was no force in his embrace. It was all tenderness.

"The coed was just a silly girl with a crush on the fiddle player," he said. "Why would I be interested in a silly girl when I've already got a smart woman?"

"You don't *have* me, cowboy," Red insisted. "I belong to myself and nobody but myself."

"Don't push me away, Red," he told her. "I know you're angry, but don't use that as an excuse to push me away."

"I'm not angry! Why would I be angry?"

He loosened his grip and turned her to face him. "Because you like having everything under control," he said. "You've made your world pretty small in order to manage that. But now the outside has come flooding in."

"That's ridiculous," she insisted, but didn't like the ring of truth that his words carried. "I'm just going to be spending more time with these kids in the next few days. The smart thing for you to do is make yourself scarce. Once this thing gets settled . . . once the kids are gone, we'll see where we are."

"I already know where I am," Cam told her. "I'm here beside you. I can help you, Red."

She pulled away. "I think I've made it clear that I don't need anybody's help."

He nodded. "Right, we're back to that. I'm just the go-to guy for sex."

"Stop looking for insults," Red told him. "Yes, I like being with you, but we both know that this is just . . . Well, it's just a here-and-now kind of thing. And today my here-and-now got a little bit too busy for being with you. And you're busy, too. Isn't the band playing in Austin next week? By the time you get back, this will probably all be behind us."

"Okay, next week I'll be gone," he agreed. "But tonight I'm here, and it's now."

He nuzzled her neck and ran his hands along her torso to her waist and down. He grasped her backside and lifted her up against him.

Her breath momentarily caught in her throat, but she managed to voice a whispered protest.

"The kids are asleep in my bed."

His answer was low pitched and lusty.

"The day I met you, I was sitting in that back booth. I wanted to do you right there, right then."

Red sighed against him.

"Tonight I'm going to polish that worn old vinyl with your sweet armadillo."

6

Between the great sex and the bad sleeping accommodations, Red began Sunday morning even more tired than she'd been on Saturday.

The kids were up and about early. Cam slipped out unnoticed and then returned an hour later, showered and shaved and carrying a sack of breakfast tacos. He received a hero's welcome from all three of them.

They sat down together on the patio. Red was hungry, but more grateful for the coffee than the food. The caffeine was just beginning to kick in when her granddaughter dropped the next bomb.

"We have to get ready to go to church," Olivia announced.

Daniel made a small sound of complaint. Red felt like doing the same, but she managed to choke back the response.

"Church?" she asked, hoping her question sounded more neutral than she felt.

Olivia gave her brother a reproving nod before answering Red. "It's Sunday," she said. "And on Sundays we go to church. That's what people do."

"It's not what all people do," Red said.

Olivia ignored that fact.

"We always go with Mom or Abuela. It's never good to miss," she said. "Usually we go to Holy Family, but sometimes we go to Little Flower. With Abuela being sick, I think we should go to Little Flower. They give out miracles there."

Red was taken aback by her granddaughter's matter-of-fact belief. She'd thought Olivia to be very much like her mother. But Bridge only had faith in herself.

Taking another sip of coffee, Red spoke carefully. "I don't go to church," she told Olivia. "Sunday is my only day off and I usually just hang around here, resting up and enjoying myself."

Olivia's little nose went up in the air a bit. "There's plenty of time for that in the afternoon," she pointed out.

From the corner of her eye, Red caught sight of Cam. He was eating his breakfast and not saying a word, but the smirk on his face was infuriating. She resisted the desire to kick him under the table.

Red kept her annoyance firmly in check.

She decided that the impasse required compromise.

Brightly, she offered a suggestion. "How about I drop the two of you off at Abuela's church and pick you up after the service is over?"

Olivia's brow furrowed and she shook her head with disapproval. "No," she stated firmly. "Mom wouldn't like that at all."

Red had not darkened a church door in a very long time. A funeral of a close friend was about the only thing that could compel her in that direction. Did she have to go? And if so, what in the devil would she wear?

She was weighing her options when her cell phone unexpectedly sang to the rescue.

Slipping it out of her back pocket, she glanced at the screen.

"It's your dad," she announced.

The response from the kids was jubilant and animated. Red hardly had time to say hello to her ex-son-in-law before Olivia and Daniel were manning the phone.

She listened to their excitement and giggling and, surprisingly, found herself feeling left out. Red pushed that strange feeling away. Having Mike in town this quick was better than she'd hoped.

Within minutes the conversation was over and the two children were wolfing down the rest of their breakfast and enthusiastically relating their plans for the day.

Mike was to pick them up in one hour. They were going to visit Abuela at the hospital and then spend the day with their dad. Their delight was obvious.

Daniel was excitedly rambling in Spanish. Red didn't recognize any of it except the name SeaWorld.

Olivia was nodding. "Daddy took us to SeaWorld once," she explained. "And Daniel got to pet the dolphins."

Once the two had scrambled up to the apartment, Red put her feet up in the chair opposite her and raised her hair off her neck.

"More coffee?" Cam asked.

She nodded and he poured her a cup.

"This is really a weight off my shoulders," she told him. "There is just no way to have a couple of kids living above the bar. I was sitting up there in the bedroom with them last night. Even with the windows all shut and the air-conditioning unit turned up, the music was blaring in at a half-jillion decibels."

"Yeah," Cam agreed. "Kids need a home in a neighborhood. That's really ideal. But just having someone who cares about them, that's an awful lot."

Mike showed up at the bar about an hour

after the call. He was driving Bridge's very distinctive Prius. Her daughter had purchased the hybrid vehicle in a pale minty color and then artfully painted it with swatches of darker green that made it look like camouflage. There was not another car like it in town. With the GO ARMY sticker on the bumper, it said a lot about her daughter.

The minute Mike opened the driver's door, both kids were running into his arms.

Miguel Lujan was tall, dark and handsome. With his easy smile, charming manners and Hollywood good looks, Red understood completely how a lot of women could fall head over heels for him. But she'd been surprised when her daughter had. Bridge had always been far more sensible about men than any ordinary female.

Red didn't know if Mike had broken her daughter's heart. Bridge never confided anything and Red was loath to believe rumors. But they'd divorced the year that Daniel was born. Red was fairly sure that neither of the children had any memory of when Mom and Dad actually lived together.

Mike grasped each child in a muscled arm and lifted them both off the ground.

"Wait a minute," he told them, feigning astonishment. "You can't be my kids. My kids are little baby kids. You guys are way too grown-up."

"We're your kids, all right," Daniel told him. "You look exactly like I always remembered you."

"You don't think I've grown up at all?" Mike asked him.

Daniel giggled. So did Olivia.

"Let's go," Daniel said. "Let's go see Abuela and the dolphins at SeaWorld and the train at Brackenridge Park and —"

"Whoa, we can't do all of that at once," Mike said.

He glanced over at Red.

"Hey, mama-in-law," he said, offering a wave as a greeting. "You're looking mighty hot to be somebody's grandma."

Olivia caught sight of the glance and frowned, apparently unwilling to share her dad's attention.

"Let's go! Let's go!"

"Come on, Livy, we have to be polite," he answered, dragging both kids closer. "It's good to see you, Red. You been doing all right?"

"Just fine," Red answered.

Mike managed to free one arm and held it out to Cam, who stood slightly behind her. He grasped it and they exchanged names.

"Are you the bartender? What happened to Karl?"

"Karl's still here," Red answered.

"I'm not the bartender," Cam offered as explanation. "I'm the boyfriend."

Mike's eyebrows went up and he looked at Red as if she'd lost her mind.

She returned his glance with one of her own that clearly conveyed the advice that he should mind his own business.

"I guess I better get out of here before I say something I shouldn't," he suggested.

Red waved him off. "Yeah, go on. Get caught up with your kids. We'll talk later."

She waved at them as they drove away. As she turned back toward her apartment, a strange feeling came over her. The relaxing, uncluttered day that she'd longed for now lay before her as an emptiness. Cam had an afternoon commitment to play at Barton Springs, so Red puttered around her place, doing laundry, straightening the apartment.

Around three o'clock she heard a knock on the back gate. Red was concerned, thinking it was Mike and the kids back already, but was more surprised to find Mrs. Ramirez, from the restaurant on Jones Street.

She was a very tiny woman in her mid-fifties. Her dark hair was liberally streaked with gray and cut into a bowl shape that was easy to manage, if not particularly attractive. She was dressed in a casual, loose-fitting dress belted at the waist, with heels that were significantly higher than comfortable for a Sunday afternoon. Carrying a plate of warm conchas — cinnamon-flavored, shell-shaped sweet rolls — her brow was furrowed and her manner concerned.

"I don't know what to do," she told Red. "Everyone has different advice for me. So I thought I'd hear what you are going to do."

Red led her to one of the patio tables in the shade. The afternoon was hot, but a nearby fan at least stirred up a breeze.

"What am I going to do about what?" Red asked her.

"The River Walk extension," Mrs. Ramirez answered. "And the redevelopment of our neighborhood."

"Oh, that," Red replied dismissively. "Yeah, I heard some talk about that. But the folks at city hall are always threatening to change things down here. It'll never happen."

Mrs. Ramirez was momentarily silenced by her response, but then appeared more anxious than before.

"But it *is* happening," she said. "The construction on the river is all the way to the Brooklyn Street bridge already."

Red remembered the bright-orange construction zone that had caught young Daniel's eye.

"They're probably just . . . just . . . well, surveying or something. I don't know what they're doing," Red admitted.

"They are making the river wider and deeper," Mrs. Ramirez told her. "They're going to bring the water-taxi service up past us, all the way to the Pearl Brewery. They've decided to remake Avenue B into houses and condos. The only restaurants they are going to want will be for tourists."

"Your café is the anchor of this neighborhood," Red assured her. "Your place will always be on that corner."

The older woman shook her head. "That is not what I hear from my landlord," she answered. "Last year he raised the rent so high on me. He said he couldn't help it, that it was property tax. This year, he said he will not renew at all. He said there's a buyer that is piecing together our entire block. My landlord is selling, and what the new owner will want from me, I do not know."

Red felt a momentary queasiness as she remembered the higher-priced lease agreement that she had refused to sign. Yes, she had heard the talk, yes, she had seen the construction, but she was still convinced that it couldn't happen. Nobody wanted this piece of town. No one ever had, no one ever would. She was certain of that.

"I'm sure the new owner is just speculating," Red told Mrs. Ramirez. "And the very fact that your landlord wants to take the money while it's offered just tells you that he doesn't think anything will happen, either."

Mrs. Ramirez nodded, but she didn't look convinced.

"My nephew, Maldito, is looking for a place for us on the west side. But there are so many restaurants over there! How could I ever make a place for myself there like I have here? My sister says I'm too old to start over."

"And when did you ever listen to your sister?" Red asked. "Don't move to the west side. Stay right here. All this will blow over and it will be the same as it always was."

Red's upbeat insistence didn't seem to do much for Mrs. Ramirez. As she continued to speculate about the future, she nervously ate all but one of the sweets she'd brought to share.

After she left, Red went through her papers and found the lease agreement that she'd failed to sign. She looked at it in a whole new light. Maybe she should have asked more questions. She'd assumed it was just a typical negotiation over money.

She looked around her little tattered business. It was a great place. A funky place. A family place. It was a place she wanted to be for the rest of her life. No one would ever want to get rid of it.

Red took some comfort in that thought and deliberately tried to push Mrs. Ramirez's revelations out of her mind.

By evening, she'd almost succeeded in not thinking about it at all. Cam showed up at seven-thirty with a sackful of barbecue. He was tired and she was hungry, so their dinner conversation lagged.

It was nearly eight when she heard Mike pull the car into the back. Red hurried to greet them at the gate. But there was not much greeting to be done. Both children, run ragged with activity and overfed on junk food, were sound asleep in the car.

"Can you get Livy?" he asked her.

Red nodded, but she didn't attempt to carry the girl. She shook her awake and led her, zombielike, across the patio and up the apartment stairs. Mike followed with a still-sleeping Daniel slung against his shoulder.

In the bedroom, Mike laid Daniel on the

bed and pulled off the boy's sneakers. "I'll . . . I'll let you do whatever needs to be done," he said and made a hasty retreat.

Red wasn't exactly sure what had to be done. She led Olivia into the bathroom, removed her clothes and made her sit on the toilet as she washed the little girl's face and hands with a washcloth. She brought her a nightgown and then led her back to the bed and tucked her in.

Red glanced across at Daniel. He was lying there so peacefully. Red was torn. She hated to disturb him, but she remembered how long Bridge had wet the bed and how much her young daughter had been humiliated and embarrassed by that failing. With a sigh, she dragged Daniel up and into the bathroom.

By the time both children were snugly in bed, Red realized that she was tired herself. But she headed downstairs, eager to hear the plans for the days ahead.

The guys were not on the patio, but she could see a light on in the bar and she followed it inside. The two men sat on either end of the bar, a bottle of Shiner Bock in front of each.

"What's the deal? Nobody drinks draft anymore?" she asked, indicating the bottles.

"Do you want me to draw you one?" Cam asked.

She waved him away as she went behind the bar. "No, thanks, I'll fix something for myself," she said.

A half minute later she heard Mike chuckle and glanced over at him.

"Are you still drinking iced tea disguised in a highball glass?" he asked her. Without giving her time to answer, he directed his words to Cam. "Did you know that about her? The woman is a genuine teetotaler. Don't touch a drop of alcohol."

Mike's words were spoken like some kind of challenge, as if to say, *You think you know this woman, but I know her better.* Red found herself hoping that it wasn't true.

"Don't act like you're an expert on me," Red told him. "It's not like you're my ex, Mike. Just my ex-son-in-law."

Mike shrugged. "Okay," he agreed. "I just wanted sonny-boy to know the lay of the land. You've thrown away more guys like him than he's ever even met."

Denial sprang to Red's tongue. She wanted to tell Mike that there was nobody like Cam and that what she had with him was very special, but she feared it wasn't true. Instead of defending herself, defending Cam, she changed the subject.

"We could talk all night about your ex-wife's mama," Red said. "But I'm more interested in your own mama. How's she doing?"

Mike nodded. "She's still not able to do any talking, but the doctors are pretty hopeful. She seemed thrilled to see the kids and they pretty much filled the room with chatter, so she didn't need to say anything."

"That's good."

"Yeah, I think so," he agreed. "They're moving her to a rehabilitation facility on Monday or Tuesday. It's by the medical center, but I'm hoping you can get the kids over there to see her while she's there."

His words momentarily caught Red up short. "How long are the kids going to be here?" she asked.

"Until Bridge gets back," Mike said. "My mother is not going to be in any shape to take them."

"I wasn't thinking about her, I was thinking about you," Red said. "Aren't you going to take them?"

Mike made a humorless chortling sound that was almost a snort.

"Yeah, I'm sure that's what Bridge is hoping," he said. "Livy probably was a genuine accident, but she knew I didn't want kids. She got pregnant with Daniel anyway. I told her then and I'd tell her now, I'm not going to be trapped into some kind of daddy thing. That's not a life I'm interested in."

Red's reaction was sharp and angry. "Those kids are crazy about you. And you act like you're crazy about them."

He shrugged. "Hey, they're great kids. I'm not saying otherwise. But I'm not a home-and-hearth kind of guy. What I want is more cheap beer and cheaper women."

Mike chuckled, but Red didn't find it at all funny.

"Look, they deduct child support from my every paycheck," he said. "I think that's penalty enough for not keeping it in my pants. Bridge was the one who was so desperate for a family she had to grow her own. I guess that's your fault, Red, so maybe granny duty is a just punishment."

To: buildabetterbridge@citymail.com
August 25 11:09 a.m.
From: Livy156@ABrats.org
Subject: I HATE HER!

I cant stand that she is my grandmother. She is the worse person in the whole world and I know now for sure why we never saw her much because you would not want usto be like her. She is so bad.

Daddy was here. It was like heaven. We went to Fiesta Texas and he rode the big roller coaster with me. Daniel was too short and he was scared too. We got to see Abuela and she squeezed my hand like she didn't want to let me go. She loves me so much. And Daddy loves me too. He is so great and he wants us so much. He has to go back to Korea and he wanted to take us with him, but the Bad Gramma said NO! I hate her so much. I will never forgive her. Ever. Ever.

When you get home I want to never come back to her stinky bar ever. I hate being here. Dont worry. I'm not running away or anything. Somebody has to take care of Daniel. The red witch cant do it. I remember how you said that you do what you must because you have to. I will do what I have to too.
Miss you.
Livy

7

Red gave the kids the news first thing the next day. The reaction to staying with her was about what she expected. Olivia called her a "mean old witch" and Daniel retreated into Spanish only, curling himself into a tiny ball on his chair. Nobody ate a bite of breakfast and morning ablutions were exceptionally noisy with all the slamming doors.

By the time Cam showed up about eleven, Red was grateful to see him.

"I've got some pretty unhappy campers," she told him. She didn't have a moment to even explain to him what had happened before Olivia piped in.

"Cam, please take us to the library," she pleaded. "Please, please."

He looked at Red for guidance.

"Do you have time?" she asked him.

"Absolutely."

"I would really appreciate it," she said.

After they were gone, Red tried to pull her thoughts and her plans together. This was really happening. She was going to have to keep these kids with her for the next four months and she needed to figure out how to do that. She was not a woman who had ever backed down from anything that had to be faced. She managed bigger challenges, just by breaking them down into smaller jobs to be accomplished.

Seated on the patio, she listened to the sound of the river nearby as she made a list of everything that was needed immediately.

Sitter
School
Home

The last she circled and drew an arrow to the top of the list. She remembered the tacky roach-infested apartment in Irish Flats where she and Bridge had lived. She needed to do better than that.

She was still thinking and tapping her pencil when Cam came back alone.

"Where are the kids?"

"I left them with Mrs. Ramirez," he said. "They were both starving and you know how she likes to feed people."

"Good," Red said, nodding.

Cam glanced at her list before he sat down. "So I guess these are your immediate needs with the kids," he said. "What can I do to help you?"

Red shook her head. "I'm still thinking that you should move along before you get yourself in deeper than you want to be."

Cam hesitated for a long moment. "I'm thinking that you are going to be a lot busier," he said. "So I am going to make myself a bit more scarce."

Red forced a smile to her face. He was bowing out after all. She'd expected it. It would be crazy for him not to. And she knew that once he was gone, he'd never find his way back to her again. There was an aching sense of loss within her that she deliberately ignored.

"It's only a few months and then Bridge will be back and things will be back to normal."

He gave a slow nod that wasn't completely convinced.

"One thing I've got to ask," he said. "Why did you let the kids think that *you* were keeping them here, instead of their dad letting them go?"

She shrugged. "I'm just their grandmother," she answered.

"What does that mean?"

"It means . . ." She tried to put her instinct into words. "It means that if they get angry with me, resent me, hate me, well, that's no big deal."

Cam let that answer soak in for a moment. "But if they get angry, resentful and hateful to their dad, it is a big deal."

"Right."

Cam shook his head. "I'm not sure Miguel Lujan deserves what you're doing for him."

Red gave an incredulous sniff of disdain. "I'm not doing anything for that sorry bastard," she said. "Or maybe I am. I'm buying him a little time to smarten up, grow up, before it's too late for any of it to matter. But that's just coincidental."

"You're doing it for the kids?"

"Children have a right to think the best of their parents," Red said. "Believe me, they always learn soon enough how flawed they really are."

"You sound like you speak from experience."

She laughed humorlessly. "From both sides. I've been the flaw finder and the flawed."

Cam's eyebrow went up slightly and Red knew that she'd revealed more than she should. She didn't want questions. Especially from a guy who was on his way out.

"I think these two kids have already got my number," she told him. "You know what Daniel calls me? Abuela Mala."

"Bad Grandmother?" Cam translated and then burst out laughing.

"You would think it's funny!" she said, although she was smiling, as well. "We'd better go down and get the kids or I definitely will have proved Daniel right."

"In a minute," he said. "First, I'd like to offer something."

Red looked at him, surprised.

"I know how you hate to take help from anybody for any reason," he said. "You certainly hate taking anything from men. So don't think this is from me to you. It's more from me to the kids."

"What do you mean?"

"Well," he said. "The truth is, I have a nice house within walking distance of a great elementary school. I'd like to loan it to you. We could just temporarily swap living arrangements. I could be the bachelor living over the bar. And you can take care of two grandkids in a three-bedroom house in a family neighborhood."

"What would your landlord say about that?" she asked.

"It's my house, Red. I don't have a landlord. I own it."

"You *own* your own house?" Her tone was incredulous.

"Yes, ma'am, I do," he answered. "And I'd be happy to let you borrow it while the kids are with you."

Red stared at her ne'er-do-well cowboy fiddler player with new eyes.

"All the months I've known you, you never said anything about owning a house," she pointed out.

Cam grinned at her and with more than a hint of teasing in his voice he answered, "You never said anything about having a daughter or grandchildren, so I guess we're even. It's my grandmother's house. She left it to me."

"Oh," Red replied, nodding, as if inheritance explained everything. "So where is this family-friendly property of yours?"

"Not far from here," he answered. "It'll be a really quick commute for you."

"And you're sure the school is okay?" Red asked, thinking again of the nearby Irish Flats neighborhood.

"It's excellent. I went to elementary there, and see how well I turned out."

He was joking, but Red detected some hedging on his part. There was something he just wasn't saying.

"We'd better catch up with the kids," he said, jumping to his feet. "I'm getting pretty hungry myself."

"I haven't said yes yet," Red pointed out, making no move to leave.

Cam reviewed the obvious. "You can't keep these kids above the bar," he said. "There's not enough room and it's too busy and noisy at night. If you're in my house, you won't actually have to move out. You can just live in my place with my stuff. It's a very good idea."

She nodded. "But there is something about this that you're not telling me."

He shrugged. "There is," he admitted. "But it's not a bad thing. It actually might be a good thing."

She waited, not even bothering to voice the question.

"My house is in Alamo Heights," he said.

"Alamo Heights?" Her tone was incredulous.

8

Alamo Heights had the distinction of being the first suburb of San Antonio. At the turn of the century the downtown streetcar line had been extended to the area and by the 1920s it was an incorporated city. For the most part, it weathered good times and bad a bit better than the city of San Antonio that surrounded it. Now it was considered a tony, upper-class enclave for architects, lawyers and old San Antonians who wanted to be close to downtown but near the country club.

"Look, I know I'm not the most sensitive or experienced grandmother in America," Red told Cam. "But even *I* know you don't plunk down a couple of little brown kids into white-bread heaven."

"It's not really like that," he insisted. "We have African-Americans. We have Hispanics."

Red nodded. "Rich African-Americans.

Rich Hispanics."

"Just see the place before you judge," he insisted.

Red didn't want to see the place. She didn't care to take the time to judge. The smart thing to do, she was certain, was reject it outright. Cam was correct in his estimation of her. She *didn't* like to accept gifts from men she was sleeping with. That sort of thing always ended badly. She was sure of that. But looking at the short-term future for herself and the kids, Cam's solution did seem like a good one.

She didn't want to have to drive too far. A temporary trade of her beloved CRX for Bridge's camo-Prius was the smart thing to do. It got good gas mileage, but still driving to and from work was going to be a new expense, along with so many others.

The Hearts Apart organization at the base had helped her locate a babysitter, a young mom with a nursing newborn. She needed a job while her husband was deployed, but wanted to bring her baby along. It was perfect for her to supervise Olivia and Daniel in the evenings when the bar was open.

And, of course, there was the upcoming school year. The Family Assistance Center had all the statistics on the local schools and Alamo Heights was highly ranked.

So a few days later, with the children still sulking, Red loaded everyone into the car and headed up Broadway.

At least Olivia was now speaking to her, though the tearful goodbye with her dad could still be heard in her every word. Daniel was only speaking Spanish, so as they drove northward, it fell to Cam to make most of the conversation.

Red was actually surprised at how well he was doing. She typically thought of him as the strong, silent type. Chattiness had never seemed to be his strong suit, but he was certainly making an effort with the kids. She was not sure, however, that asking lots of questions about their big day with their dad was exactly the way to go. As she drove through the small, retro commercial area that was downtown Alamo Heights, she tried to change the subject.

"This place sure has a lot of mom-and-pop stores. How do they stay in business?"

Cam shrugged. "Some of them don't," he said. "It's hard to keep the prices comparable to what they charge in big box stores. But I think people like to buy local if they can. Turn left here."

Red followed his directions and turned down an expansive boulevard that curved through lush green trees and grass. Initially she thought it was a park, until she noticed the driveways. The hair stood up on the back of Red's neck. This place was very different from the world in which she'd made herself comfortable. And it was also very different from the west-side *barrio* of the children's *abuela* or even the military housing they'd shared with their mother.

Cam was so familiar with the neighborhood that he apparently didn't notice. The kids were focused on their own discontent and not paying attention. But Red was sharply aware that, despite the short drive, this neighborhood was a very long way from the corner of Eight and B. The profusion of plants and flowers and the elegant homes set back from the street gave her the strange sense that the location was uninhabited. As they rounded a curve, however, that notion was put to rest.

A large, robust man of later years, wearing a golf shirt and shorts, was ambling along the sidewalk with a pair of primped and prissy Pekingese. With a broad smile and a raised hand, he offered a greeting.

"Who was that?" Red asked.

"Huh?" Cam looked up and then glanced back toward the man they'd passed. "I don't know," he said.

"He waved at us."

Cam shrugged. "Everybody knows everybody," he answered. "Of course he waved. He probably couldn't even see us."

Somehow that didn't give her comfort.

The roadway continued to curve like the dry creek bed it had once been. Cam finally directed her to turn off on a side street and then an even narrower avenue. At least here the houses and yards were smaller.

"This is it, here on the left," he said. "Just pull in to the driveway."

The house he indicated, like the ones on either side, was far from new, but its butter-yellow paint and unscarred white trim kept it looking fresh and cheery. The front door was centered in a wide covered porch that wrapped around one corner and sported an array of wicker furniture, as well as a swing.

"This is it," Cam announced. "My home sweet home."

"It looks kind of like Abuela's house," Olivia said.

Red didn't really see the comparison. Granted, it was quite modest in comparison to some of the magnificent homes they'd passed and the style was similar to many homes on the west side. But it was clean and scrubbed-looking, to the point of drabness. Still, if the kids found something positive or familiar about that, then so much the better.

They got out of the car and went inside. Cam fumbled momentarily with the keys and Red had the distinct impression that he was a bit nervous, as if stepping over this threshold was more than just going into his house.

Red refused to see it as anything else as he held the door and she walked inside. She glanced around the living room, taking it in.

"My decor is sort of my stuff, mixed with the old things I've inherited," he told Red. "So it's not exactly the kind of bachelor crib that kicks, ah . . . armadillo."

He chuckled at his own little joke.

Red didn't laugh. She was still trying to get her mind around the living room. She hadn't really thought about what Cam's place might look like, but if she had imagined something, she would have thought sleek and sparse. It would either be all industrial stainless steel or it would be unobtrusively modern. Instead, the cozy stuffed sofa and upholstered reading chairs were traditional and homey. Where Red might have anticipated old concert posters and oversize flags to cover bare walls, tastefully framed art was displayed instead.

"Uh . . . nice," she said inadequately.

The adjacent dining room was also visible, its drop-leaf mahogany table an obvious leftover from earlier occupants. Beyond that, Red could glimpse one corner of a gleaming white kitchen.

"The stereo stuff is all in here," Cam said, opening a cabinet on the interior wall. "The CDs are alphabetical by artist. You guys are welcome to use all this," he said to the children. "And . . . I guess we'll have to move the TV." He opened the top cabinet to reveal a small television inside.

"Why do you have the television up there?" Red asked.

"It keeps me from wasting too much time," he answered. "You'd be surprised how few things on the air are compelling enough to make you stand up to watch."

Red saw Olivia and Daniel share a glance that clearly indicated their opinion.

"The main bedroom is in here." Cam led them into the hallway, indicating the first doorway. "This is perfect for you, Red. When you come in from work, you won't wake up Livy and Daniel."

Red glanced around the room. It was obviously a masculine room, but it was classy-looking, she thought. There was no sense of it being a bachelor's passion pit. It was cozy, and while her eyes viewed that favorably, she couldn't help comparing it to the stark utility of her own bedroom over the bar. The only expense she'd been willing to incur for decoration had been the ugly but effective blackout curtains.

"It's got a pretty good closet and I thought we'd do halves," Cam said. "I'll take half of my clothes to the apartment and you can bring half of your clothes here."

Red didn't comment.

Cam quickly clarified. "I didn't mean it as a way to comingle our stuff," he said. "I'm just thinking about cutting down on the moving."

She nodded slowly.

"You guys are down this way," Cam said, addressing the children. "You can each have your own room. But they're right next to each other."

Red followed them past the bathroom to the far end of the hallway, where one corner had two open doors.

"I thought this room would be good for you, Daniel," he said. "It's my guest room, where all my buddies hang out when they stay over. You kind of fall into that group."

Daniel's chin rose a little higher and he puffed his chest out slightly.

"We're going to clean out these shelves and drawers and bring all your things from your *abuela*'s house to put there," he continued. "This used to be my room when I was your age."

Red was surprised at that statement. "You lived here when you were growing up?"

He nodded. "My mom and I lived here for about ten years," he said.

"Your parents were divorced, like ours?" Olivia asked, sounding almost excited at the prospect.

"No," Cam answered. "My mom was sick for a while, so we lived here."

It was a simple explanation and he smiled as he said it, but Red detected more to the story than was being said.

"Olivia, I want you to have the music room," he said, stepping into the door on his left. "This is where I practice. I can move most of this out of here to give you space, and there's a bed I can bring down from the attic. It has little fairies painted all over it. Kind of girlie, but it looks pretty cool."

Red watched Olivia take in her surroundings. She ignored the uncomfortable-looking folding chairs, the music stands and the various guitars, violins and the electronic keyboard. Instead, the girl seemed drawn to the small computer desk near the window. She'd hardly spoken since they walked into the house, but she did now.

"Are you taking this with you?" she asked.

"The computer?" Cam shrugged. "I have a laptop. I can leave it here, if it won't be in your way."

"It won't be in my way if I can use it," she said.

Her comment bordered on rudeness and it was on the tip of Red's tongue to scold her. But Cam seemed more amused than offended.

"If it's sitting here, I wouldn't want it to become just a giant paperweight," he answered.

"Do you have Internet?"

"Sure."

Olivia nodded. "Okay, leave it here," she said.

Cam laughed and attempted a joke. "So you like the Internet?" he teased. "Should I start calling you Surfer Girl?"

Olivia didn't appreciate the humor, but she didn't comment on it, either.

"Okay," she said, as if making an announcement. "Daniel and I can live here."

Her presumption that such a decision was hers to make was defiantly meant to needle Red.

Cam turned with a stern expression and a teasing glint in his eye to the children's grandmother. "Does that work for you, Abuela Mala?" he asked.

Red huffed in lieu of a reply.

To: buildabetterbridge@citymail.com
September 3 7:12 p.m.
From: Livy156@ABrats.org
Subject: The New Place

Hi Mom! Thanks for the emails. It is great logging in and seeing all these from you. We moved into the boyfriends house. And guess what? I am righting to you on his desktop. This is what we got to get, Mom. We got to get are own internet at home so I can always right to you. I guess tho when your home I dont have to right you ha! ha!

My room is nice and I have all my bears and my clothes now. I got a bed that somebody painted with tiny fairies like the size of bugs all over. Its weird but I like it.

I like the house mostly. We have a backyard with trees and stuff. But some old lady in the yard behind us keeps snooping on us. She yelled at Daniel to get out of the yard, but I told her it was our yard and none of her business. I know that was rude Mom but she scared Daniel so she deserved it!

We drove by the school. It is brown. That is all I know about it. School starts next week so I guess I will find out. I won't miss my friends from last spring cause I hardly knew them. But I still remember my school before.

Our babysitter is named Kelly. She has a baby girl name Kendra. I guess Kendra misses her dad like I miss you. Dont worry about Daniel and me. I am taking care of us fine.

Livy

9

Red stood in front of the full-length mirror in Cam's Alamo Heights bedroom and assessed her appearance. The ill-fitting gray suit she'd bought at the discount store disguised her appearance to the point of dumpiness and washed out the complexion that was already suffering from considerably less makeup application. She'd constrained her gorgeous red hair into a tight updo. It was not a good look for her, although she did appear slightly taller, even in very sensible low-heeled pumps. It gave her face a narrowness that somehow seemed unhappy, repressed.

That's exactly what's required, she reminded herself. Her intention was to blend in. In a scrubbed-clean little neighborhood like this one, she was pretty sure that joy should be carefully contained.

Wham! Wham! Wham!

"We're going to be late!" Olivia insisted as

she knocked loudly at the door.

"It's only five minutes away. How late can we be?" Red answered.

"It's the last afternoon of the last day of pre-enrollment," Olivia shot back through the doorway. "So we're almost already late."

She took one last long look in the mirror. The reflection was unpleasant, but she did look sufficiently grandmotherly, she assured herself. She grabbed the file of papers atop the bureau and headed out with all the enthusiasm of facing a firing squad.

Red had put off this day as long as she could. Moving into the house, getting settled in and establishing a routine for her work and the children was her priority. Her interaction with her new surroundings had been minimal. But classes began on Monday and if she wanted Olivia and Daniel to start school on time, she had no choice but to make the effort to enroll them.

She was not alone in her reluctance. Every time the word *school* was mentioned, Daniel shrank into a protective ball. He didn't want to go anywhere or see anyone.

Olivia, on the other hand, could hardly wait for the school bell to ring. She'd talked eagerly about it to her *abuela* on their last visit. The old woman still couldn't speak, but Olivia didn't appear to need any help with the conversation. Red had waited out in the rehab-facility corridor while the girl had giggled and gushed hopefully about the future. Only the silence in the car on the ride home suggested that perhaps not all of her optimism was genuine.

"Okay, I'm ready," Red announced as she stepped into the living room.

Daniel looked very small, curled in one corner of the oversize reading chair. Olivia was pacing.

"Let's go," the girl responded. She couldn't get the door open fast enough. She motioned for her little brother, who obediently followed her, albeit with much reluctance.

The school was only a few short blocks away and Red insisted on walking so that she could be sure Olivia and Daniel knew the way. That it took more time was only a side benefit.

The three walked together up the sidewalk to the corner doorway of Cambridge Elementary. Red couldn't remember the last time she'd been inside a school building, but from the moment she stepped across the threshold, the familiar smells of blackboard chalk and library paste brought back memories that were young and happy and hopeful. Deliberately she cast those thoughts off. It was never good to start remembering. She had the real world to face.

"This looks like the office," she said of a doorway on the left. She held the door open allowing the children to go first. Olivia walked through without a qualm, while Daniel clung to his sister's hand.

"May I help you?" the woman at the desk inquired, without raising her eyes from the computer screen she was viewing.

A small wooden plaque on the woman's desk identified her as Ms. Sorenson.

"I'm here to enroll my grandchildren in school," Red answered. "I have an appointment with Ms. Kilheeny."

She smiled as if to welcome them, but never even glanced in their direction. "Take a seat," she told them. "I'll let her know that you're here."

Red glanced around and spotted the row of chairs. All three took seats, though the children sat as far as possible from their grandmother.

Red heard Daniel whisper something in Spanish to Olivia. His sister replied a bit sharply.

"What did he say?" Red asked.

"He wanted to know if this is where you sit when you're in trouble," she answered.

"I told him we weren't *ever* going to find out."

Red almost smiled, but found that she was still too edgy to manage it.

They waited only a few minutes before Ms. Kilheeny appeared. She ushered them into an office stacked with files. Fit, trim and all business, she looked over the paperwork that Red had gotten from the base, as well as the children's past school records. She hardly looked in Red's direction, who wondered why she'd taken such pains with her wardrobe.

Ms. Kilheeny directed several general questions to the children. Olivia answered politely and respectfully and earned an approving smile.

The questions for Daniel were also answered, but in whispered Spanish.

The woman looked directly at Red for the first time. "He doesn't speak English?"

"Yes, yes, of course he does," she answered and glanced over at her grandson. Once again he'd drawn his knees up to his chest and scrunched his shoulders down into a hiding position.

"Sit up straight!" Ms. Kilheeny said a little too sharply.

Red stiffened her own spine, as if the admonition was meant for her.

"He understands perfectly," Red assured the woman. "He is just choosing to speak Spanish."

The woman appeared skeptical.

"We can put him in an ESL class," she said. "English as a second language."

"English isn't his second language," Red insisted. "This isn't about language, it's about . . ."

Red's explanation trailed off. She didn't know what it was about. She didn't know these kids or what their problems were.

"Look, it's a summer thing," she said, leaning forward to add sincerity to the lie she was forming to tell. "I wanted him to improve his Spanish, so I bet him he couldn't speak just Spanish all summer long. If he makes it until class starts on Monday, he wins."

From the corner of her eye she detected both Olivia and Daniel staring at her in openmouthed disbelief. Ms. Kilheeny, however, was delighted.

"Oh, I love at-home educational motivation!" she gushed. "I'm sure these children are going to fit in here just perfectly."

Red smiled back at the woman, pleased. As Ms. Kilheeny continued through the paperwork, Red relaxed back in the chair and caught the children looking at her.

Daniel's expression was confusion. But Olivia's spoke volumes of silent disapproval.

Red gave a slight shrug. Maybe she should have tried to explain why a boy with a mother at war, a father far away and a grandmother who'd had a stroke could choose not to speak his first language. But Red lived a life where she tried not to owe people explanations. She had no desire to change that now.

"So all of this seems fine," Ms. Kilheeny said, still shuffling through the papers. "I'll put Olivia in class with Ms. Gomez. And Daniel . . . let's see . . . Daniel, we'll put you in Mrs. Reardon's first grade. There's a shortage of boys there, you can make up the numbers."

"Great," Red said.

"So that looks like everything . . . Oh, wait." Ms. Kilheeny glanced up at Red. "I'll need your proof of residence."

"Oh sure," Red answered, pulling open her purse and fishing through it for her driver's license. She handed the card over and the administrator glanced at it.

"No, this has your old address on it," she said. "I need something that proves you reside within the school district. Your mortgage papers or rental contract, even a water or electric bill will do."

Red stared at the woman for a moment. "I don't have a written contract," she said. "And my . . . uh . . . my landlord pays the utilities. But we live right up the street here. We're within walking distance."

Ms. Kilheeny nodded and smiled. "Yes, of course, Mrs. Cullens, I just need something official to verify that."

"I don't have anything official."

"Well, we have to have something or we can't enroll the children."

"We have to be enrolled!" Olivia insisted. "It's no good starting late. If you're not there the first day, then you're a new kid and that's twice as hard."

Red didn't know if Olivia's desperate plea was meant for Ms. Kilheeny or herself, but the woman continued to simply look at her for an answer.

"Could I . . . uh . . . could I go outside and make a phone call?" she asked.

"Yes, you do that," Ms. Kilheeny said, "and I'll dot the i's and cross the t's on the rest of the paperwork." Her smile was still pleasant, but Red knew that she'd messed up by not having some piece of paper from Cam. She was sure that other grandmothers would never fail to have everything that was required.

"You kids wait right here, I'll be right

back," she said.

Red hurried out of the office and through the front door. Her cell phone didn't actually require outside use, but she was in dire need of fresh air.

The phone rang twice before he picked up. She quickly explained her problem to him.

"So, do you have any ideas? Can you write me up some kind of rental agreement or something?"

"Sure, I'll run by there," he said. "I'm on my way out of town, but I can swing by."

"Out of town? Where are you going?"

"We're playing Schroeder Hall tonight. I told you that."

"Oh yeah, right. You did tell me that."

He chuckled ruefully. "You know, Brian's girlfriends always keep up with where he's supposed to be and make sure he's there," Cam said. "I guess they're checking up to see he's not running around on them."

Red knew he was teasing her, but she was in no mood for it. "We're supposed to be seeing each other less," she reminded him. "So you being able to see someone else would be pretty much standard. I don't need fidelity, just a rental contract."

There was a hesitation on the other end of the line.

"I'll be there in ten minutes," he said before hanging up.

Red snapped her phone closed and walked back inside. In the outer office, once again Ms. Sorenson didn't notice her and she walked directly into Ms. Kilheeny's office.

"My . . . my landlord said he would be here in ten minutes."

"Fine," the school administrator said.

Olivia let out her breath as if she'd been holding it the whole time.

"While we're waiting, why don't I give you a little tour of the school. The children can see their classrooms. And you can learn your way around, as well."

"Okay," Red said.

The school was bigger than Red had imagined from looking at the outside. It was clean and neat and inviting. As they walked through the hallways, Ms. Kilheeny pointed out the amenities of the ninety-year-old building. Although her words were mostly directed to Red, it was Olivia who asked all the questions and made all the comments. They visited the library, the cafeteria and the gym as well as the classrooms for both Olivia and Daniel.

At Olivia's room, Ms. Kilheeny explained at great length all the new equipment and all the technical savvy that was fostered and encouraged.

"This is our new 'Elmo,' " the woman said with a girlish giggle, indicating a mechanical arm attached to the ceiling. "That's short for elevated monitor. It lets our teachers share what's on their computer with the whole class."

She directed her conversation to Red, possibly because Olivia wasn't paying attention to her anymore.

The girl walked around the room, silent, focused, intent. She surveyed everything critically, noting how the desks were arranged and what kind of markers were at the computer stations. She looked at all the bulletin-board presentations and the books on the shelves, the empty cage for the class pet and the stack of hall passes on the edge of the teacher's desk.

Long after Ms. Kilheeny fell silent, Olivia was still looking the place over. Finally she headed for the door.

"Fine," she declared, as if the adults were waiting upon her critique. "I can learn here."

In Daniel's classroom they discovered his teacher, Mrs. Reardon, on her hands and knees surrounded by plastic containers in primary colors.

"This is Daniel," Ms. Kilheeny announced. "He's going to be in your class on Monday."

The woman's attention immediately went to the little boy, and her smile was broad.

"Hi there, Daniel!" she said, louder and with more enthusiasm than was truly necessary. "I'm just putting together some task boxes. You want to help me?"

The child gave only one uncertain glance toward his sister before stepping forward and settling in on the floor next to his teacher.

"Mrs. Reardon has been teaching first grade here for fourteen years," Ms. Kilheeny assured Red. "And twice she's been our school's choice for Teacher of the Year. You won't have to worry about your grandson. Kids are crazy about her." This last statement was added in a whisper.

They hung around the brightly decorated room for several minutes as Daniel helped his teacher. He did whatever she told him without comment. Red was grateful that the language issue didn't come up.

Olivia got bored and was tapping her foot before they finally left, but Daniel seemed happier and more open. As they made their way down the hallway, both children appeared reassured and eager for Monday morning.

Red was eager, too. She figured that with their day schedule and her evening schedule, she would hardly see them at all. And that would be for the best for everyone.

She was just settling into the satisfaction of this thought when a familiar chuckle drifted around the corridor. When they turned the corner, Red could see Cam standing in the entrance hall with Ms. Sorenson. The two were obviously old friends.

"Do you remember that night we decided to float Dolph Carniby's fishing dingy through Brackenridge Park?"

Cam laughed. "Do I remember? I have perfect recall. Running like hell from the park police. But, you were far too drunk to remember anything about that night. There's got to be a rule for strawberry margaritas. You drink one. Only a true drinking novice would suck down ten."

"It wasn't ten, it was only eight."

"Only eight? Oh, well then, that was fine."

Ms. Sorenson laughed so hard she snorted in a very unprofessional manner.

Beside Red, Ms. Kilheeny, who had certainly heard every word as clearly as Red herself, cleared her throat loudly.

The two younger people glanced up in their direction. Ms. Sorenson looked caught. Cam, on the other hand, smiled, completely comfortable. Then his eyes lowered from Red's own to the children with her.

"Hey, guys! So, whatcha think about my school?"

The two ran up to him as if he was actually somebody to them. Daniel was chattering in indecipherable Spanish and Olivia was giving her own rundown as she translated.

Cam squatted to be on their eye level and listened with both interest and intent. Red envied his easy quality with them.

"So, it's all going to work out great, you're thinking?"

Daniel nodded, but Olivia had a caveat.

"We need proof of residency before they can officially enroll us," she explained gravely.

He nodded. "I hear ya," he answered. "Red and I are going to work this out with the folks here and you're going to school on Monday, I promise. Now, have you seen my favorite part of the school?"

They both shook their heads with questions in their eyes.

"It's down that sidewalk and around the corner," Cam answered.

"What's down there?" Olivia asked.

"The playground, of course."

The children giggled.

"Why don't you two run over there and check it out," he suggested. "Olivia, you'll have to watch out for your brother, but then you always do. Red and I will catch up with you in a couple of minutes."

The kids agreed and scampered off, excited.

As he rose to a standing position, Ms. Sorenson voiced the same thought that was in Red's mind.

"Cam, I had no idea you are so good with kids," she said. "You ought to get around to having some."

He gave her that gorgeous grin that always made Red weak in the knees.

"Aw, you people with kids are always trying to lure the rest of us into your camp," he said. "I'm going to leave all the procreation stuff up to you and Cody. You two are really good at it. For me, well, it's much more fun to be a kid with the kids than be a parent to anyone."

His explanation sounded exactly like something he would say, but Red was beginning to have real doubts about the simple-cowboy explanations of himself that he was always throwing around.

As if to quickly move on to a new subject, he reached out his hand to Ms. Kilheeny. "Excuse me, I don't believe we've met."

There was a flutter of hasty, embarrassed introductions.

"Campbell Early? Are you Phyllis Early's nephew?"

His smile never wavered. "Yes, I am."

"I've heard wonderful things about you," Ms. Kilheeny told him. "Phyllis and I are in DRT together."

When the woman caught sight of Red's blank look, she quickly offered an explanation. "Daughters of the Republic of Texas. Phyllis Early and I are both part of the organization. Of course, I'm only an associate member."

This last was stated with a slight discomfiture that Red had no clue about, so she merely smiled and nodded.

Ms. Kilheeny hurried on. "Phyllis tells me that you're a musician. A violinist."

"I'm a fiddler," Cam replied.

"Oh, I'm sure you're being too modest," the woman insisted.

Ms. Sorenson agreed. "He was first chair in the youth symphony for three years. Nobody ever does that."

Cam's expression did not alter in the slightest, but he changed the subject abruptly.

"So, what exactly do you need from me to establish residence for the children?"

124

"Oh, a copy of the rental agreement should be fine."

"Truth is, there isn't a rental agreement," Cam answered.

Red was very aware of her lover's body language. He was loose and casual and comfortable and she knew he was going to say too much.

"We . . . we should write one up," she piped in immediately. "It's something that we should have done earlier, but we can certainly do it now."

Cam was oblivious to her statement. "Oh, she's not really renting," he continued to explain. "While her daughter is deployed and she has the kids, we've just swapped houses. Her place doesn't have a yard or even an extra bedroom."

Ms. Kilheeny took a startled intake of breath.

"Cam, that is just so like you," Ms. Sorenson said. "When we were kids, he was always the one we could count on to feed the strays and carry the injured birds to the vet."

"That is *so* generous," Ms. Kilheeny agreed. "And patriotic, too, when you think about it. Phyllis is right, you are an exceptional young man."

Cam was shaking his head and opened his

mouth to contradict her. Instead, Red jumped into the conversation again.

"He truly is," she agreed. "And for that very reason, I must have a lawyer draw up some kind of paper for damage or liability at least."

"Yes, absolutely," Ms. Kilheeny concurred. "Although I don't know where you could find a lawyer to do that this afternoon."

"We don't need a lawyer," Cam assured them both with a laugh. He reached out and took Red's hand, pulling her close beside him, before wrapping his arm around her waist. "You've got the wrong idea about this. I'm not doing some favor for a stranger because her daughter is overseas. Red is my girlfriend. We're a couple."

Ms. Sorenson's reaction was to burst out laughing, assuming it was a joke. But then slowly, as the punch line never arrived, her slack-jawed, poleaxed expression of horror mirrored Ms. Kilheeny's.

Less than ten minutes later, having conducted the rest of their business in a very quiet, professional manner, Cam and Red were outside the school and walking down the sidewalk toward the playground.

"I can't believe you did that!"

"What?" Cam's expression was genuinely puzzled.

"You blathered about our . . . our hookup in front of those women."

He shook his head. "Don't worry about it. It's a small town, so everybody would have figured it out. But it's also in a big city, so nobody is going to be scandalized. We might as well get it out there, so those who worry about that kind of thing can start getting over it."

"Those who worry about that kind of thing would more than likely have never guessed," Red said angrily. "I'm old enough to be your mother and those women would have never even suspected. Now you've blown them away with your confession and they won't be able to shut up about it for weeks."

"Since when do you care what people think or talk about? You've been giving the Bronx salute to that stuff since I've known you," Cam said. "And you're not old enough to be my mother."

"I most certainly am. I have a daughter who is twenty-nine."

"So? I'm thirty-one, thirty-one and a half really."

Red stopped abruptly and turned to face him, her expression a mix of humor and incredulity.

"Thirty-one and a half?"

Cam didn't reply, but his face reddened.

"I was fifteen years old the day you were born," Red pointed out. "Do you think that I wasn't sexually active at fifteen?"

Cam's brow furrowed and his jaw set angrily. "I don't know," he answered with even-toned honesty. "How could I know? You don't share anything about yourself. You didn't even tell me about your daughter."

"You don't tell much, either," Red retorted. "I'm finding out all kinds of things about you."

"There's a difference," he answered. "You don't know about me because you were never interested enough to ask."

He glanced ahead at the playground and waved at the kids, then looked back at his van sitting at the curb.

"I've got to go," he said. "I should have been on the road to Schroeder an hour ago. Tell the kids I'll come by to see them this weekend."

"Okay," Red answered, wondering if he would be coming by to see her, too.

"Try not to worry about these people so much," he advised. "They're just people, Red. Just like all the other people you know."

She shook her head to disagree, but she

didn't comment.

He began walking away and then turned back for one more comment.

"And what is with your hair?" he asked. "You look like you're taking styling tips from those polygamous wives."

10

Saturday night, Red stood on her usual perch behind the cash register. But the smile on her face was as fake as the bosoms on the obnoxious drunk currently making a fool of herself with the guys around the billiard table.

Red was dead tired, but she tried hard not to let it show. The place was very crowded tonight and the band, a group of aging Merle Haggard wannabes called Twice-Baked Taters, wasn't quite good enough at their music to keep the audience engaged. She'd be as glad as Olivia when school started on Monday. Then maybe she could get back to getting a few decent hours of sleep. For the last few weeks she was getting to bed at her usual 2:30 to 3:00 a.m., only to wake up when the kids started moving around at seven. She was foggy and cranky, but she couldn't show it. It was her job to be cheerful, but it wasn't easy.

"Do you want me to show her the door?"

"Huh?"

"The cougar," Karl said as he stepped closer, making himself heard over the noise of the crowd and the band out back. "I'd be happy to show her out and she'll thank you in the morning. Nothing more humiliating than having a couple of beers too many and thinking you're just as young as the fellows that look good to you."

Red was immediately defensive. Although she was no regular, there was something about the woman that seemed familiar. Red assumed it was because she was not so different from Red herself.

"Give her a break," she defended. "She's just having a good time. I don't see anything wrong with a gal enjoying herself on a Saturday night."

Karl shrugged. "Except when she's annoying the other customers," he answered. "But it's your call."

It *was* Red's call and she should have made it right then, because less than fifteen minutes later, the woman began to turn sullen and angry. She threw a beer mug at one of the boys and the glass shattered against the wall. It was a miracle that nobody was hurt. Customers immediately headed for the door. Red put her arm around the woman and half led, half dragged her outside.

"Let me go!" the gal demanded. "Get your hands off me!" Her complaints were punctuated by lavish amounts of coarse language and every epithet imaginable. She finally pulled free of Red, but the force of her action threw her off balance and she fell to the sidewalk.

The woman began to cry and Red helped her up. Once back on her feet, she tried to make her way up the street.

"My car's up that way," she said.

"You're not going to be able to drive," Red told her. "Karl's called you a cab. We'll get you a ride home and you can come back and get your car tomorrow."

"It's my car, and I can damn well drive it if I want to," the woman insisted.

"You can drive it tomorrow. Tonight, you're going to let somebody drive you."

"Don't you be telling me what to do!" the woman snarled. "You think you're better than me, but you're not."

"Believe me, I don't think I'm better than anybody."

"You think you're so high and mighty, telling me what I can and can't do. Throwing me out of that trashy place like I'm not good enough. But I know who you are!"

The woman's anger had her reeling and she would have fallen to the sidewalk again if Red hadn't grabbed for her.

"Don't touch me!" the drunk screamed, and aimed an angry slap that Red managed to dodge easily.

"Let's just get you in a cab and get you home," Red answered, wishing that she'd let Karl handle this.

"I know who you are," the woman yelled again. "Do you think you're that far from Piney Woods?"

Red froze.

"You think you're something, but you're just a cheap barmaid in a cheaper honky-tonk. I know who you are. I know all about you. You're just a slutty piece of small-town trash. Did Grayson buy you this place? Hell, at least I did him for free. Of course, he wasn't my brother."

In one motion of anger, adrenaline and self-preservation, Red hurled herself at the woman, slamming her against the wall of the building. She shoved her forearm against the woman's throat, effectively cutting off her ability to speak and most of her ability to breathe. The woman's eyes were wide now, her expression terrified.

"Kenny Grayson was not my brother," Red told the woman through clenched teeth. "He is nothing to me. And he never gave me anything. This place, my life, everything I have I got for myself. Do you understand that?"

The woman made a gasping sound as she tried to speak. Failing that, she nodded in agreement.

"Now, there's a cab coming to get you. You're going to get in it and go home. Tomorrow, you're coming back here to get your car. And then you will never come to this bar again. You won't even drive down this street again. You're not going to mention my name to anybody. You're not even going to say it aloud to yourself. Do you understand me?"

The woman nodded furiously.

"You've got me all wrong," Red assured her. "I am not some fragile East Texas flower. I can take care of myself and my own. If you give me one more word of trouble, I'll sure take care of you. Do you understand my meaning?"

The woman's eyes were huge as she nodded again. This time Red let her go. They stood on the sidewalk together for a couple of minutes without a word passing between them. Red didn't even look in her direction.

When the taxi came around the corner,

Red said matter-of-factly, "Here's your ride."

She walked back into the bar without even making sure that the woman managed to get in the car.

Red went to her perch, but didn't get up on it. "Cover for me," she told Karl.

"Are you all right?" he asked. "Did she give you trouble?"

"I just need to wash the stink of her off my hands," Red answered.

She made her way through the bar, not bothering to smile or talk to anyone. Outside, she went up the stairs without even a glance toward the crowd or the band.

Once in the apartment, she went straight to the bathroom and vomited into the toilet. Then, dropping to her knees on the cold tiles, she began to cry.

In the harsh, unflattering light of the tiny bathroom, her brain begged her, *Don't think about it! Don't think about it!* But the onslaught of memories would not be held back.

Don't think about it! Don't think about it!

Red couldn't think of anything else.

"The whole town knows what a little tramp you are," her mother had screamed at her. "There are men all over town now bragging about doing you."

135

"It's not true. I haven't done it with anyone but him."

"Oh, well, that's okay, then," she had snarled sarcastically. "You're not the town whore, just an everyday, ordinary slut. You are trash. Dirty, worthless trash. He used you like a snot rag, just something to wipe his nose. Now he's thrown you away and laughing about it. The whole town is laughing about it. I will not be dragged down to your level. Let them laugh at you, I won't allow them to laugh at me."

Hundreds of miles and a lifetime away, the words still cut her to the quick. She sobbed fresh pain, not just from the memory of it.

"You are just like your father," her mother had spewed with distaste. "Too low class to ever be a credit to me. I'm better off just cutting my losses."

Red's tears were not for the mother who'd turned her back on her or the private shame and public humiliation she'd suffered. She wasn't crying from the loss of a happy life that might have been so different. Her tears were for Emmaline Cullens, that clever, inquisitive farm girl who'd been the apple of her daddy's eye.

"Red? Are you sick?"

Red gave a startled shriek at the unexpected sight of Cam in the doorway. She sat up straight and scooted herself back against the wall.

"What are you doing here?" Her statement was so accusatory that his tone turned immediately from concerned to defensive.

"I live here, remember," he answered.

Then, clearly deciding action would be better than words, he grabbed a washcloth from the cabinet and dampened it under the hot-water tap. Wringing it out, he knelt on the floor as he handed it to her.

"Wash your face."

"I've got on makeup," she protested.

"What's left of it is nothing to brag about," he answered. "Wash, you'll feel better."

She did and he was right.

Cam got up, rinsed and wrung out the rag again and then seated himself next to her. Red leaned back against the wall and laid the wet cloth across her forehead, heaving a great sigh of relief.

The two of them sat in welcome silence as Red regained her composure.

"Did you get some bad food or do you think you've caught a stomach bug?" he asked finally.

Red opened one eye to glance over at him. His face showed no anxiety, only concern.

"Maybe I'm pregnant," she suggested.

He laughed. "Nope, that's not it."

"You think I'm too old to get pregnant?"

"No. I just know I won't get you pregnant and I trust you not to two-time me."

"Accidents happen."

His grin widened. "I even trust you not to *accidentally* two-time me."

His humor wasn't that funny, but she appreciated levity. That, at least, would keep the subject far from things she never wanted to discuss with anyone.

"I didn't think you were home," she said. "I thought you were playing the Cove tonight."

"I did. We were the warm-up act," he said. "As soon as we finished, I came on back here. I've got to get up early in the morning. I'm going fishing."

"Fishing?"

"Yes, indeed."

"I didn't know you were a fishing guy."

"All guys are fishing guys," he answered. "Just some of us are less drawn to water than others."

"Ah."

"The truth is, Daniel told me that he'd never been. And I don't think you can have a childhood without it."

Red's thoughts flashed back to a creek bank from long ago, her father at her side.

Despite herself, she smiled.

"See," Cam said, reaching out to touch the edge of her curving lip with his thumb. "Every kid needs to have that smile somewhere when he's grown up and things are going wrong."

Red nodded. "Thanks for taking him."

"You're welcome," he said. "In fact, I'll take Olivia with us, too. She didn't seem much interested, but she'll go. And that way you can sleep in late in the morning and catch up on some rest. Maybe avoid coming down with something."

Red sighed again and shook her head. "Cam, someday you're going to make some lucky woman a very good boyfriend."

He raised an eyebrow. "I already make a lucky woman a very good boyfriend."

Red didn't comment one way or the other.

"I've got to get downstairs before Karl sends someone to look for me," she said as she moved to get up.

Cam stayed her with a hand on her thigh. "Wait."

He leaned forward to kiss her, but she pulled away. "I'll taste awful."

He planted his kiss on her temple.

"I just want you to promise me something," he said.

Red stiffened.

"I don't make a lot of promises," she reminded him.

"I know that," he said. "And I know that there are things you just won't tell me. I'm okay with that. I don't understand it, but I'm learning to be okay. But if you're sick, I don't want you to keep it from me."

"I'm not sick," she assured him.

"Good. But if you ever are, I want you to promise me that you'll tell me."

"Sure," she answered, shrugging it off.

Cam continued. "I know there are guys that can't deal with illness. I'm very familiar with that. But I'm not one of those guys."

"Okay." Red dragged the word out until it was almost a question.

"My mom got sick when I was about seven," he told her. "My father didn't want to be around it. So she and I moved in with my grandma. I continued to see him pretty often, but for the next six and a half years, he only came by to see her twice."

"Did he live far away?"

Cam shook his head. "He lived in that house across the back alley from mine," he answered.

As soon as Red realized that her jaw had dropped, she cleared her throat and tried to look unfazed.

"I'm not like that," Cam repeated. "When

things get tough, I want to be there for you. Kids don't scare me. Tough times don't scare me. And sickness doesn't scare me. I'll be here for you, Red. As long as we're together, I'm in a hundred percent."

To: buildabetterbridge@citymail.com
September 5 9:30 a.m.
From: Livy156@ABrats.org
Subject: Gess where I am?

Mom, gess where I am? U will never gess. I am sitting by a tree next to the river. Not the river that is in back of the bar, but farther up nearer to the park. Cam brought us here fishing. I told him I don't like to fish, at least I dont think I do. So he brought his laptop with WIFI and he is letting me use it while him and Daniel fish.

Daniel is not so good at fishing. He keeps getting up and running around. Cam doesn't get mad tho. He is a pretty good friend to Daniel.

School starts tomorrow. That will be so great. Much better than being with the babysitter or Abuela Mala. I think Daniel's teacher will be good. She likes him. And she speaks some Spanish so Daniel wont have to say English unless he want to. Daniel slips into English some times with Cam. Cam acts like he doesnt notice so its cool. For sure the Red person still gets fusstrayted with him. But at least she doesnt yell. She looks like a yeller but so far no.

I am back. Daniel caught a fish and I had to go look at it. He is so happy. I wish you could see him. It would make U happy 2. Cam says it's a perch. He will cook it up for lunch. Is that weird! We can catch it in the river and eat it. Cam says it will be good and he doesnt lie.

I got to go. I told Cam that we cant miss church on Sunday so we are leaving here to go to second mass.

I love you Mom. Dont worry about us. I am taking care of us fine.

Livy

11

School started as it always does and Red found herself sighing with relief at the structure it provided. She managed to drag herself out of bed every morning before eight. She would sit on the front porch, bleary-eyed and dressed in her bathrobe as she sipped coffee and watched the two kids walk the blocks down the street before they turned toward the school.

She always wished them a good day and waved goodbye. It was the only apparent requirement from her. Olivia took care of everything. She got up on her own and made sure Daniel was up, too. She fixed cereal with bananas or berries and toast for their breakfast. And she critiqued her little brother's washing and dressing, insuring that he was clean and appropriate. Then she'd double-check their backpacks, read Daniel the lunch menu so he could opt for peanut butter and jelly if necessary, and keep one young, keen eye on the clock to get to their classes before the bell went off.

The first few days, Red had tried to help. She figured out pretty quickly that her assistance was unwanted and unneeded. Olivia took on the responsibility for the two of them as a duty. She saw Red's attempts to bear some of that weight as an intrusion, a slight against her abilities.

Red was fairly certain that the child had not been so self-sufficient while living with her mother, or her *abuela*. She hated the idea that Olivia felt it necessary. But Red found herself running into nostalgia, as well.

Bridge had been so much the same way.

Theoretically, Red meant to go back to bed after the kids were gone. A couple more hours of sleep would have been welcome. But she discovered from the first day that it wasn't going to happen. So she puttered around the house, cleaning, doing laundry. If she couldn't help Olivia directly, she could at least make her responsibilities a bit lighter.

More often than not, she'd sit out on the little back porch, taking in the sights and sounds and smells of the morning. It was a time of day that she'd almost forgotten about. The neighbor behind her was some sort of bird fanatic. She had little birdhouses all over the yard and red hummingbird feeders hanging from several tree limbs. It was too late in the year for anything but sparrows; still, Red found herself spending some of her morning watching with fascination. How wonderful it must feel to be that person, she thought. To own a handsome, comfortable house and spend nice mornings sitting on the deck and sipping coffee as she watched the day-to-day lives of small industrious birds.

Of course, Red was doing exactly that. But her sojourn in the land of lawns and birdhouses was a very temporary one. She knew better than to get too cozy in it. When she caught herself mentally planning flower beds and backyard shrubbery, she got furious with herself. How easy it was to settle into a myth of the future that was clearly not within the realm of her possibilities.

Routinely, she now arrived at the bar by ten o'clock, two hours before she opened. That gave her more time to take care of paperwork and, more often than not, to see Cam.

On Tuesday of the second week of school, she finally went through the mail. It was a mess. She'd allowed the mail from the bar to pile up in the last few days, and she'd brought everything from Cam's front-porch mailbox, as well.

She began sorting it into piles. The biggest pile was, of course, the junk mail destined for the trash. Her business stuff from the bar was easy to spot. But she was most interested in things addressed to Cam. Red had decided that she would pay the utilities for the house. It was the very least she could do to offset the expense of living there. Not to mention the inconvenience to him of staying in her apartment.

She easily picked out the electric bill and the one from the Alamo Heights waterworks. She noticed a couple of envelopes with the same look and the same return address, Schavetti Music Company. Momentarily she wondered if he was buying something, a violin maybe, on a payment plan. That was something she could do — she could pay for something he wanted. It would have the effect of a gift, without all the emotional land mines of handing the object to him.

Red pulled a knife out of the flatware drawer and, with a quick, efficient motion, cut open the end of the envelope. Because her motives weren't negative, she didn't even think of it as snooping.

But it wasn't a bill. It was a check. A check for six hundred and eighty-five dollars. Red frowned. The stub indicated hours and numbers of something called Tangrelo Opus 17 editing.

Curious now, she opened the other envelope that was just like it. It was also a check, this one eleven hundred dollars, and it was for Waverly Petty Opera editing.

Red shrugged. She didn't know all that much about the music business. She paid her bands after every night's work, but maybe some places sent checks. Though she hadn't heard of any places called Tangrelo or Waverly. And it was surprising that anyone would pay a fiddler so much.

She asked him as much when he came downstairs a few minutes later. He was shirtless, wearing jeans and sleep-tousled. He looked so young, she thought, and so completely desirable.

"So, I opened these," she said, handing them over. "They're checks."

He glanced at them and nodded, pouring himself a cup of coffee. "Oh good," he responded almost absently.

Red hesitated, wondering if he was going to say more. When he didn't, she prodded.

"I guess I shouldn't have opened them, but I thought they might be bills."

He looked at her for a long moment over the rim of his coffee cup.

"You're welcome to open my checks," he said. "You're welcome to open my bills. I'm not the one with the secrets here. I'll tell you anything you want to know."

Red deftly avoided the gibe.

"Okay," she said. "Tell me about the checks."

"It's my day job," he answered.

"Your day job? What day job?"

"I do music editing," he said.

She was more confused. "In a studio? When do you have time to do that?"

"I don't edit recordings," he corrected her. "I'd love to do that, but I don't have the room for a decent studio. I edit sheet music. The company e-mails the compositions or arrangements and I go through them for errors. I'm actually very good at it."

"I never see you working," she told him.

Cam shook his head. "You see me on the computer all the time."

Red nodded. "I thought you were playing Grand Theft Auto or something."

He laughed. "I'm really not so much the smashing-cars kind of guy."

She shrugged. "So this is like a regular job?"

"No," he said. "It's freelance. I get paid by the measure. I've been doing it since college. One of my professors, who thought I was headed for a life in academia, helped me get the job, and the quality of my work has kept the company coming back to me for ten years."

Red was shaking her head. "It seems really strange."

"With me having a house and a car and money in my pocket, you must have realized I had some kind of day job."

"I thought you had money from your family," she admitted.

"What?" He laughed. "That's a good one. Sometimes you're just completely without a clue. For months you think I'm a hand-to-mouth musician. Then, you turn a hundred and eighty degrees and decide I'm a trust-fund legacy. I'm just a regular guy, Red. Oh, and by the way, I'm a regular guy who is crazy about you."

"Oh . . . thanks."

"Ah . . . you're welcome."

Red was embarrassed and felt slightly cornered. She hated men making declarations, because she'd decided long ago never to reciprocate. She believed that, almost universally, they were lying, but that most didn't even realize it. They just spoke the words they thought she wanted to hear, never imagining that those words had been spoiled for her. They only recalled bad memories. By the time the words came up, she was usually done with the men already. But she still liked Cam and he hadn't really said the BIG words and anyway, she couldn't break up with him while she was living in his house. Explaining that, explaining how little she had to offer him, was not a topic she really wanted to discuss. Fortunately she was saved from the prospect by the very loud sound of machinery coming from the patio.

"What the devil is that?"

Cam didn't answer, but started running in that direction. Red was right behind him.

Through the patio doorway, the sight that greeted them was startling. The brick patio that meandered its way toward the river was now cordoned off at the far end by a vivid orange net. And parked just behind the stage was a giant earthmover.

"Hey! *Hey!* What are you doing?" Red screamed at the man sitting in the big machine.

Apparently he couldn't hear her over the sound of the engine, but two other men in hard hats emerged from around the corner and spotted her.

One waved her over to the orange net. She moved as quickly as her high heels would allow.

"What's going on here?" she hollered over the noise.

"Morning, ma'am," the older of the two men said with a big smile. "I'm Ernie."

"What's going on?" she repeated.

Cam walked up behind her and Ernie offered his hand. "Morning."

"Good morning."

"You know, some of your pavers are in the easement. Those are going to have to come out. And this structure —" Ernie indicated the stage "— it needs to be moved to three feet from the property line. You should have got that done already."

"Don't talk to him, talk to me," Red snapped. "This is my place. And why would I want to move anything?"

Ernie's eyebrows went up. Red wasn't sure what part of her statement he found so amazing, but his response was no-nonsense. "Ma'am, we're beginning excavation into your section today. I'm sure you got all the particulars in your letter."

"What letter?" Red asked. "I didn't get any letter."

The workman looked skeptical. "All the property owners got letters. Registered letters."

"I lease this place," she told him.

Ernie nodded, as if that explained everything. "Then you'll need to get in touch with your landlord, and the sooner the better. We can dig around you for a bit, but we're going to need everything out of our way or we'll have to bring it down with a dozer."

Over the next few hours, the fresh coffee that had tasted so good when she'd sipped it that morning turned sour in her stomach as she tried to get answers.

First, her landlord wasn't in his office. The receptionist offered to have him call her back, but Red wasn't willing to wait. After several transfers to different people who knew different aspects of almost nothing, she finally got to a "contracts accountant." After several minutes on hold, she came back with startling information.

"Mr. Garza no longer owns that property," she told Red.

"How can he no longer own it? I've been paying him rent every month."

"Yes, I see that here," the woman answered. "And we've been forwarding payment to the new owners."

"Who are the new owners?"

"Merton, Wythe and Stone Development Properties."

"I've never heard of them."

"They're in Dallas."

Red was still trying to track someone down when the bar opened for business. The noise of machinery in the back made the place less than relaxing, but all the regulars were extremely interested. Red thought their curiosity must be similar to rubbernecking at car accidents.

It certainly felt like a smashup to her.

Cam called some friends with the intent of using their free labor to move the stage.

"These guys are okay as strong backs," he told Red. "But we'll need a real electrician. And you'll have to pay a premium to get one here on such short notice. There are so many lines and wires on that place, it'll take a half a day just to figure out what goes to what."

"Señor Puentes installed all that," Red told him.

"The old guy that's a regular?" Cam asked, surprised. "Good grief, he must have retired back when dirt was the new thing. I can't imagine that he would still be licensed to work."

"Call him anyway," Red said. "Maybe he'll recommend someone."

"Sure, I can do that."

"And could you try to get in touch with the band that's scheduled for tonight?" she added. "They're just some young kids, but they'll be disappointed at not getting to play. Tell them that I'll have them back and pay them anyway."

Again and again she tried to find someone on the end of the phone at the office of her new landlord that could help her.

"Now, who exactly are you again?" one woman asked.

"I'm Red Cullen. The name of the business is Red's Hot Honky-Tonk Bar."

The woman cleared her throat unpleasantly. "Our company doesn't own any businesses such as that."

"No, I own the business, you own the building," Red corrected her.

"I don't believe our company leases to any businesses such as that," she said. "We do very exclusive property development."

"I called my landlord and they said that they sold the property to you."

"Then your landlord must be mistaken."

"They've been sending you my rent checks," Red pointed out. "How mistaken can that be?"

Red finally hung up on her and called again, hoping to get somebody more amenable on the end of the line.

It was after three when she finally talked to some frightened, mousy-sounding young clerk who reluctantly agreed to research the issue and get back to her. It was the best she could do.

She went out to the patio. Old Señor Puentes was lying on his back underneath the stage as he directed his grandson, who was probably nearing thirty, as to which lines to disconnect. Within a half hour, they'd moved the breaker box to a free-standing pole, shut down everything live attached to the stage and the old man declared it safe to move the stage. The orange-vested crew and their noisy machines had fallen silent, waiting.

Red went outside to find out what was going on and was surprised to see so many of her regulars standing around. Hector and Casey were there and the Grisholm brothers. Loop was there, too, and even Alfred, who had brought his mama with him. J.B. was standing closest to her, so she directed the more universal question to him.

"What are you doing here in the middle of the afternoon?"

J.B. shrugged. "We heard you needed some help," he answered. "I guess we all wanted to be in on it."

She was certainly glad. When Cam and his friends gathered around the platform to move it, the willing bystanders were the ones with the best idea. The construction crew offered their help, as well.

They managed to get plywood sheets underneath the stage and scooted it onto the bricks of the patio and past the chalk mark that Ernie and Cam had come up with together.

The guys shouted in triumph at their success and the audience of patrons of the bar applauded their efforts.

Red smiled as best she could and thanked everyone profusely, but she couldn't help noticing that her patio space had diminished significantly. The stage now seemed oversize for its proximity to the customers.

"Karl, could you draw these fellows a beer on the house, please?"

"I sure can," he answered. "Belly up to the bar, boys. The redheaded gal is buying."

That produced more jokes and laughter as everyone filed inside. Karl turned to her.

"Shouldn't you be going?" he asked.

"Going?" She looked at him, clueless.

"You told me that you needed to be off tonight."

"Oh, damn," she said. "I forgot. It's Howdy Night."

12

Howdy Night was the first big school event of the year. It involved a parade down Broadway of kids and teachers and school groups led by the Alamo Heights High School band. That was followed by a carnival, with parents and teachers manning booths where students could toss beanbags, knock over milk bottles or play musical chairs.

Olivia was frantic when Red arrived home late.

"I was getting ready to go without you!" she threatened angrily.

"I would have called if I couldn't make it," Red assured her, hoping it wasn't that much of a lie. "And Kelly would have taken you."

"We're not supposed to go with our babysitter. We're supposed to go with our parents."

Daniel was also jumping in place with

excitement he couldn't contain and chattering in a mix of English and Spanish. Red picked up the word *parade* and a reference to his teacher, Mrs. Reardon.

"What's with Daniel?"

"His teacher picked him to ride on the first-grade float, but we're probably going to be so late he'll miss it."

At his sister's words, Daniel suddenly went still, his expression crushed.

"We're not going to be late," Red assured him quickly. "And we're leaving right now." As if to emphasize that plan of action, she marched over to the door and opened it wide. "Let's go!"

After a mere instant of hesitation, the kids rushed out. Red was not unaware that she was still dressed in her uniform of the day, skintight capri pants and a green glitter tube top. She grabbed the first blouse she saw in the closet and hurried after the children, putting it on as she trotted down the street.

There was nothing much she could do with her hair. She didn't have a pin or a scrunchie or a rubber band. She didn't even have a shoelace. She pulled it all forward down her left shoulder and began braiding it as tightly as no mirror and fast walking would allow.

They made it to the parade rendezvous

just as the line was starting to move. Olivia and Daniel were racing down the length of it, frantic to find his teacher's group. Red had no choice but to run, as well. She was completely out of breath when the kids finally stopped in front of a flatbed trailer, festooned with trim in primary colors. The homemade float had a huge painted cardboard book opened at one end. Red couldn't tell if the image portrayed was supposed to be the kids going into the book or spilling out of it.

Finally there, Daniel froze, as if he was preparing to have his hopes dashed again. When Mrs. Reardon caught sight of him, she smiled and called out to the driver to hold up. When he was at full stop, she held out her hand.

"Oh, Daniel! There you are. Our float wouldn't be complete without you."

Red could see her grandson's shoulders relax as he reached for his teacher's hand and hurried to take his place.

"We'll be bringing all the children to the school grounds after the parade," Mrs. Reardon told Red. "Meet us under the blue-striped awning. And please be on time," she admonished firmly. "I don't want any of the children to miss the fun because they're stuck waiting for their supervision to show up."

Red nodded. "I'll be there."

"Now, hurry on," she said, much more lightly, adding Olivia to her audience. "You need to find a great vantage point for the parade."

Red barely had time to assure herself that Daniel was indeed seated and his float was moving. She waved at him, but he didn't even notice.

She turned to see Olivia had disappeared. Red headed frantically in the direction they'd come, only slowing when she spotted her granddaughter ahead.

Olivia wormed her way through the crowd to find a perfect spot. Red trailed after her. It was not a great mass of people, but there were enough parents, grandparents and students to create an unbroken line along the few blocks of the parade route.

All around her there was talking and laughter. It imbued Red with a sense of camaraderie. They were all there to cheer for the kids. By the time she could hear the band music floating up Broadway, Red was as excited and eager as the children.

The procession turned out to be exactly what it purported to be — a line of crepe-paper-strewn trucks, antique cars, marching

Boy Scout troops and rows of pint-size twirlers in red lamé and sequins.

The members of the board of education rode in convertibles supplied by the local Camaro club. The Little League champs were in the fire truck. And the high school's cheerleaders led their mascot mule, who seemed much more interested in the bag of oats over his nose than the cheering fans on the street.

When the first-grade trailer went by, Red looked for Daniel. She didn't see him right away. Then she realized that the laughing, happy, animated little boy who was throwing candy to the crowd was the same cautious ball of uncertainty that lived in the house with her.

She waved at him and felt a strange clutch in her heart when, grinning, he waved back.

Maybe he was waving at Olivia, she thought. That must be it.

When the last float passed, the crowd surged into the street, everyone headed for the school grounds. Red didn't want to lose Olivia this time and grabbed for her hand. Her granddaughter looked up at her sharply, brow furrowed, but she didn't let go.

At the school grounds, it was as if a tent city had sprung up overnight. There were booths of all kinds, with games to play and food to eat. Participants were scrambling to get everything set up even as the crowds arrived.

"Look!" Olivia pointed out a particular site. "Face painting. I want to get my face painted. I want something really pretty, like a butterfly or a rainbow or something with all the glitter on it."

Her effervescence genuinely surprised Red. Bridge had been such a completely responsible little person. She'd begun to think of Olivia as exactly the same, but Bridge would never have allowed herself the frivolity of a butterfly on her cheek.

"Sounds great," Red answered. "But we have to go meet your brother first."

Olivia nodded, her tone more sober. "Yes, you're right. We have to do that," she agreed. "I hope the line doesn't get too long."

The return of the dutiful big sister was deflating. Red wanted to fix that.

"We both don't have to waste time at the blue-striped awning," she said. "You go ahead and get your face painted. I'll find your brother."

Olivia looked up, uncertain.

"Can you do that?"

"How hard is it to wait for a six-year-old?" Red asked rhetorically.

"Okay," Olivia said. "I won't leave the school grounds. I won't go off with anybody I don't know. And I'll stay with a group as best I can."

"Sounds like a plan," Red agreed. "Do you need cash?"

Olivia looked incredulous. "Oh no. I save my allowance for this sort of thing."

"Of course you do," Red said, managing not to smile. "Have fun. Make some friends. Daniel and I will catch up with you later."

Olivia raced off and Red continued through the grounds, looking for the blue-striped awning. She almost thought that she'd missed it, when she spotted it up ahead. There were numerous parents standing around, but the children had yet to show up.

There were a few fathers in the group. They varied widely in age and appearance. Some were handsome, tanned and in golfing shirts. Others had obviously just come from the office, sleeves rolled up and ties loosened. There was one guy in surgical scrubs. And another in military fatigues; an officer, she noted.

The women were closer in age than the men. Although they varied in height, weight, race and complexion, they somehow managed to all look very much alike. Appropriately dressed for the occasion, each woman was wearing perfectly creased capri pants of khaki or some other neutral. These were topped by designer button-downs from Talbots or Nordstrom. Hair that had been carefully and expensively highlighted was pulled back in ponytails with deliberate unconcern. Tory Burch flip-flops and understated jewelry completed the look that might have been described as somehow desperately casual.

Red straightened her blouse and surreptitiously adjusted the neckline to hide the green-glitter tube top that was peeking out. Then, a bit more confident, she went to the corner of the awning and stepped just inside.

"Is this Ms. Reardon's first-grade pick-up spot?" she asked a mother with a sleeping infant in a stroller.

The woman nodded.

Red gave a slight smile as a thank-you and then deliberately turned to face outward. It was easier to pretend a great interest in what was going on around them than to have to make eye contact with the Stepford Moms.

After a couple of long moments, as Red stared out at the crowd and resisted the impulse to tap her foot, the woman behind her spoke up.

"Do you have a child in Mrs. Reardon's class?" she asked.

Red turned to her. "A grandson, Daniel Lujan."

"My daughter is Mia, Mia Carson," the woman said. "I'm Sarah, and this is Elliot."

The child in the stroller was still sound asleep and listing to one side.

"Elliot doesn't seem too impressed with the festivities."

The mom laughed. "I've learned not to get too used to it. It can end really abruptly."

She seemed to relax and Red did, too.

"So, what committee is your daughter on? Or is it daughter-in-law?"

"Daughter. Committee? I don't know what you mean."

"For the class," Sarah said. "Everybody's got to be on a committee for the class."

"My daughter can't be on a committee," Red told her. "She's overseas in the military."

"So the children are with you?"

"Ah . . . yes, we're living in a house just a few blocks up —"

"Are you on a committee?" she interrupted.

"Me? No, I —"

Sarah stepped closer and grabbed Red's arm. "Oh, please be on the Cupcake Committee," she whispered frantically. "Please, please, please."

Red was momentarily speechless.

"There's no one on it but me and Tasha Shakelford. Please, please."

"I . . . ah, I don't know how to bake, really."

"You don't have to bake," Sarah insisted. "We'll buy everything from Cupcake Cabin." Her voice softened to a whisper. "I can't be on the committee by myself with Tasha. She hates me. Please, I'm desperate. For sure Mrs. Reardon will get you on a committee. Be on Cupcake Committee with me. I promise, you won't have to do anything."

"Well, I . . . ah . . ."

"Here they come," someone said behind them and all attention was suddenly focused on the line of wide-eyed but well-behaved six-year-olds being led through the crowd.

Under the blue-striped awning, chaos erupted. Not from the children, who were orderly and obedient and eager to follow directions, but from the parents who all surged forward to retrieve their child, assuming that everyone else would allow them to be first.

Mrs. Reardon, who was so sweet and soft-spoken with the first graders, was extremely firm with their moms and dads, insisting that she personally hand off the students to their respective adult.

Sarah was the third person called. As she hurried to pick up Mia, she glanced back toward Red. Using her hand to mimic a phone, she indicated that she would call.

When Daniel was turned over to her, Red took his hand and smiled at him, hoping to see that great, happy grin once more. But Daniel looked decidedly uncertain, not saying a word but glancing around nervously.

"Olivia is getting her face painted," Red told him. "We're going to catch up with her. Does that sound okay?"

Daniel nodded, apparently reassured.

They made their way through the crowd. Daniel loved it. Occasionally he would see something that compelled him to spew a slew of excited Spanish, but mostly he just pointed and smiled.

They spotted Olivia easily, though she now sported a huge pink-and-purple butterfly on the left side of her face that included her glitter-decorated eyebrow as part of the design. She was standing in a group of chattering girls about her age. As they walked up, Red could not avoid hearing the conversation.

A tall blond girl wearing very short shorts

and an elaborate French braid pointed to Olivia's feet.

"Cute shoes. Where'd you get 'em?"

"Uh . . . my mom bought them for me at the PX."

"Oh." The girl frowned as if that was the strangest thing she'd ever heard. "Mine are Nine West Kids."

"Hi, girls!" Red said as she and Daniel stepped up to the group.

Daniel was blurting out a big explanation of some sort to his sister.

Olivia answered him offhandedly.

"You speak Spanish?" one of the other girls asked. "Me, too. I was in Spanish immersion, back before I tested into Gifted and Talented."

Olivia chose to ignore that piece of information and instead fell back on good manners.

"This is my grandmother and my brother, Daniel," she said. "This is Mixon, Carly, Jocelyn and Kaya. Kaya's in my class."

"Hi," the four girls responded in unison.

"Daniel and I are going to get something to eat and then he wants to ride the pony. Are you hungry, Olivia, or do you want to just hang here with your friends?"

"I'm starving," Olivia answered and turned to offer a quick goodbye to the girls.

"I'll catch up with you later."

They headed toward the food booths, which to Red's surprise seemed to be less about hot dogs and hamburgers and more about turkey franks and vegan sprout wraps.

The three finally agreed on spinach tamales with chipotle salsa. Red got them settled at a picnic table, with food, drinks and plenty of napkins.

"I'm sorry to take you away from your friends," she said to Olivia. "Did you have a good time?"

"Yeah, it was all right," she said. "They're not really my friends. The only one of them that I really know is Kaya and all she can talk about is the Jonas Brothers."

"Are they in your class, too?"

Olivia and Daniel shared a quick, shocked looked and then burst out laughing.

"What?" Red asked. "What?"

"The Jonas Brothers are a band," Olivia told her.

Daniel was still laughing, his mouth wide open. "Abuela Tanta!" he said.

"I understood that, Daniel Lujan," Red told him. "I know what *abuela tanta* means." Her tone feigned a threat, but she was laughing with them.

Her terrible day had somehow dissolved into a distant annoyance. And it felt strangely like progress for Bad Grandma to have become Silly Grandma.

To: buildabetterbridge@citymail.com
September 16 4:24 p.m.
From: Livy156@ABrats.org
Subject: School

hi Mom! I love you 2! Thanks 4 the email. I always remember how busy you are, but if I don't hear from U, well its bad. But I did so its good. Daniel sends his love 2. Course he'd never say anything, cause he just doesn't. He still cries at night sometimes but dont worry. He wouldn't let nobody hear him. He tries to be a big boy like you told him.

School is great. Its like the school on the base but bigger and different. My teacher is very cool. Her name is Ms. Gomez. She looks like she could be someone on tv. She has the most awesomist clothes ever. Mixon says she must have a rich husband because teachers don't make enough money to afford hot cature. Hot cature means fashion. Mixon knows a lot about fashion. She is not in my class, but everybody knows her. She pretty much runs the school. At least among the girls. The boys are enemies so they don't count. Mixon doesn't like my clothes much. And I don't think she likes me. But she REALLY likes Ms. Gomez and Ms. Gomez likes me so its all even-steven.

The bad grandma is doing some better. We don't see her so much now that we have school. But why does she half to dress like that. Its embearussing. I miss Abuela. I miss U 2!

Keep drinking your orange juice and email me when you can. Dont worry about us. I am taking care of Daniel and me fine.

Livy

13

When Merton, Wythe and Stone Development Properties finally got back to Red, the news was even worse than she'd imagined.

"The mixup seems to be that the property you're leasing was listed as unoccupied," Claire Richmond, associate contracts representative, told her.

"Unoccupied? I've been here for nine years," Red told her.

"Yes," Ms. Richmond said. "But as there is no current lease agreement in effect, it was assumed that the building was empty."

"I've been paying my rent every month," Red pointed out. "I don't miss, I'm not ever even late."

"Yes, that's what I understand from Receivables. I'd be happy to make a note of that here on the record."

"Ah . . . thanks," Red answered, "but I don't see how that affects the price of pork bellies."

"I beg your pardon?"

"How does that help me?" Red explained without the sarcastic idiom. "I've got a ton of heavy equipment out back making a whole lot of noise and ripping up the river access to my patio. Both of those things are bad for my business. Can you make them stop?"

"Well, no," Ms. Richmond answered. "We don't want them to stop. Your building was purchased in a bundled block for redevelopment. The potential for that redevelopment is tied directly to the River North expansion."

"They've been talking about that River North expansion for years," Red told her. "It's not ever going to happen."

There was a long silence on the other end of the line.

"You're the one who is saying that the construction is up to your back door," Ms. Richmond observed.

The woman had a point, one that Red was not at all crazy about.

After more discussion, Ms. Richmond suggested that someone from Project Management call her with an update on the building's status.

Red acquiesced to that, but not happily.

After hanging up the phone, she walked

outside onto her much-abbreviated patio. The place was amazingly quiet. All she could hear was the sound of Cam's fiddle drifting down from the apartment. The tune was not a familiar one, but it was intense and sweet, stirring her heart.

The heavy equipment was sitting in silence and none of the orange-vested workers were around. Red didn't know if they'd taken off for lunch or for a week. It was one of the notorious truths of San Antonio construction that the crews for tearing things up and the crews for putting them back together were often not well coordinated. A well-traveled street could be torn into a nasty detour that strangled traffic for months before the repairs even got started.

Red desperately hoped that wouldn't be true here. As it was, things were bad. Between the truncation of the patio and the relocation of the stage so far inside the property line, she'd lost three tables. That added up to a loss of at least a thousand dollars in receipts every week. If she could let one of the waitresses go, it would lower the overhead. But that would put too many tables on the staff that was left. And she couldn't know yet how moving the stage closer would impact the inside business. Those customers who came more to socialize than for the music might not be able to hear themselves talk.

Red felt her insides tightening up with the uncertainty. When things got tough, this patio and the view of the river had always calmed her. But nothing about backhoes and orange tape was calming.

She closed her eyes, trying to see it again as it was. The shady morning patio, the sounds of the rippling water, the rustling of the trees on the opposite bank. But the scene in her mind was no longer the San Antonio River but Cayou Creek, near Piney Woods, and her daddy was sitting beside her.

"Did Mama just not love us anymore?" she asked him.

"Oh no, that wasn't it," he answered. "Your mama is just not like all the other mamas. She needs different things. Things I couldn't give her."

"You gave her what you had," Red defended.

Her father shrugged. "That's all in the past. She has a new husband now and you and I are going to have to be happy about that. We're going to be happy for her. You think we can do it?"

Red nodded. "I can be happy about it. Now she won't be here yelling all the time."

"Your mom loves you. She just has a hard time showing it."

"Are you sure, Daddy?"

"I'm as sure about it as anything, my little Red."

"You shouldn't call me Red. Red's a color, not a person. It's silly."

He laughed. "I like being silly," he told her. "And I like being with you."

"You won't ever go away, like Mama?"

"I won't ever go anywhere," he assured her. "You can count on it. Day and night I'm going to be right here on this farm, loving and protecting my favorite redheaded girl."

That hadn't been true, of course. He'd died. She didn't blame him for that. But once he was gone, nobody had ever been there to protect Red again.

Lost in thought, Red was startled as a pair of arms wrapped around her waist. It was Cam. The warmth of him, the strength of him was so welcome that she relaxed in his arms, still pliant from the memory of her father.

"I heard you upstairs playing your fiddle," she said.

He pulled her back tight against his chest and gave her a kiss on the throat. "I was just practicing."

"It was real pretty," she said. "What's it called?"

The side of his face was against her temple and she could feel him smiling. *"Concerto for Violin number 2 in D Major."*

She laughed lightly. "Not exactly a catchy title."

"Yeah, a honky-tonker would have come up with a better one, for sure."

"Is it one of the songs from your day job?" she asked. "Something you're editing?"

"It's Mozart. He doesn't need all that much editing these days."

"How come you practice Mozart, if you're going to be playing Willie Nelson?"

"That's Woody Guthrie's fault," he answered.

"Woody Guthrie?"

"Where were you just now?" he asked her, changing the subject. "I didn't mean to sneak up on you, but when I walked up here, you looked to be a million miles away."

"Not a million," she answered. "Just a few hundred . . . and about four decades."

She felt him go very still. Immediately Red was on her guard. The gentle moment grew tense.

"What?"

"Nothing," he answered. "I thought you were about to tell me something."

179

"Tell you what?"

"I don't know," he said. "Something. Anything."

"No," Red assured him. "Nothing."

Cam gave a light chuckle. "When I met you, you were so different from any woman I'd ever gone out with. Those girlfriends were constantly telling me everything that came into their heads and trying to pry out every thought I'd ever had. You never asked me anything. You never told me anything."

"And you liked that," Red pointed out.

"I did," Cam admitted. "I did like it. But I don't anymore. I want to tell you things, I want you to tell me things. Why don't we do that? Why can't we do that?"

Red freed herself from his grasp.

"If you want to play Twenty Questions, go find some twentysomething. I'm past those kinds of games."

"I don't want to play games, either," he assured her. "And the last thing I'm interested in is some little chickie. But for just an instant there, it was like you were about to say something, reveal something, give me a hint of who you are and how you got to be that way."

Red secured her defenses and switched tactics. "I'll tell you what I am. I'm horny. And I'll tell you how I got that way. You haven't jumped my bones in nearly two weeks. Do you think I'm some bored wife, perfectly satisfied with a five-minute poke once a month. I've got to get me a little. And if you're not available, I may have to start trolling the other cowboys who come into this place."

Cam delivered a sharp, flat-handed slap to her backside.

"Ow!"

"Just swatting the armadillo, ma'am," he said. "It's getting a bit rowdy."

"That's not going to help," she said. "It needs to get bounced on a bed till it's too tired to wiggle."

"You'd better be careful," he warned. "You may get more than you can handle."

"Oh, you just trust me, cowboy, I can handle you and you'll love every minute of it."

"Don't you have to open the front door in fifteen minutes?" he asked.

"Some things can wait and some can't," she told him. She ran her hand down the front of his jeans. "And it seems to me that we've got an emergency situation growing here."

"You are really going to get it."

"Please, oh please, pretty please."

Cam bent down, grabbed her behind he

knees and hoisted her over his shoulder like a sack of feed. Red laughed as he carried her across the patio and up the stairs.

In the apartment, Cam tossed her on the bed.

Red reached to her waist to unbutton her tight jeans. To her surprise, Cam grabbed her hands and pulled them high over her head as he lay down on top of her, fully clothed.

His face was directly above hers, his mouth only inches away. She parted her own lips in expectation. When the kiss didn't come, she opened her eyes to see him looking at her.

"You almost managed to pull it off again," he said.

"What?"

"I know what you're doing," he whispered.

Red frowned. "What I'm doing about what?"

"About me," Cam answered. "About getting close to me. I've figured out how this works for you."

Red frowned. "I don't know what you're talking about," she said.

"Oh, yes you do," he said. "Or at least unconsciously you do. I'd be willing to let you get by with saying it's not intentional."

"What is not intentional?"

"This," he answered.

Red still didn't get his meaning.

"Every time we're getting close, every time you are about to tell me something, every time your heart is exposed, it ends up like this. Us on a bed or a chair or a table, rocking our brains out."

Red laughed. "Sounds like heaven to me."

Cam rolled over to lie beside her, but kept her hands gripped tightly in his own.

"I get it," he said. There was no humor in him. His tone was factual. "A lot of women throw up defenses against sex. Your defense *is* sex. It's like a secret weapon for you."

"I don't use sex as a weapon."

"Oh, yes you do. You know perfectly well that it's the one thing that answers all the questions in a guy's head. It's the one move that always changes the subject."

Red started to wiggle away. Cam clutched her body with one muscular thigh.

"Years ago I was at an old honky-tonk in a near-dead oil-boom town," he told her. "There was a tableful of poker players and the money pot was getting pretty full. All of a sudden one of the players, a moderately attractive woman, just pulled her shirt off. She's sitting there bare-breasted at a tableful of men, with money on the line. And every last one of them dropped his poker face. She won the pot because they couldn't keep their heads in the game."

Red shrugged. "Men think with their dicks. It's not news."

"No, it's not," Cam said. "But it's not me." He let go of her hands and sat up on the bed. "I love having sex with you, Red. Making me want you? Heck, all you have to do is walk into the room. But I think I've made it clear, I'm not a disinterested sex buddy. I want to do you because we're both craving each other. I want to satisfy you from that red hair on your head to the soles of your feet. But I want it to be because you want me. Not because you're feeling threatened enough to throw up a big distraction."

Red rose to her knees on the bed and huffed in frustration. "What is the deal with you?" she asked. "Why can't you be like other guys?"

"Because my Red deserves a lot better."

Cam leaned forward and kissed her on the bridge of the nose, then stood up and walked to the door.

"Where are you going?"

"Downstairs," he answered. "Take your time, comb your hair. I'll unlock the door and man the bar until you get there."

"Uh . . . thank you."

"You're welcome," he answered. "And just

so we're clear, nothing I do for you is ever owed to me or paid for by services rendered. Understood?"

She nodded.

"Good," he replied. "Now, put your pretty armadillo on ice for a few hours and I promise to grill it to well-done later."

As he walked out of the room, Red found herself surprisingly turned on. There was something about a man who wouldn't be manipulated that was amazingly sexy.

She ran her hand across the jean-covered tattoo on her backside.

"You are so lucky," she told her armadillo. "Cam is the best boyfriend you've ever had, both in bed and out of it."

He was going to make some woman a great husband. It wasn't the first time she'd had that thought, but it was the first time that she was bothered by it. He *would* make a good husband. And the way he was with Olivia and Daniel, he was going to make an excellent father, too. That's what he deserved. And, she realized with sadness, that was what she wanted for him.

As that realization settled in on her, the source of her sadness became suddenly clear. She was in love with him.

14

Red was standing at a long bar. A very long bar. She couldn't see the end of it. But then, she was focused on the beer spigot. She was drawing glass after glass of golden draft. Pull down the lever. Watch the mug fill. Set it on the counter. Grab another glass. Pull down the lever. Watch the mug fill.

A buzzing jerked her momentarily awake. She was dreaming. And it was the very worst kind. Dreaming about working always made her wake up tired.

She wanted to dream about something else. Something bright and sunny. Maybe something with Cam's arms around her. That thought had her smiling languidly.

The buzzer went off again and she realized that it hadn't been in her dream; it was someone at the front door. Her first thought was to just ignore it. Then it occurred to her that it might be Cam. If so, the kids would normally open the door. Maybe they were asleep, too. Or more likely playing in the backyard.

Groaning, she rolled over to where she could reach the window shade. She pulled it back slightly and peeked out. Standing on her porch was a skinny, buttoned-down old lady in beige slacks, tailored blouse and Gucci loafers.

"Real-estate agent or neighborhood petition?" Red wondered under her breath.

She was not in the mood.

"Go away!"

The woman startled at the response. Red quickly let the shade drop.

She should have just kept quiet. She knew that. She'd spent way too many years living over the bar. In more civil localities you weren't supposed to yell at people on the porch.

The buzzing began again, this time more insistently.

"Oh cripes!" Red complained as she pulled the pillow over her head to drown out the noise.

Mentally she went through the list of who this person might be and what good reasons there could be for getting up and opening the door.

Could it be someone from the school? No, not on Saturday morning. Anyone from the military would be in uniform. No, it was undoubtedly a do-gooder or a door-to-door saleslady. Red was certain that no person she had any need to talk to would show up on the porch. It was one of the frustrating realities of working late nights. Most of the world assumed that if they are awake, you should be too.

She stayed right where she was and ignored the buzzer. Eventually she heard unhappy footsteps retreating to the curb. Red stretched. She wanted to go back to sleep, but she was completely awake now.

The idea of coffee began to sound good to her, so she rolled out of bed and headed for the kitchen.

The morning sun shone through the windows, giving the room a glow that was surprisingly welcoming. Red didn't like mornings, but one like this could win almost anybody over.

The quiet of the place felt unfamiliar. Red found the rattling of the spoon against the coffee can to be like a clanging bell in the silent house.

Hadn't her home been silent for years?

It wasn't silent these days. Olivia was constantly haranguing her about something. And even Daniel was more verbal these days, constantly chattering to his sister in

Spanish, though he'd yet to say even one word directly to Red.

She poured the water through the coffee-maker and waited.

The kitchen could be correctly described as a mess. The sticky evidence of toaster waffles for breakfast was everywhere. Red avoided sitting at the table, which had pancake syrup dribbled in several places. Instead, she stood at the kitchen sink, gazing out into the backyard.

Olivia was jumping rope. She was apparently trying to perfect the backward criss-cross, and she was doing a pretty good job.

Daniel had piled up a small pyramid of stones and was lobbing them like grenades at a paper target that he'd hung on the back fence. Red was glad to see him engaged in a very boylike activity. He was such an anxious, frightened little guy. She worried about him. She hated seeing him curl into that ball, trying to make himself disappear. But he was a likable kid and he was going to be as good-looking as his dad. Fortunately, unlike Mike, Daniel was smart and generous and thoughtful. And being raised almost exclusively among women could be a good thing.

As Red stood there watching, suddenly all hell broke loose. The woman Red had seen on her front porch came charging into the yard, waving a broom like a weapon and screaming like a banshee.

Red was out the back door like a shot, racing toward the intruder. From the corner of her eye she saw Olivia, stunned and frozen to the spot.

Daniel was not frozen. His eyes wide with terror, he was running as if all the demons in hell were after him. He grabbed on to Red's leg as if she was a lifeline and then hid behind her.

"What the devil are you doing in my yard?" Red yelled angrily at the woman.

She continued to approach, unintimidated. She was perhaps twenty years older than Red. Her perfectly coiffed updo and line-free Botoxed forehead were in sharp contrast to her angry narrowed eyes and the line of her mouth as she answered through clenched teeth.

"*Your* yard?" she said with drawn-out sarcasm. "I don't believe so."

"If you're not out of here in one minute," Red threatened, "then I'm calling the police."

"No, *I'm* the one calling the police," the woman countered. "That hellion of yours has been throwing stones at my birdhouses. It's a miracle that he hasn't killed one of the bluebirds or the little wrens."

"There's nothing in your backyard but sparrows," Red informed her. "And he's not a good enough shot to kill anything."

"But he tried," the woman ranted. "He's an undisciplined child with apparently no upbringing at all. I've watched them over here, day after day, doing whatever they like with virtually no supervision at all. Growing up to be no better than the irresponsible people who created them. I don't know why they allow people like you to even have children. You carelessly breed like rats and then ignore your offspring, drinking all night and sleeping all day. You foist these wild children on the community and they end up as menaces or criminals."

"These children are not menaces or criminals!"

The woman gave a hmmph of disdain. "Attempting to murder innocent animals certainly qualifies as being a menace."

Beside her, Daniel was tugging frantically on Red's nightgown. She looked down to see an expression of remorse on his face, which was awash with tears. Red couldn't resist the need to comfort him. She dropped to her knees and pulled his shaking body into her arms. The warmth of him, the smell of his hair, the small vulnerable form against

191

her, awakened something she hadn't allowed herself to feel in years.

"I wouldn't hurt a bird, Grandma," he whispered, using the first English he'd ever spoken to her. "I threw the rocks, but I never meant to hurt a bird."

"Of course you wouldn't," she told him. "And you didn't hurt anything or anyone." Red squeezed him tightly to her for a moment and then held him at arm's length. "Now, can you do something for me?"

He nodded, still frightened but wanting to be brave.

"Could you go get Olivia and take her inside?" Red said. "I think this mean old witch is scaring her."

"Okay . . . okay."

Red watched as the boy grabbed his sister's hand and ran toward the house. She turned back to the intruder. The woman was glaring at Red as if she were a cockroach that had suddenly appeared atop a white linen tablecloth. Red knew that look. She'd lived through it once before. Then, she had been cowed. Today, she was livid. She took two steps forward and jerked the broom out of the woman's hands.

"GET OUT OF MY YARD!"

Startled, the woman stepped backward. But it wasn't fast enough for Red. She began swatting her across the back of her Ann Taylor slacks as the woman ran toward the gate. Three, four, five times Red managed to land a blow before the yelping intruder was safe on the far side of the fence. Red threw the broom into her backyard with the last word.

"And stay out!"

Red turned and walked back to the house, filled with great satisfaction. Surprised, she felt light enough to walk on air. She was actually grinning by the time she caught sight of the kids' noses pressed up against the glass of the kitchen window.

When she stepped inside, the kids were wide-eyed and stunned into silence.

Red self-consciously cleared her throat. She was pretty certain that this was not the way Bridge would have handled the situation. And it was undoubtedly not a good example of conflict resolution for the children. Red didn't know how to fix that, so she didn't try.

"Okay," she said to Olivia and Daniel as they stared at her in awe. "I don't think she'll be back. Still, it's probably a smart idea to set up any targets you're going to throw at in the middle of the yard. We don't want to bother our neighbors, and we certainly don't want to accidentally hurt any animals."

The two children nodded solemnly.

"So . . . uh . . . I think I'll get some coffee and . . . ah . . . why don't we clean up this kitchen?"

To her surprise, the kids jumped right into it. The three of them worked together congenially for the next twenty minutes. It took only about five of that before they were reliving the backyard encounter with much humor. Daniel retrieved their broom from the pantry closet, feigning a need to sweep the kitchen floor and then delightedly demonstrated Red's attack on the neighbor by bashing the chairs with it. His expression, clearly meant to convey a raving maniac, had Red and Olivia laughing until both were holding aching sides.

It was the most fun Red had had with the kids. They were smart, entertaining, resourceful and full of life. And she enjoyed every moment of being with them.

When the doorbell rang and Cam walked in, it felt like a cherry had been added to the top of a hot-fudge sundae.

"You'll never believe what happened this morning," Daniel blurted out as soon as Cam crossed the threshold.

Cam smiled, but somehow it didn't seem totally genuine.

"I want to hear everything," Cam assured him. "But first I need to talk to Red for a couple of minutes." He turned to her. "Have you got another cup of that coffee?"

"Sure," she answered and turned to pour him a cup.

Daniel couldn't keep his story quiet another minute and was talking a blue streak about the backyard encounter, utilizing the broom as a prop in the demonstration.

"Hey, did you learn English last night?" Cam interrupted him. "I swear you were a Spanish speaker when I saw you yesterday."

Daniel giggled and shrugged.

Red handed Cam his coffee. "Do you want to sit out on the patio?" she suggested.

Cam glanced through the kitchen window at the backyard and beyond.

"Maybe we should sit on the front porch," he said.

She followed him back through the house and out the front door. The morning heat was beginning to pick up and the sun flooded the area of the wicker furniture, but Cam took a seat there anyway.

He looked good to her this morning, really good. Red was certain that had to be in the eye of the beholder, because he'd clearly just rolled out of bed. His usually well-groomed hair had been jerked back into an untidy ponytail. He wore a T-shirt with cutoffs, and instead of cowboy boots he had on flip-flops. A stubble of beard added to the unkempt allure.

For an instant she was tempted to plant her behind right in his lap. That was where she wanted to be. But the reserve in his demeanor discouraged that.

Red sat on the swing and watched as he took a sip of coffee. Something was up. She wasn't sure what, but it wasn't good.

Their eyes met across the width of the porch.

"Okay, I'm listening," she told him.

"No," he replied. "I'm the one who's listening. I want to hear your side of the story."

"What story?"

"The one that got my morning off to such an abrupt start," he answered. "Something about assaulting my aunt and ordering her off the property."

"Your *aunt?*"

Cam nodded and took another sip of coffee before he spoke.

"I know you're not the type to try to suck up to my relatives. Still, she's the only family that I have, so it would be nice if you didn't go out of your way to make her hate you."

"That bitch is your aunt?"

"Uh . . . yeah," he replied. "I'm sure I told you that my dad lived across the backyard. Phyllis Early is my father's sister."

"You may have mentioned something about your dad," Red recalled. "But you never said anything about this aunt."

He shrugged. "Or maybe you just weren't listening," he suggested.

Cam's words held the sting of truth. She didn't always listen to him. The less she knew, the easier it was to move on.

"You never told me. I'm sure of that," she lied with conviction.

"Okay," he said a bit too calmly. "The scoop is, my parents grew up across the backyard from each other. My grandfather put in the gate between the yards when they were children. Until today, everyone has always just gone back and forth without much fuss about it."

Red felt the color rise in her cheeks. "I had no idea that she was your aunt," she told him. "And she started it! But you'd probably never believe that."

Cam raised an eyebrow. "If you say that's the way it was, then I believe it," he answered.

"Good. Then that's settled."

Red rose with the hope of making a quick retreat, but Cam wasn't letting her off that easy.

"Sit!" he commanded, pointing to the chair.

"I am not an Irish setter."

He nodded agreement. "*Please* sit," he revised. "I still have a few questions."

"Okay," she replied, reluctantly complying.

"I don't want to argue with you," Cam said. "And I don't want to second-guess you. I just need your side of this so I can figure out how to smooth things over."

"Don't bother on my account," Red told him. "I don't need anything smoothed over. The woman is a bitch and if she comes into the backyard again while I'm living here, I'll kick her fancy-pants butt and enjoy the experience."

Cam templed his fingers against the bridge of his nose.

"Not a hopeful start, Red," he pointed out. "While you're here in the neighborhood, you need to get along. Aunt Phyl can make trouble for you, and I don't want that to happen."

Red snorted. "That whiny sack of designer

clothes couldn't begin to make trouble for me."

"You'd be surprised. Aunt Phyl and her posse pretty much run this town."

"Her posse?"

He shrugged. "My description, not hers. Aunt Phyl has this little clique of Alamo Heights matrons who get together at the Argyle for coffee and gossip a couple of times a week. If you're under discussion, you might as well hire a billboard because everybody in town will know about it in no time."

"Like I would care?" Red shook her head dismissively.

Cam eyed her critically. "Of course you wouldn't," he said. "But it's not all about you anymore, is it?"

"Oh, I guess you don't want me tarnishing your reputation among your peeps."

"I wasn't thinking about myself," he said. "Despite your occasional need to talk down to me, I'm an adult male, perfectly capable of taking responsibility for my own choices. I was thinking about Olivia and Daniel. Isn't this time hard enough for them? Their mom is in the middle of a war. Their grandmother is ill. And they are making a life in a new school with all new people. I think they should get to do that without the added burden of social ostracism."

"I'd rather see them ostracized than caught up in all that social-climbing crap."

The vehemence of her response caught his attention and Red knew that she'd said too much. Quickly she attempted to deflect the questions that her reaction might have provoked.

"Your stupid aunt accused Daniel of throwing rocks at her birdhouses. Can you imagine anything less likely?"

"He was throwing rocks, though."

"I'm sure she told you that," Red said. "He was aiming at a target on the fence. Maybe a couple went over, but I seriously doubt there was any danger involved."

"She told me that the children were running wild, unsupervised. She was concerned for their safety. And that she came over to let you know about it and you refused to get out of bed and ordered her off the front porch."

Red was hardly in a position to deny that.

"Aunt Phyl felt she had no other choice but to speak to the children herself."

"Speak to them?" Red was incredulous. "She was screaming at them. She called them 'menaces and criminals.' "

Cam chuckled.

"You think that's funny?"

"No, I think it's Aunt Phyl," he answered. "The only kid she has ever been around was me. And I definitely fell into the criminal-menace category."

He got up from his chair and seated himself beside her on the swing. Cam slid his arm across the top of her shoulders and pulled her close, planting a tiny kiss on her temple.

"I'll talk to Aunt Phyl," he promised. "I'll convince her to stay out of sight, or at least out of our backyard."

"Good."

"But I need you to promise not to antagonize her," Cam said. "She loves me and has been good to me. And I'm certain that if she ever got to know you or the kids, she would love you as much as I do."

Red opened her mouth to dispute that. She knew all about women like Cam's Aunt Phyl, high-class ladies who were so concerned with their social position and community standing. Red's mother was like that. And if she couldn't put her own daughter first, no one else could ever be expected to do so.

None of this came out of Red's mouth. Instead, she was silenced by the dawning revelation of Cam's comment. He had just said that he loved her.

To: buildabetterbridge@citymail.com
September 28 7:41 p.m.
From: Livy156@ABrats.org

hiya Mom-ster 2 emails waiting 4 me! That is totally the best. And U are going to be so happy. I know, cause I am. The big news is TA-DAH!!!! I have a best friend. I haven't had a BFF for like 3 schools or something. An she is SO COOL. Much cooler than Mixon, tho Mixon is way popular. Nayra, my BFF, is smart like me. I met her in music class. We are both taking violin for the 1st time this year. She is changing from piano. I took it cause Cam said that it helps the brain do math. I don't know how, but Cam always knows what he talks about and he loaned me one of his violins anyway. Nayra and I are IMing or on the phone every night. I talk 2 Kaya 2. But Kaya always says what R U going to wear tomorrow and I don't care much. Nayra and I talk better stuff. And sometimes we practice together over the phone. I want her to sleepover on Saturday, but Red says that's her busyest night, so I told her Cam would stay with us if she asked him, but she won't. POOT!

I wish U were home. U would let me have a sleepover. But SHE won't.

Daniel is ok too. He likes school and he can read now. Truly. He wasn't so into *Curious George* and *Babar* like I was. So Cam took him to Red Balloon Bookshop its not far from us and told him he could have any books he wanted to read. He chose a bunch of Scooby-Doo with vampires in them. I don't like scary stuff but Daniel can read them all by himself. Thats pretty good huh. Cam lets us go to the bookstore any time we want and buy whatever we want. He says the library is great but some books you just gotta have forever. He's right.

I luv U Mom. An I miss U so much. Please come home as soon as U can. Daniel and I are fine. But we want U.

Livy

15

As the weeks went by, Red settled into a new routine that included both the kids and the construction. Daniel turned out to be quite talkative about school and vampires and who's who in professional wrestling. Olivia became as much a phone diva as an Internet surfer. And the guys from the crew site all wanted coffee the minute she opened and a beer as soon as they clocked out for the day.

Sunday and Monday were nights off for Kelly, the babysitter. Red found that worked just fine. The bar was closed on Sunday, and Monday was the slowest night of the week. Karl actually seemed pleased to be given a chance to run the place on his own.

They visited the children's *abuela* almost every week, and she was improving. Her speech was still a huge challenge and Red couldn't help but admire how patient Olivia and Daniel were as the old woman struggled to get out the words she wanted to say. She was still mostly wheelchair bound, but was making progress in therapy on a walker.

Bridge called as often as she could. Because of the time difference, it was decided that Saturday mornings was the best time to call. Ten o'clock in San Antonio was 8:00 p.m. in Kabul. Bridge tried to make that, but sometimes work or phone availability got in the way. The weekends when no call came were always quiet ones for the kids.

Red hadn't caught a glimpse of Aunt Phyl since the day of the brooming, but Cam was around all the time. He spent more time with the kids than he did with Red, but it was hard to resent that. Daniel more or less idolized him. The little boy followed at his heels like a puppy. Cam took great care to talk to Daniel about whatever he was doing and to listen to all the silly stories from his day at school.

He spent time with Olivia, as well. Cam tutored her on the violin, and once she decided she could not be separated from her best friend, Nayra, he expanded the one-on-one to include both of them.

Managing to do all this was aided in part by having more time on his hands, though it was not his own choice. The band was suffering through a soap opera that threatened its future.

Brian had gotten one of his groupie/fans pregnant.

"I think that's what guys your age are supposed to do," Red told Cam. "Be fruitful and multiply."

Cam, seated across the bar, rolled his eyes at her. Of course, it was much more complicated. The young woman was only twenty and earning minimum wage at the counter of Whataburger. Although Brian was in his thirties, with a bit of money in the bank, he was still living with his parents. He'd spent the last ten years totally absorbed in the band.

"So what does he *want* to do?" Red asked.

"I think he wants to marry her," Cam said.

"That is so totally retro," she said. "I didn't think guys like you and Brian ever even considered the ball-and-chain life."

Cam gave her a long look. "Honestly," he replied, "I decided back in high school that marriage just wasn't in the cards for me. But I'm beginning to rethink that."

Red felt the blood drain from her face. It was what she wanted for him. It was what he deserved. Standing behind the bar, she grabbed a towel and began wiping down the pristine surface so that she wouldn't have to look him in the eye.

"No hurry," she told him. "It's not like guys have the biological clock that gals do."

He reached across the bar and grasped her wrist, stopping her deliberate distraction and forcing her to look up at him.

"Different people have different kinds of clocks, Red," he told her. "I think we both set ours running when we still should have been in that timeless-childhood place."

She looked askance at him and defended her feelings by lashing out.

"Well, I know I had to grow up in a hurry," she said. "But it seems to me that you're still just a big kid."

An unhappy line appeared on his forehead, and she knew that she'd hurt him. She'd meant to do it. Now she wanted to take it back. The phone rang and saved her from attempting to.

"Red's Hot Honky-Tonk."

"Uh . . . hello. I'm . . . I'm looking for Daniel Lujan's grandmother. I was given this number. . . ."

"I'm his grandmother."

"Oh, great! Hi! It's Sarah. Sarah Carson. Mia and Elliot's mom. I met you at Howdy Night."

"Oh yeah, sure," Red answered, vaguely recalling the woman with the baby in a stroller.

"I've had a terrible time getting in touch with you," she said. "Nobody answers your phone in the mornings and in the afternoon and evenings, it's always the babysitter, and she is as closemouthed as the CIA. I swear, if you hadn't become, like, the latest gossip in town, I never could have tracked you down."

The last statement was accompanied by a fairly frantic giggle.

Red didn't know how to respond to that. Cam had warned her that she was going to get talked about. She'd been the subject of gossip once before and she didn't like it.

"Is that why you called?" Red asked. "To let me know that my name is being dragged around Alamo Heights?"

"Oh no, no," Sarah assured her quickly. "I called about the Cupcake Committee. I went ahead and signed you up and . . . well . . . Could I come in?"

"Huh?"

"I'm actually parked outside," Sarah said. "I didn't want to come in unless . . . unless you really are inside."

"Come on in," Red told her. "It's usually pretty safe this time of day."

She slammed down the phone shaking her head.

"What's up?" Cam asked.

"We're being invaded by your homeys," she answered.

Red walked around the bar and over to the front entrance, assessing the cleanliness of her skintight jeans and her low-cut lace camisole. She held the door open and waved her visitor inside.

Sarah looked much the same as she had on Howdy Night. Dressed in designer slacks with coordinating blouse and expensive shoes, her accessories included a Fendi bag on one arm and a six-month-old boy on the other.

"Hi, oh my God! Your hair! It's, like, incredible hair."

Self-consciously, Red attempted to smooth it down. "I guess it must be humid today."

"No, no, it looks great. Is it natural? Oh, it must be. I am so jealous."

"Uh . . . thanks."

"I'm so sorry to barge in on you. I hope you're not too busy."

"It's fine," Red said. "Not much happening this time of day." She indicated the less than half-dozen customers scattered around the room.

Sarah glanced at them, but her gaze was caught immediately by Cam.

"Oh wow!" she exclaimed with a giggle to Red. "So it really is true. You two *are* a couple. That is so cool!"

Red didn't get a second to answer that as Sarah immediately stepped forward to offer Cam her hand.

"I'm sure you don't remember me," she said. "I used to be Sarah Endicott. I was a junior when you were a senior. Go Mules! I married Brad Carson. I think you were in Boy Scouts with him."

"Oh yeah," Cam answered, nodding vaguely.

"You were in Boy Scouts?" Red asked rhetorically.

Cam ignored that. "It's nice to see you again, Sarah," he said. "What's Brad up to these days? I haven't seen him since high school."

"Oh, he's a real-estate attorney with Isaccson and McNulty. He just made part-ner."

"Sounds good. Those Eagle Scouts always turn out well. Say hi to him for me."

"Oh, I can't," Sarah protested with a whisper. "He'd have a fit if he knew I was down here. But as soon as I heard about this place, I was dying to come here."

Cam flashed a smile that was definitely feigned as he shared a glance with Red.

"So, now that you're here, what do you think?" Red asked.

"Oh, it's great. I used to go to places like this when I was in college," she confessed. "Drinking too much and listening to honky-tonk. There was nothing I liked better."

"Well, you are welcome to drink too much and listen to music here anytime," Red said.

Sarah giggled again and it was all Red could do not to roll her eyes.

"What did you want to talk to me about?" Red asked.

"Is there someplace we can sit?"

Red glanced at Cam.

"Go ahead, I'll take care of the customers," he said.

Red led Sarah toward the back of the building. Normally, she would have taken her out to the patio, but the construction workers were noisy. Instead, she took the corner booth. It was a good distance from everyone else and slightly secluded from the other patrons.

"How's this?"

Sarah nodded agreement. "Do you have a high chair?" she asked. "I could strap Elliot in and give him some crackers and he'd be just as happy here as anywhere else."

Red shook her head. "Sorry, no high chair. I do my best not to serve these guys that really do look underage."

She reached out and touched the chubby

fellow's cheek. To her surprise, he offered her a great big toothless grin.

"I'll just sit him on my lap," Sarah said, scooting along the seat.

"He seems like a pretty easygoing guy," Red said.

"And thank God for that," she replied. "Mia has always been such a drama queen. I deserve a child that's, like, more centered. Elliot is practically Buddha compared to her."

Red thought the comparison might be apt. He was fat and happy and bald. And, at least initially, he seemed content to sit on Sarah's lap, beating crackers into small pieces and then stuffing them into his mouth.

"I hope you don't mind me dropping by, but I did have to see you and I was really curious about this place," Sarah said. "It's really pretty amazing. And this is yours? It's your business?"

"Yes."

"Was it, like, a family business or did you get it from your husband or something?"

The young woman's questions seemed strangely genuine, as if she was really interested. For once Red decided not to evade the answers. If she did, Sarah would undoubtedly keep asking. Red figured one really stark, honest reply would be stunning enough to shut her up.

"No, I built it myself," Red told her. "I had a kid and figured I needed something more steady than lap dancing. I saved my money and opened this place. You might say I pulled myself up by my G-string."

Sarah's eyes got huge. But rather than being shocked into silence, she was stunned into speech.

"Oh my God, that is so . . . so heroic," she said. "I mean it. You are just my hero. It's like . . . like, real feminism."

"Feminism?"

"Absolutely," Sarah replied. "You went into a man's world and turned a den of misogynist exploitation into something that empowered you and your child. I so admire that."

"Misogynist exploitation?"

"Absolutely," Sarah said. "It is so hard to swim against the tide. And when I see a woman succeeding at it, I'm just so impressed."

"Well, thank you," Red replied, uncertain.

"I tried something like that, you know," Sarah told her with a sigh. "When I went off to college I was determined to major in Women's Studies. My mom was just horrified! She said that only lesbians do that.

And that I'd lose my chance with Brad. He'd been my escort the year I was Duchess of the Sublime Virtues at Fiesta. And you know your escort is really your family's first choice for you. Mom didn't want me to mess that up. And I just said to her, I'm not a lesbian, but I am going to study this and you just might as well get over yourself."

"I guess you told her," Red replied, a bit confused as to where Sarah was going with this.

"And it all worked out well for me anyway," she said. "Brad and I got back together just before graduation and had a beautiful wedding just like my mom had hoped. So all's well that ends well."

"Congratulations."

Sarah giggled again. It was not a particularly attractive behavior, but Elliot seemed to like it and began to giggle, as well.

"So I was thinking about that," Sarah said. "And when I heard the gossip about you and Cam, I thought this is going to be even so much better than I thought."

"What are you talking about?"

"Oh, the Cupcake Committee, didn't I make that clear?"

"No, not quite."

"Well, I really need someone to help," she said. "I signed up for it before I knew who was going to be the committee chair and now no one else will sign up. But as soon as I heard about you and Cam, I said, this is somebody who won't be afraid to take on Tasha Shakelford."

"Who?"

"Tasha Shakelford. She was Tasha Godfrey."

Red continued to look at Sarah, completely clueless.

Sarah leaned forward dramatically, causing some complaint from Elliot.

"Tasha Godfrey was Cam's high-school steady," Sarah revealed. "He was *her* Fiesta escort and her family was completely sold on him. Then they mysteriously broke up and no one would say why. I don't think she ever got over him. Shake Shakelford went to Edison, for heaven's sake. Alamo Heights girls might *date* guys from Edison, but they never marry them."

The would-be rebel was so clearly horrified at the thought that Red had to disguise a chuckle as a cough and hide a smile behind her hand.

Elliot began to dislike the whole crackers-in-a-booth thing. And Sarah had to rush to get through the rest of her talk as quickly as possible. The bottom line was that the Cupcake Committee, including Red, would be serving up the refreshments at Harvest Party on October 31.

"We can't call it Halloween," Sarah explained, "because we don't do religious holidays. Of course, it's really kind of an anti-religious holiday, I guess. Unless maybe you're, like, a Wiccan or whatever. Well, anyway, we call it Harvest instead of Halloween, but it's still orange and black. We do mostly pumpkins. No ghosts or witches or black cats. That could scare the children."

"Okay," Red answered, suddenly wondering about Daniel's fascination with vampires.

"I'll take care of getting everything ordered," Sarah said. "If you'll just be there to help me set up and serve, then Tasha won't be on my case. You know, she just can't stand me."

A few minutes later she was rushing out with all the starry-eyed enthusiasm she came in with, stopping for only a moment at the bar to speak to Cam.

"Oh, I really like her, Cam," Sarah said. "I don't care what anyone says, you two are just perfect for each other."

While he was still searching his brain for an appropriate response, Sarah turned and attempted to hug Red, half squashing Elliot in the process.

"See you soon. See you both real soon."

Once Sarah and child were outside, Cam turned to Red.

"What was that all about?"

She shrugged and then answered with dramatic emphasis. "I'm secretly being inducted into the Society of the Cupcake Committee."

"Oh, really?" Cam answered.

"And you'll never imagine why."

"Okay, why?"

"Because I am the potential nemesis of your past flame, Tasha Godfrey."

"Tasha? That was about a hundred years ago," he answered.

"That's not as long ago as you think," Red told him. "Apparently, she's never recovered from when you broke up with her."

Cam laughed and shook his head. "The way I remember it, she broke up with me."

"Really? Why would she do that?"

The emotions that flashed momentarily on his features were startling, serious, sobering. But they disappeared so quickly and completely Red wondered if she'd imagined them.

Cam smiled broadly, deliberately. "I guess she wasn't just perfect for me, the way you are."

16

The hole being dug behind the honky-tonk got deeper and deeper.

"Are you guys planning to bury a convoy of Mexican buses down there or what?" Red asked Ernie one morning over coffee.

The foreman chuckled. "We're going down about twenty feet," he said. "So we're making it wide and we're making it deep."

"Twenty feet!"

"Twenty feet down from the natural bank," he clarified. "Twenty-five from behind this property."

"That's ridiculous," Red told him. "Why would the river need to be so wide and deep here?"

"Oh, the river won't be much wider than it is downtown," he said. "And the depth will only be about six feet. But we've got to get low enough that we can move river traffic this far uphill. The only way to do that without a lock system is to get everything down on the same level."

"But that will create a giant bluff off the back of this property."

Ernie nodded and took another sip of coffee. "It'll be all rocked up real pretty," he assured her. "The masonry fellows on this crew are just exceptional. There'll be stairs at the Eight Street corner to get down to the walkway. And just a few hundred yards north, they're planning a dock where you can catch a river taxi."

"I don't want a river taxi," Red told him with disgust. "I want a view of the river."

He laughed. "Then you're going to have to buy one of the fancy residential units they're putting on this street. Avenue B will be mostly two-story row houses, with a couple of high-rise condominiums thrown in for perspective."

"I've heard all that," Red answered, waving away his words. "They've been talking about that for years. But changing a whole neighborhood owned by hundreds of different people. It'll just never happen."

Ernie shrugged. "Maybe not," he admitted. "Though developers keep picking it off piece by piece. Some said the river would never get up this far, but you can look out your back door and see how that has come to pass."

He was right about that, Red worried. She'd still not received any contract from the new owners of her building. She wanted to kick herself for the mistake she'd made with the last owners. Instead of fighting the higher price, she should have pushed for a long-term lease. She should have asked for ten years!

But of course, she knew why she hadn't. A ten-year lease gave the landlord an excuse to allow a building to run down. And her building already had plenty of problems. She'd thought she'd needed the option to walk away to keep him on top of things. Now, everything was different.

"I'm going to quit thinking of the back area as a patio. It's going to be more like a terrace," she told Cam. "I need to put up a wall along the back. At night, with people drinking, it's just a matter of time until somebody stumbles through that construction netting and falls into the big hole."

Cam nodded in agreement.

"I could put up something temporary, but that would just add to the cost," she said. "I should go ahead and solve the problem now. If I put it off or come up with some semisolution, it will just waste my time and money."

Red considered that thought for a long

moment before adding, "Of course, the two things I absolutely don't have are time and money."

"Maybe you could take out a small business loan?"

She shook her head. "Banks are notoriously stingy with alcohol-related businesses," she said. "Besides, you'd have to be an idiot to loan money to someone who doesn't have a lease agreement or any kind of long-term guarantee. No one is going to want to invest in a business that could be shut down tomorrow."

"I would," Cam told her.

They were lying in bed in the upstairs apartment, sneaking a few moments together before she had to open up.

"I've got some cash saved up," he said. "It's not a fortune, but it would be enough to do some renovation on the patio."

Red was touched. But she was uncomfortable, as well. Men did not rescue her, they abandoned her. That was a reality that she couldn't afford to lose track of. Cam was melting her heart and she fought back with humor.

"Cowboy, you're confused. You're supposed to offer the woman money *before* you get her panties off. Not when you've ridden her so hard, she hasn't got the strength to even look for them."

He grinned and wrapped an arm around her, pulling her close. "To paraphrase a line from *The Graduate,* 'Mrs. Robinson, you're trying to distract me,' " he teased.

"Is it working?"

He kissed her and then replied, "Think about it, Red. A thousand bucks could do a lot, especially if we round up some buddies to work for a few free beers. I want to help."

"You've helped too much already," she answered.

"If you won't let me give it to you, it can be a loan or a share in the bar."

"I don't share my bar."

"Think about it," he insisted. "You're too smart a businesswoman not to even consider the option."

She didn't get much time for consideration. The changes just kept coming.

That very afternoon, a beautiful fall day with a scent in the air that reminded one of pep rallies and football games, a safety inspector walked across her patio and closed it to public access.

Red was shocked almost to disbelief.

"I haven't condemned it," the little man, with a pen in his hand and another behind his ear, told her. "You can still use it for access to the stairway and for storage, you just can't serve people out there or have musicians working."

He slapped a handwritten sign on the inside of the back door that read:

EMERGENCY EXIT ONLY
NO CUSTOMERS BEYOND THIS POINT!

"My God, haven't you people done enough to me?" Red complained. "Are you *trying* to kill my business?"

"I have no interest in your business one way or another," the man assured her. "You're welcome to appeal. Call city hall and get on the waiting list for reconsideration. But until my decision is overturned, don't even be tempted to open that space to the public. We do random checks and a violation won't just result in a stiff fine. We can get your license pulled. And that *will* kill your business."

After he left, Red felt physically sick. She walked out on the patio to get some fresh air and ended up sitting in one chair with her feet propped up on another. A gorgeous blue sky arched overhead. She pulled her hair away from her neck and back and held it atop her head as she stared across the devastation that had once been her serene sanctuary. She could no longer see the river. Across the wide divide, the trees that had once lined the far bank were all gone. What was left was a muddy slope decorated with bulldozer treads.

Red closed her eyes and tried to listen for the water, the buzzing of bees, the wind in the leaves. The only sounds she could hear were those of workers and construction vehicles.

Deliberately, although with some effort, she quieted those sounds in her mind and drifted back to the peace of the faraway farm that had always been there for her.

The little girl that she once was sat beside her daddy, happy and content as they listened to the rushing water of a farm creek and watched the afternoon sun slip beyond the trees.

"I wish every day could be just like today," she told him.

"No, Red," her dad answered. "It just can't be that way."

"Why not?"

"We've got to have our bad days to make us notice the good ones, I guess," he said. "Though I have to admit, this one has been too fine for anyone to ignore. I'm happier sitting on this grassy bank with my red-headed girl than doing anything else in life."

He hugged her close and smiled down at her. Red could see that smile in memory as clearly as if it had happened an hour ago, instead of forty years earlier.

"This is something I won't forget," her dad told her. "Not even when you're grown up with a husband and children and living far away from me. I'll hold this precious time when it was just me and my girl in my heart, to get me through every lonely hour after you're gone."

Red felt a hand on her shoulder and snapped upright, her eyes wide open. Cam was beside her. He seated himself in the chair where her feet had been.

"Whoops, I didn't mean to scare you. I came out here to give you a hug and hold your hand," he said. "I thought you might be crying, but I see you're a million miles away again, sitting here with a smile on your face."

She started to dispute his words, to get mad or make a joke, something, anything to throw him off the track. But, surprising both of them, she didn't.

"I was thinking about my dad," she said.

"Ah . . ." he said, nodding slowly. "You have a dad."

"Had," she answered. "He died when I was a teenager."

There was a quiet moment between them.

"Then we have that in common," Cam said. "Mine was killed in a traffic pileup on Interstate 10. What about yours?"

"Heart attack," Red said. "He was driving a hay mower and just keeled over. Folks said that he was dead before he hit the ground."

"I'm so sorry for your loss," Cam said.

Red laughed, but it came out so strained, it was almost a choking sound.

"Thank you. It was a long time ago," she said.

"Yeah," he agreed. "But it's never that far away, is it?"

She thought about that and then nodded.

"I guess it's not," she agreed. "He was a great guy. You would have really liked him. And, you know, I think he would have liked you."

"Thanks," Cam said. "You were really close to him, huh?"

"Oh yeah," she said. "He and my mom were divorced. He was . . . he was my whole life. What about you? Were you close to your dad?"

"Not so much. My mom had been sick and I was so involved with her that I didn't even have an ounce of anything to spare for him. She died first, slowly, really painfully. And I was still so angry, grieving so much, that losing my dad a year later was almost a nonevent. I felt like he'd been gone forever and his funeral just made it all official."

Red felt a strong pang of sympathy for the young man that Cam once was. She reached up to lay her hand against his cheek. He turned his face enough to plant a kiss on her palm.

"Is your mom dead, too?" he asked.

Red immediately withdrew her hand. "No, I'm sure she's alive and well. Though I haven't actually checked on that in about thirty years."

"I'm sorry."

"I'm not," Red answered. "Sometimes you just have to cut your losses and move on."

She started to get up, but Cam stopped her by laying an arm across the chair.

"What?"

"I just wanted to thank you for sharing with me," he said. "It wasn't so bad, was it?"

"No," she admitted, a bit surprised at the truth. "I thought I couldn't talk about it, but it was fine."

"Good."

He let her go and she rose to her feet.

"So, what are you thinking about all this?" he asked. "Is this one of those times when you just cut your losses and move on?"

"No," she answered with a determined sigh. "This is one of those times where we figure out how to set up a postage-stamp-size stage inside the bar with the least amount of equipment we can get by on."

To: buildabetterbridge@citymail.com
October 7 9:16 a.m.
From: Livy156@ABrats.org
Subject: Hi Mom!

U will never guess what I got 2 do! Nayra and I went to the High School football game. SO COOL! Nayra's m&d took us but they didn't make us sit with them. We sat with some other kids from school. Kaya and Jocelyn. Jocelyn is not too bad really. Nayra and I think she could be a friend. She has a great personality and that is why we like her. Mixon does not have any personality at all. She is maybe the prettiest girl in school but I agree with Nayra. Mixon is a horses bottom! (Nayra didn't say bottom, but she was not talking to her Mom like I am. ha-ha)

Mixon wore a cheerleader skirt to the game and her blouse had little blue and yellow pom-poms and megga-fones on it. She thinks she is so much. She waved at us but she sat with her sister's friends from Junior School. I bet her sister got sick of that.

Daniel wined because I got to go and he didn't. So today Cam is taking both of us to a rodeo in Hunt where his band is playing at noon. I don't know if the Red person will go with us or not. A lot of stuff is going on at the bar. She is moving the tables around to make it small or something.

I luv U and miss you. Daniel does 2. We are ok and having a good school year. So don't worry about us. Get all the sleep U can and email me anytime.

Livy

17

The new lease contract arrived from Merton, Wythe and Stone Development Properties on the same afternoon as the moving party at the Ramirez's restaurant. Red didn't have time to look at it. Instead, she stuffed it under the cash drawer, vowing to go over every word when she had the time.

She'd brought the kids down to the bar with her and they were hanging out on the patio. She went outside to join them.

The place looked completely different than it had only a few weeks ago. She'd left only two tables on the much-shrunken patio. The old stage was now utilized for storage of all of the tables and chairs that used to make money for her every night. Her seating capacity had gone from a hundred thirty-two patrons to ninety-two. Of course, people could still stand, but without the open area on the patio, there was just a feeling of crowdedness that made standing less desirable. A big chunk of her business now walked through the door, only to turn around and walk back out again. Red knew that even the most loyal customer, turned away more than once or twice, would just find somewhere else to go.

Her beer sales had dropped by fifty percent, as well, and she had let Graciela go. She'd hated to do it, but the business could no longer support three waitresses. As things turned out, some good actually came out of it. Nata, already dealing with his job moving across town, was so thrown by the possibility of losing track of Graciela that he suddenly found the courage to declare himself and pop the question. Mrs. Ramirez was hopeful that, in the new location, there would be a job for Graciela, as well.

Red couldn't resist a smile as her gaze focused on the three occupants of the patio area. Cam was sitting at one of the tables, and Daniel was kneeling on the chair beside him. They were both busy using colored chalk on the bar's blackboard.

"What's going on?" Red asked.

"We're working on signage," Cam answered.

Red leaned over the table to examine it critically. The message was written in the crisp, clean strokes of Cam's penmanship.

Closed for a party
  Join us
Ramirez Restaurant
  3 blks north

The words were surrounded by artistic depictions of colorful streamers, stars, flowers and what looked to be fish.

"Why the fish?" Red asked.

"For my favorite, fish tacos," Daniel replied earnestly. "That's what I'll miss most."

"It's not that we won't go to their new restaurant," Olivia informed her brother.

The young girl was standing behind Cam with a rattail comb and a determined frown. She was about halfway through the elaborate process of French braiding Cam's hair.

"And you're getting a new hairdo for the party?" Red's tone was teasing. "The princess look really suits you."

Cam stuck his tongue out at her, but refused to take offense. "You know, Livy," he said to his would-be stylist, "it's your grandmother that you ought to be practicing on. She's really got the hair to carry this off."

Olivia glanced up, giving Red a look of professional hair assessment.

"Yeah, she'd be great," Olivia agreed. "But

she'll never sit still for long enough."

"Ah . . ." Cam agreed. "So I was chosen for my sedentary qualities, rather than my luscious locks."

"Thinner hair is better to learn on," Olivia said very matter-of-factly. "Your hair is kind of strange, especially here in the front."

Red leaned closer to assess what Olivia was talking about. The girl ran her fingers curiously along his hairline.

"I think what you have here is the beginning of a new world for Cam," she said.

"What do you mean?"

"Yeah," Cam asked. "Am I going to have to change my look to a French braid on a permanent basis?"

"No, that won't be the answer," Red said. "I think the technical term for what Olivia's detected here is male-pattern baldness."

The two children both had sharp intakes of breath.

"Baldness? Cam is going to be bald?" Daniel asked.

"Oh no, this is terrible," Olivia said. "Your beautiful hair!"

To Red's surprise, Cam laughed.

"Hey, I'm not kidding," Red said.

He grinned up at her. "I know you're not," he said. "It's one of the things I really like about you. You never try to pretty up the

234

realities." He reached over and wrapped an arm around her hip, pulling her closer. "I guess I'll just have to leave the gorgeous hair to you, Red. Are you still going to love me when my nickname is 'Cueball'?"

"I don't believe I've ever said that I love you," Red pointed out.

He nodded. "I know, you're always playing hard to get." Then he pinched her backside.

"Ouch!"

"Sorry, didn't mean to pinch you, I was aiming for the armadillo."

"You were aiming for the armadillo?" Daniel asked, confused. "What does that mean?"

"Nothing," Cam assured him. "Grownups are just crazy, crazy, CRAZY!"

"I think losing his hair is making his brains spill out," Red told the children. They both laughed.

A few minutes later, with Cam's elegant hairstyle completed and the blackboard sign hung on the front door, Red locked up and they walked up Avenue B toward the restaurant. The ill-maintained sidewalk had weeds growing through its cracked and buckled concrete, and the pavement itself was an obstacle course of potholes. Except for VFW Post 76, housed in an old Victorian house set back on Tenth Street, the buildings were either boarded up or festooned in burglar bars. The kids ran ahead, Daniel acting positively goofy. Olivia was a bit more circumspect, but she was having fun, too.

Typically, Cam would have been hanging with the kids, being as crazy and silly as they were. But today, he walked sedately at Red's side and clasped her hand.

Red wasn't much of a hand-holder. She preferred to relegate physical contact to the bedroom, where it belonged. But strangely, she wanted this memory, walking down the street with a man who loved her and cared about her, in the wake of two happy children. If someone glanced in their direction and maybe squinted slightly, they might mistake them for a happy young family.

If things had gone just a little bit different, Red might have had a chance at something like that. But life had gone as it had. Nothing could change that now.

"What?" Cam said beside her.

"What what?" she responded.

"You were just looking very relaxed, very content, and then something came across your face. What kind of shadows are we working with here, Red?"

"No shadows at all," she lied. "Hurry up, slacker. The kids are getting too far ahead of us. You can always count on a musician to be running late."

He grinned. "I think a better way to look at it is that fiddlers always take their time. And I believe that's one of the things you've always liked about me."

Red teased him right back. "How about later, you see if you can remind me why I've liked you?" she suggested. "When we've got a bit more privacy."

He stopped walking and abruptly pulled her into his arms. "I love you, Red," he told her just before his lips came down on her own.

"Cam and Grandm a standing in the street, K-I-S-S-I-N-G!"

Red pulled away from him. "You're going to embarrass the kids," she said.

Cam gave a quick glance in their direction. "They don't seem embarrassed," he pointed out.

He was right. Daniel was grinning ear to ear and Olivia was giving her a thumbs-up.

"The kids aren't embarrassed at all," Cam repeated. "It's you who's doing all the blushing."

It was true. And for Red it was a bit humiliating. She should be way too old, too hardened, too cynical to allow a sweet kiss and the trifecta of the romantic words, "I

237

love you," to make her heart flutter. It *was* embarrassing and she was sure that she looked ridiculous. Deliberately she pulled her hand out of his grasp and toughened her tone.

"It's the advantage of the redheaded complexion. I used to get paid good money for that," Red told him. "The old men especially loved to see me blush like a virgin while I lap danced like a nympho atop their stiff little wieners. It was always good for an extra twenty in my G-string."

Cam's smile thinned into one straight line, but he purposely took her hand once more.

"I don't care what you did ten years ago or twenty years ago," he said. "You can't push me away with your past, so you might as well stop trying."

They reached the Ramirez Restaurant and went inside. The place was already full of well-wishers and good cheer. And the smells of the food were mouthwatering. But Red found it difficult to throw off a feeling of sadness. All the Mexican pottery that had decorated the walls had been taken down and transported to the new place. The old photographs of the Ramirez family, her parents' wedding picture, she and her sister in matching fiesta dresses, the seventies vintage photo of the restaurant when it first

238

opened, were all packed away. The faint squares on the bare walls where they had hung for so long were a testament to the loss Red felt. Avenue B wouldn't be the same with this place gone.

She smiled as much as she could and tried to pull herself into the festive mood of those around her. There was plenty of laughing and talking. Once the mariachis arrived and conversation became impossible over the music, the crowd got down to the very serious business of eating. Mrs. Ramirez had made her usual platters of quesadillas and enchiladas for the kids. The grown-ups groaned in culinary delight at her more rarely served but beloved *cortadillo,* beef tips in red sauce and the *cochinita pibil,* roast pork flavored with achiote seed and wrapped in banana leaves.

The great food improved Red's mood and before long she was genuinely enjoying herself. She didn't know everyone in the crowd. Except for a couple of the sons and daughters, Red didn't know any of the dozens of Ramirez family members. Mrs. Ramirez's sister, *la gorda,* was easy to spot and hard to miss. She was ordering people here and there in a manner that suggested the place was as much hers as her sister's.

There were people from the church that

Red had never met, as well as many of the family's neighbors. But the majority of the celebrators were people who also patronized the bar.

Red sat for several minutes talking with Alfred and his mama. Alfred was probably about Red's age. He still lived at home and except for his job and his night or two per week at the bar, his whole life revolved around taking care of "Mama." Mama was a charming old lady. She had a quick smile that crinkled her whole face and when she laughed, her whole body quaked. But she was hard to feed. Alfred brought her sample after sample of the food what was available and none of it suited her. Her slight, skin-on-bones frame suggested to Red that she had simply lost her appetite completely.

Red also ran into Elena with her new beau. Cesar was very, very handsome, she thought. Dark hair, dark eyes and a fit, muscular body. But he was very short — Red was a few inches taller than he was. It was not all that common an occurrence for her to be able to look down on anyone.

"What do you think?" Elena surreptitiously questioned as Cam engaged Cesar in a discussion about Spurs preseason basketball.

"Cute," Red whispered.

"I know he's short," Elena told her. "But not anyplace where it matters."

The last was offered with a meaningful wink and the two women laughed together.

As the evening got later the crowd was shoulder to shoulder. It was amazing that Mrs. Ramirez managed to get through the crush carrying a huge *tres leches* cake.

Her sister began cutting it into little pieces as her son helped Mrs. Ramirez up on a chair and quieted the crowd.

"Bienvenidos a todo!" she said. "Welcome! Welcome all of you. I am so glad that everyone is here with us tonight to say good-bye to the old place."

She paused for a moment, surveying the room.

"This place has so many memories for me. My husband and I were so very young when we opened up," she said. "All five of our children learned to crawl on this floor and toddled around these tables. We've celebrated birthdays and anniversaries, graduations and baptisms here in this place. It has been my life and I know it has been a part of your life, too. I will miss it."

There were nods all around the room.

"Things change and sometimes we must change with them. Some people say that's good. Some people say that's bad. I don't know which one it is, or if it is neither. But I know that change is as natural to life as breathing, so we cannot stop."

Mrs. Ramirez looked around the room, a determined smile on her face.

"Tonight, we're not fighting this change, we're taking it . . . we're taking it *abrazo.* Embracing it," she said. "The new place is very nice, roomy with a wonderful kitchen. I don't want any of you to become strangers just because we will be so far away. I promise to make the cooking worth the drive."

Laughter floated through the room.

"I'd drive to El Paso and back for your *menudo!*" someone hollered from the back.

"Thursday," Mrs. Ramirez answered him. "Give me a few days to settle in and I'll have a big pot of *menudo* ready to serve by Thursday."

"But tonight we have cake," Mrs. Ramirez's sister announced, abruptly ending any further speech. "Here, start passing this back."

The cake was excellent. The music started up again and the party revved back into high gear. It was perhaps an hour later when Red noticed Daniel was asleep in a chair. She looked around until she spotted Cam and then waved him over.

"I guess this means it's time for us to go," he said, glancing at the little boy.

"Let me find Olivia," Red said.

"Last time I saw her she was playing out back."

Red found her easily. She and another girl about her age were supervising the younger children through a game of *bebé leche,* a kind of hopscotch.

"Your brother's fallen asleep. Are you ready to go?"

Olivia quickly said her goodbyes and followed Red out the gate and around the building, instead of making their way back through the crowd.

Cam was standing by the front door, a sleeping Daniel slung over his shoulder. He was talking to another couple who seemed to be leaving, too. As Red got closer, she recognized J.B. and his wife, Carol. J.B. was a regular at the bar a couple of times a week, but Carol neither drank beer nor was a music fan, so Red rarely saw her. She gladly took the opportunity to give the woman a hug.

"Carol, it's so good to see you. You're looking great."

The woman shook her head. "I don't know how you can say that," Carol answered. "My backside is getting so broad

J.B. is threatening to bring home the Wide Load sign from his truck for me to wear on my jeans."

"She's lying," J.B. accused. "I like a woman with a button her."

"Oh, you pretty much like all women," Carol corrected.

They all laughed.

"Well, *I* don't like all women," Red told her. "But I do like you and I think you look great. So just take the compliment and quit finding fault with yourself."

"Yes, ma'am," Carol said, giving her a mock salute.

Then, a more serious expression came over the woman's face and she glanced around, making note of Olivia several feet away, and Cam, talking with J.B. She leaned closer to Red.

"I just wanted you to know that there's a woman in town who is spreading stories about you," she said.

For an instant Red was surprised and then she laughed.

"Cam, listen to this," Red said.

Both he and J.B. turned in their direction.

"Some woman is spreading stories about me," Red explained, still finding it humorous. "It's got to be your sweet aunt Phyl again. The mean old battle-ax."

Carol's brow was furrowed. "I don't think this woman was related to Cam," she said. "She's someone who says she's from your hometown. She's saying really ugly things."

Carol stopped and glanced up again at Cam uncertainly.

"She's saying you seduced your own brother and that your parents threw you out of the house because of it."

For an instant Red's whole body was paralyzed. She was so stunned, she wasn't sure she'd be able to speak at all. But from the depths of strength that had kept her life moving forward this far, she dredged up a biting wit and a nonchalant attitude.

"Oh, well, I'd say that's a good story to make up if you can get away with it," she said to Carol, faking a laugh. "She's probably some cowboy's ex-girlfriend still out for a grudge match because I fucked her true love."

Everyone laughed.

"The losers do have it in for you," Carol agreed.

"Yeah," J.B. said. "Remember that bow-legged gal that spray painted the word *bitch* on the front of your building?"

"Oh yeah, who could ever forget that."

"I guess that was before my time," Cam pointed out.

245

"You're lucky you missed it," Red said. "I was mad enough to spit nails."

"You made her boyfriend paint it over," J.B. said. "And it had to have been a hundred and ten degrees outside that day."

"Yeah," Red laughed. "The SOB never spoke to me again. But I heard he went back to her and paddled her scrawny backside for a week. That was good enough for me."

After a couple more laughs and some friendly goodbyes, Cam and Red made their way down Avenue B to the bar. When they arrived, he got the kids into the van while she made sure the bar was all locked up and the alarm set.

When she finally got to the van, both kids were asleep in the backseat.

"We didn't leave a minute too soon," she said.

Cam reached over and grasped her hand.

"You don't have to tell me anything," he told her. "The past is truly the past as far as I'm concerned."

"How did you know?" she asked.

"You never resort to the F word on anything less than a direct threat."

Red realized he was probably right.

"Don't worry," Cam said. "I don't think Carol or J.B. know you as well as I do."

She nodded.

246

He started up the car and backed out of the driveway. In silence they drove up Eight Street and turned north on Broadway. It was a few blocks later before Red finally spoke.

"I didn't seduce him," she said. "And he wasn't my brother."

It was all she intended to say about it.

18

The night of the Harvest Party was as Halloweenlike as a night could get with surprisingly chilly fall air, a full moon and hundreds of little ghouls and goblins out in the neighborhood with their trick-or-treat bags before it even got dark.

Kelly had put Kendra in the stroller and agreed to walk Daniel and Olivia around the neighborhood before bringing them to the party at school.

Red carefully dressed in a button-down shirt tucked into conservative slacks. She'd tried to twist her mile of hair into some kind of respectable updo. After the third failure, she finally settled on braids that crisscrossed and looped around her head.

"Pippi Longstocking grows up to be Mrs. Olsen," she said to herself in the mirror with disgust.

Fearing lateness would be worse than bad hair, she hurried to make her way down to the school.

Inside the gym at Cambridge Elementary, the scene was controlled chaos. There were games going on, art displays and science projects. The dance floor boasted no actual dancers, but there were a fair number of goblins milling about. And a DJ was playing such seasonal favorites as "One-Eyed, One-Horned, Flying Purple People Eater."

Red looked around and realized that she'd missed one important detail about the party. Even the adults came in costume. She should have come as herself, she thought, and she might have been less conspicuous.

With a few directions from a helpful Klingon, Red managed to locate the first-grade cupcake table. Sarah was nowhere in sight, but there was a woman behind the table. She was tall and willowy, like a dancer, and her straight blond hair was pulled back into a ponytail of casual perfection. Her focus was intent and she was busily rearranging everything on the table.

"Hi, I guess this is first-grade cupcake," Red said.

The woman looked up. Her eyes were dark brown, heavily fringed, and her skin was flawless. She gave Red a long look.

"Cullens?"

"Yes."

"I'm Tasha Shakelford," she said. "And you're late."

Red glanced quickly at her watch. It read 6:01.

"Sorry, I got held up by a crowd of pudgy Pokémoners."

Tasha didn't seem amused.

"Carson is a no-show, so the onus is on you."

"Huh?"

"Carson. Sarah Carson," Tasha clarified. "She's not coming. She says that Elliot is sick. But then she always manages some kind of excuse for everything. I've got to handle membership fees at MiniMules. So you'll have to distribute the cupcakes yourself."

That sounded fine to Red. In fact, it was extremely preferable to the alternative of working next to this brusque, unsmiling, former girlfriend of Cam's.

"Sure," Red said with confidence. "I'd be happy to do that."

"Then get over here and let me show you the setup."

How hard can it be? Red thought to herself, but made her way to the workers' side of the table hastily. Despite what Sarah might have been hoping for, Red wasn't interested in any way in fomenting a power struggle with Cam's ex.

The cupcakes were adorable. They had mostly orange or white icing with jack-o'-lantern faces. There were several different patterns, but they were all delightfully cute. Red envisioned children walking up and making their choice with the very least encouragement from her.

"I've drawn up a schematic," Tasha said, handing her a piece of paper that looked as complicated as a house plan.

"Okay."

"The basic is that we have white, chocolate and strawberry," Tasha said. "The white are the ordinary face. The chocolate have the little hair swirl and the top of the face and the strawberry have the square nose."

Red took quick notice of the subtle differences.

"Each type comes with nuts or without," Tasha continued. "We have to be very careful of nut allergies. They are very dangerous. If one of these kids has a reaction and EMS has to be called, I don't want the offending nut coming from this table. Do you understand me?"

"Sure."

"Don't assume anything. Ask every child if he or she can have nuts or not."

"I can do that."

"Good," Tasha said. "That's the most important caveat. This section right here —" she indicated about half of the table "— is for the speciality cupcakes."

"Specialty?"

Tasha nodded. "We have sugar-free in all flavors. The faces with smiles are sweetened with Sucralose. The frowns have aspartame."

"Okay."

"We have dairy-free in white and strawberry," she continued. "As well as dairy-free/sugar-free in white."

Red nodded.

"Gluten-free is available in strawberry only," Tasha explained. "And if they ask, tell the parents that it's a rice-flour and flax combination."

"Rice-flour and flax," Red repeated to herself.

"These are the organic whole wheat." Tasha pointed to a slightly oversize group of cupcakes near the front of the table. "They are, like the bleached wheat, available in sugar-free and dairy-free."

"Okay."

"And we have egg-free vegan in all three types," Tasha continued. "Assure anybody who asks that the ingredients are as local as possible. And that all the chocolate is fair trade from areas without child labor."

Red wasn't even sure she knew what that meant, but she nodded anyway.

"This bin at the front of the table is for the paper cupcake cups," she said. "Please have the children dispose of them here rather than in the trash. We'll add these to compost and that will help to keep down our carbon footprint."

"Cupcakes have a carbon footprint?" Red asked with a smile.

Tasha looked at her as if she'd just arrived from an other planet.

"Everything has a carbon footprint," she answered in a hushed and horrified tone. "And our first graders know that."

Red was grateful when Tasha was forced to leave for her duties at another table. When the hordes of kids arrived in the gym, however, she would have welcomed help from almost anyone.

The younger children showed up with pushy parents who always seemed intent on countering the children's well-trained regimentation of standing in line and waiting their turn.

Red also had to guard against older children who would swoop through and just grab something, without waiting for questions about their allergies or dietary regimen.

She was slow and she had to refer to the dreaded schematic more times than she would have liked to admit. She was only certain of making one mistake, she handed out a dairy-free to a child who was supposed to get vegan. She recognized the error a minute later and told the little girl's mother, who was horrified.

While the child stomped her foot, screaming, the mom forced open the girl's mouth, cleaned out the wad of half-eaten cake and then wiped her tongue with a napkin.

"I'm so very, very sorry," Red apologized profusely.

The woman answered with a dirty look before accepting the guaranteed-hundred-percent vegan cupcake.

It was a welcome relief when the next couple of kids in front of her were familiar faces, even full "princess makeup" with their dark hair coated with pink glitter hair spray.

"Hey, girls, what'll ya have?" she asked Olivia and Nayra.

"Chocolate," they agreed. "We'll both have chocolate with nuts."

As Red handled the request, she added, "Nayra, do you have any allergies?"

"Only mustard," Nayra answered. "It gives

me hives. Yuk of the universe, for sure."

"I don't think there's any mustard in this," Red said, handing the girl her choice. Then, glancing at Olivia, a thought occurred to Red. "What about you?" she asked. "Do you have allergies?"

Olivia looked at her grandmother with the kind of undisguised disgust that only a preteen girl can truly pull off. "Isn't it a little late to ask?"

She grabbed her cupcake out of Red's hand and stomped off, her little nose decidedly in the air.

Daniel came by later. Kelly, with her baby in the stroller, was ostensibly watching him, but the little guy was too wound up for the sitter to manage more than just eyeballing.

"I want strawberry!" he told her.

"Daniel, are you allergic to anything?" Red asked.

The boy's brow furrowed and he looked confused.

"Does any kind of food make you sick?" she clarified.

He was thoughtful for a moment. "I don't think so," he replied. "But asparagus probably could if I had to eat it a lot."

Red smiled at him. "Message received," she answered. "We'll avoid asparagus as much as possible."

The noise level was beginning to wind down, when she looked up to find Cam in front of her table. She was surprised to see him.

"I thought you were playing a party out at Floores Country Store?"

He nodded. "We played a set at five-thirty and we're not going on again until midnight. I thought I'd come and see what you were up to, give Kelly and the baby a chance to go home early."

"I'm sure she'll appreciate that," Red told him. "I sure do. Would you like a cupcake? Not much of a reward, but they look pretty good."

He grinned at her. "You look pretty good, too. Except for the hairstyle. Is that like a modified Princess Leia? I'll just take my reward from you, next time we've got a half hour."

Red didn't get a chance to respond. Tasha Shakelford suddenly appeared out of nowhere. The young woman's face was completely changed by the gorgeous smile that spread across her face.

"Tash!" Cam exclaimed and casually enveloped her into a hug that was so natural it seemed like they must have done it a million times. She was the perfect height and their bodies fit together like a matched set.

When they stepped apart, she continued to hold both his hands.

"It's good to see you," he said.

"When I saw you here," she gushed, "I just had to come over and say hello."

"Well, I'm glad you did," Cam replied. "Have you met Red?"

She barely glanced in her direction. "Uh . . . yes, of course. We're on the Cupcake Committee together."

"How's Shake?"

"Oh, he's fine. The same."

"And your son?" Cam said. "You do have a boy, right?"

"I have two boys now," she said with a slight something in her voice that Red couldn't quite interpret. It seemed part pride and part gloating. "You're not keeping up, Cam," she chastened. "Nearly all of us, your old friends, we're still right here in town and we never see you."

He shrugged. "I work mostly nights," he said. "The rest of the world works mostly days."

She nodded as if she accepted his excuse, but Red was pretty sure she didn't.

They stood looking at each other for another long, slightly uncomfortable half minute before Cam broke the spell.

"It was great to run into you, Tash," he

said and then turned to Red. "I'd better go find Daniel and the girls. I'll see you back at home."

A minute later he disappeared into the crowd and Tasha made a hasty excuse to return to the MiniMules table.

So that was the wife he might have had, Red thought to herself. Tasha was indisputably attractive. She was also young and smart and stylish and well-educated. But she wasn't exactly the spontaneous type. She wouldn't be very suited to the honky-tonk musician's lifestyle. And she didn't seem as if she would be very much fun.

Red felt a very self-satisfied smile spreading across her face. Their breakup may have been a teenage heartbreak, but it was a great stroke of luck for them both.

Red returned to her cupcake-pushing crusade. For a bespectacled redheaded kid who reminded her of herself at that age, she managed to find the very last of the sugar-free/salt-free/gluten-free non-dairy. The girl looked at it as if it were the miracle she'd always been waiting for.

By the end of the evening, most of the cupcakes were gone and the kids who came by for seconds were not among the more picky variety. EMS had not been called to the scene for anyone and Red considered that a personal victory.

At ten minutes before nine, Tasha came over and ordered Red to "close up and break down the table."

She decided to translate that directive on her own terms and began loading up the few leftover cupcakes in the pastry boxes they had come in.

By the time she got down to the decorations, Tasha had returned and was efficiently breaking them down and boxing them up.

"These are mostly Carson's," she said. "Do you want me to drop them by her house or do you want to take them to her?"

"I don't know where she lives," Red answered.

Tasha raised an eyebrow as if the answer surprised her. "I thought you two were friends," she said.

Red wasn't quite sure how to answer that, so she tried to go mostly with honesty is the best policy.

"I'm not really 'friends' with anyone in this town," she said. "I know a few people, but not very well."

"Except for Campbell Early," Tasha said.

"Yes," Red answered simply.

A moment of silence stretched very broadly between them as Red snatched up the tablecloth and began folding it. She needed to be careful. Just because Cam was no longer in love with this woman and because she could never have been happy with him didn't mean that she couldn't be a lot of trouble for Red. A wounded raccoon was sometimes as dangerous as a bear.

"I'm sure Carson was quick to let you know that Cam was once my steady boyfriend."

"I think she did mention that," Red answered, deliberately smiling. "But I believe she got the story all wrong."

"Wrong?" Tasha was looking straight at her, her brow furrowed.

"Sarah seemed to think that Cam broke up with you," Red said. "But when I asked him about it, he said that you broke up with him."

"Oh yes, I did break up with him," Tasha agreed.

"It's so long ago, it's a miracle that either of you even remember."

Red thought she'd handed her the perfect end-of-conversation line. All she needed to do was make a joke about days of old and an ancient former obsession with Pearl Jam. They would both share a little chuckle and the topic would never come up again.

"I broke up with him," Tasha said. "But it was his fault."

"Yeah, well, in some way it always is," Red tried again, with the oft-used, tried-and-true, men-are-pigs diversion.

She didn't take that lifeline, either.

"I still very much care for Cam," she stated instead. "But I love my sons. Trent and Tyler are the best thing that ever happened to me."

Red wasn't sure what that had to do with it, but she didn't ask. She didn't need to, Tasha seemed determined to tell her anyway.

"I am so glad that he's finally found someone like you," she said.

Red was immediately on guard. Her back stiffened and her eyes narrowed. She was ready to mop the floor with this snotty twit.

"What exactly do you mean, 'someone like me'?" she asked with deliberate, dangerous evenness.

"Someone who's already had a family," Tasha replied. "I mean, it was all easy to understand with his mother and what he went through. But getting a vasectomy at eighteen, well that is just more than almost any teenage girl can get her mind around."

To: buildabetterbridge@citymail.com
November 2 10:14 a.m.
From: Livy156@ABrats.org
Subject: Disaster!

Mom you will not believe what my father did. I am SO angry. ANGRY ANGRY ANGRY. We went to see Abuela this morning and she was not there. She finished her rehab and Dad had her moved to some nursing home in the Valley. THATS THREE HOURS AWAY. Why would he do that? STUPID STUPID STUPID.

The Red person just made excuses for him. She said that he must have tried to call us and didn't get us and then forgot that he didn't tell us. That he must have thought since we are busy in school that she would be better off down there close to her sister and her sister's family.

That's maybe what SHE would have done. I can't stand her. Dad probably called and she forgot to tell us and now she blames it on him.

No. She wouldn't of taken us out there if she knew Abuela wasn't there anymore. It is Dad. He is the one who messed up and makes me SO MAD!!!!!!!!!

Daniel cried. Right there in the rehab place in front of nurses and people. It was awful. At least Red didn't shush him or nothing like that. She hugged him and patted him. I guess trying to be Abuela. No way. She told him we could drive down the the Valley tomorrow. That is Sunday and if we go we will miss church. Red said that God will understand. But I don't think she knows much about that. I will let you know.

Livy

19

The days after the Harvest Party were so busy that Red hardly had time to think. It was hard enough to keep up with the kids' schedules, frequent trips to the grocery store and her usual workday. She now added to that Sunday car trips to the valley to see the children's grandmother.

From Red's perspective, however, being busy had its advantages. It gave her a lot less time to think. Most of what was on her mind, she didn't want to think about.

Cam was busy, too. Brian had decided to "make it legal with his baby mama." This created two almost conflicting imperatives for the band. Brian would be leaving to take a "real" job to support his family. Without him, the band really ceased to be a band. So the other musicians would need to find a place for themselves with other groups. They all understood that and were looking to make the transition sooner rather than later.

But Brian needed to put as much cash together as he could to pay for his wedding and to get settled into a place. So he was piling on extra gigs wherever he could. They were winding up at the same time they were winding down.

Cam had been approached to play studio back-up in Austin for a young performer that appeared to be ripe for some success. He liked the guy and his music, so he didn't even consider turning it down. Red teased that he'd become a pinball with a fiddle; she never knew when he was going to bounce in next.

She did manage to catch him one morning for a quick cup of coffee together.

"I haven't signed the lease contract yet," she told him.

He was surprised. "Why not? You were so anxious to get it."

She nodded. "I was," she said. "I was thinking a lease would give me some protection. But I've read it a half-dozen times and it just doesn't offer much of anything at all. I'm here and I can pay rent and as soon as they want the building, I have thirty days to get out. That doesn't seem like much of a lease."

He nodded sympathetically. "That doesn't sound very good."

"Would you read it over?" she asked. "You went to college. Maybe you can see something I can't."

"I can read it," Cam agreed. "But I'm a fiddler, Red. What you need is a lawyer."

"I don't know any lawyers," she said. "And with business like it is, I couldn't afford one."

"With business like it is, you can't afford not to have one," Cam said. "What about Brad Carson?"

"Who?"

"Brad Carson," he repeated. "Didn't Sarah say he was a real-estate attorney?"

"Yeah, I guess she did. But I couldn't ask him."

"Why not?"

"Because I barely know her, and I don't know him at all."

"And if you did, would that make a difference?"

Red opened her mouth to say that it would, but she saw Cam's eyebrow raised and knew he would recognize a lie when he heard it.

"I don't like taking help from anyone," she said.

"Especially from men," Cam pointed out.

"Yes, especially from men. Look, in a business like this with the woman up front, it's almost expected that some man is pulling the strings."

"I know that you've got to guard against that," Cam said. "I understand it and I'm okay with it. But sometimes you've just got to take a chance on letting friends help."

"I do," Red insisted. "The last few months, I've been letting you give me a house and you help me with babysitting and things here at the bar, as well."

"Yeah, and I'm glad about that," Cam said. "I can help and I want to. That's what people who are in love with people want to do."

Red ignored that.

"And I've let the regulars at the bar do things, too."

"That's right," Cam said. "And why do you think you've been willing to do that?"

"Because . . . because the people who come in here, we're all struggling to make it. And we all know that if I need you today, maybe you'll need me tomorrow."

"Exactly," Cam said. "And you should apply that same philosophy to Sarah and Brad."

Red shook her head. "No way. That's different."

"How is it different?"

"*They're* different," she said. "Or maybe I'm different."

"And you don't think the people in Alamo Heights do the same thing as folks here at the bar? That in the heavenlike '09 zip code there is no tit for tat or I'll scratch your back, you scratch mine. And, God forbid, no community pulling together to help each other."

"Oh puh-lease! I'm sure they do for each other, but nobody there needs my help."

Cam shook his head. "Everybody needs help sometimes. Having a nice house in a good neighborhood doesn't make anyone immune to disaster."

"Okay, Mr. Do-Gooder Genius, if I did accept a favor from them, how would I ever pay it back?"

"Hey, you already told Sarah that she could get drunk and listen to music here anytime."

Red shook her head and laughed.

"Do it," Cam persisted. "People are people and you can't make assumptions about them based on some huge generalization about what they do for a living or how much money they make. Give them a chance."

"I'm more experienced in this than you think," Red told him. "I've given people like that a chance and lived to regret it."

"But you did live," Cam pointed out. "This is a great bar, Red. And right now it's dying. If you don't get something going with your new landlord pretty quick, you're not going to have anything left to save."

She knew he was right. She hated it but she had to agree with it.

After he left, Red swallowed her pride with the dregs of her coffee and gave Sarah a call.

"I'm so glad to hear from you," she told Red. "I've been afraid that you might be mad at me for deserting you at the cupcake table. You had to take on Tasha without any backup!"

"It was fine," Red assured her. "She and I will probably never be friends, but we got along fine."

"Oh, I *knew* you could handle her," Sarah said. "You really are my hero. Did she mention Cam at all?"

"Cam came by to take the kids home," Red answered. "They hugged each other and it was all friendly and everything."

"Oh my God! I would have loved to have been there," Sarah said. "Why do my kids always need me just when something really exciting is going on? I'm sure Tasha wanted to rip your throat out. She didn't do anything or say anything?"

Red was not about to share the very startling revelation about Tasha and Cam's breakup. It was a fact revealed to diminish Red and to test the waters to see how close she and Cam might be. Red felt as if she'd handled it well, in that she'd offered no comment at all and managed to keep her expression as blank as possible. However, she wasn't interested in bragging about that to Sarah. The woman might see the incident as a personal version of *One Life to Live.* But for Red, this soap opera was not ready for prime time.

"I actually called to see if I could get you to help me," Red said. "Or rather, to see if your husband, Brad, can help me."

Red briefly explained her concerns and Sarah was very eager for her husband to help.

"So, if you'll give me a number where I can call and maybe get an appointment with him."

"I'll call him myself," Sarah said. "Don't worry another minute about it. Brad will take care of this."

Red had her doubts, but fifteen minutes later he called. He seemed like a pretty reasonable, no-nonsense kind of guy.

"You're not alone in this," Brad assured her. "Businesses in these gentrifying neighborhoods are being pushed up or pushed out. There's a limit to what you can do about that, but I do have some experience and I'll try to get you the best deal that I can."

He asked Red to make a copy of the contract. He would stop by and pick it up on his way home from work.

Red was surprised at how she felt after hanging up the phone. Nothing had changed, but somehow she felt better.

The afternoon rain apparently ran off the construction crew and a pleasant quiet settled inside. The interior was drastically changed from just a few weeks before. She'd had the pool table carted out into the garage and wrapped in plastic. She hated to give up her devoted players — every quarter that went into the slot went into her till — but she wanted to keep the music, and the music was overhead. To pay the overhead, she needed customer seating.

Of course, the music itself had been forced to change. Outside in the open air, she'd had large groups, loud and raucous. Within the confines of the bar, she'd opted to go with smaller groups and more acoustic performances. That created a real scramble with the schedule. Some of the bands she signed just had to be canceled as inappropriate for the current venue. The bar now required a much more intimate performance, much less structured.

"It reminds me of Luckenbach," Casey told her one evening. "Just a bunch of people who love music getting together to make some."

Red hadn't yet decided if that sold more beer or less, but she was aware of the change in the clientele. Most of the regulars still showed up as usual. But she seemed to have lost most of her party-hearty crowd. To her surprise she was seeing some new people — music people. And they appeared to be quite willing to stand shoulder to shoulder all evening to hear a good band.

Karl showed up a little after six.

"I'm sorry I'm late," he said, but Red waved him off.

"As much as you've had to cover for me in the last few months," she told him, "I could wear out my apologies completely."

Karl nodded acceptance.

Red retrieved the leasing contract from beneath the cash drawer.

"I need to run down to the Quick Print and get a copy of this for a guy who is coming by," she said. "His name is Brad Carson. If he gets here before I get back, give him a beer and have him wait on me."

"Sure thing."

Red hurried out. The small business center was just a few blocks downtown. Once there, she copied the twelve-page contract fairly quickly. But by the time she managed to return to the bar, Brad was already waiting. She recognized him easily. Dark suit, dark hair, but the same baby face Red had kissed on Elliot. She walked right up to him.

"Hi, Brad."

The guy rose respectfully to his feet. Not the usual behavior of guys on bar stools when the barmaid walks up.

To say he looked shocked was putting it very mildly. His eyes were as big as saucers and his jaw actually dropped.

"You're . . . you're Sarah's friend?"

"We're on Cupcake Committee together," Red answered. If he was disapproving, at least he couldn't blame Sarah for seeking her out. "Sit, sit," she said to him and popped herself up on the adjacent stool. "I see you've already got a beer."

"Yes."

Karl walked over and set her usual iced-tea highball in front of her.

Red gave him a nod of thanks and took a generous sip before turning her full attention to Brad.

"I was out getting this copied for you," she said, handing over the contract papers. "I hope you can help me make sense of it."

In the less-than-perfect light of the bar, Brad looked over the contract and asked Red a few questions.

There was something strange about their conversation, and at first Red couldn't figure out what it was. Once she did, she had to hide a smile. When Brad Carson talked to her, he looked her directly in the eyes. He looked only in her eyes. Even when he was forced to gaze down at the papers, he did so quickly, without so much as a glance below her chin.

Red did not have the most amazing cleavage on the planet, not even the most amazing cleavage in town. But she did have a nice cleavage and showing it off was just part of the uniform. Very few men passed up the opportunity to get a good look.

Brad did. He managed in fifteen minutes of discussion not to peek even once. She admired that about him. And her estimation of Sarah went up, as well. Her mother might have picked Brad out, but Sarah ultimately signed off on him and she apparently had high standards.

"I feel confident that we can get some compromises in your favor on this agreement," he told her. "Just because they seem to have you in a squeeze, that doesn't mean we can't convince them to sign on to a win-win agreement."

"That would be great," Red told him. "But I think we need to discuss your fee. With the situation like it is, I don't want to be running up a bill that I can't afford to pay."

Brad stated his hourly rate.

Red quickly drank a gulp of tea to keep from choking on the figure.

"I understand the uncertainty of your situation here," Brad told her. "I would never want to encourage anyone to get in over their head. However, I believe I'll be able to save you as much money as I'm going to cost you."

Red quickly ran through her options and decided she didn't have any. At least if it cost an arm and a leg, it didn't feel so much like a favor.

"I appreciate your help," she said. "Please do what you can."

Brad promised to get back to her within a few days and, downing the last of his beer, he said goodbye with the same businesslike manner that he'd maintained during the discussion.

The crowd and the noise level was beginning to pick up. The band had just arrived and were unloading out back and carrying their equipment from the patio.

Red took her place on the box behind the cash register where she could keep an eye on things.

Karl walked over.

"You got a call while you were gone," he said. "The guy left his number."

He handed her a cocktail napkin with the name and phone number scrawled upon it. The number she recognized only as a Dallas area code. The name written underneath was one she'd tried to put out of her mind for thirty years.

Kenneth Grayson.

20

Red sat on the corner of the couch in the living room of the bungalow, her knees drawn up tightly to her chest. She rested her chin upon them. It was very late and the house was quiet, but her thoughts were not.

She had thought that she loved him. But more important, she believed that he'd loved her. She remembered it all so vividly. The first time she'd seen him, she'd been sitting in her lonely bedroom window seat as he pulled his Corvette into the driveway. He looked much like his photographs, square-jawed, athletic, rugged, handsome. She'd been told that he was coming. He was a junior at A & M in College Station, but he worked every summer at his father's car dealership and this summer would be no different. Except this summer, Red was living there.

"I don't think we can ever feel like brother

and sister," he told her that very evening. "Your mother is married to my father, but that means nothing to us." Kenny reached over and took her hand. "What I hope is that you and I can be friends."

Red had badly needed a friend. After her father's death, she'd been forced to move into town. The home of her mother and stepfather was one of the nicest in Piney Woods. Not as nice perhaps as the home that Grayson's first wife lived in across town, but much nicer than anyplace Red had lived.

Her stepfather was a complete stranger to her and her mother was almost as distant. Patsy Grayson was busy every day with her clubs and her charities, trying to become so generous, so beloved of the community that they would forget that she used to be a receptionist at Grayson Automotive and that she'd broken up two marriages to get the old man's ring on her finger.

She had no time or interest in comprehending Red's grief or her loss. She offered no encouraging words. No shoulder to cry on.

Kenny had understood that completely. He'd offered both and more.

He had talked to her. Listened to her. Made her laugh. He'd treated her as if she was important. No lonely, miserable, gawky sixteen-year-old with red hair and freckles would have been able to resist him. From hand-holding to hugs to kisses, it had all proceeded so naturally. And when the kisses evolved into make-out sessions in her bedroom late at night, it was just a matter of time before it became sex.

"I'm scared," she told him. "I've never done anything like this before."

"You trust me, don't you, Emmaline?" he'd asked.

"I love you," she'd answered.

"Then you have to let me."

She hadn't liked it much. The first few times it hurt. And even after that, it seemed more unpleasant than pleasurable. But Kenny really liked to do it. It made him happy and that's all that she'd wanted.

One afternoon toward the end of the summer he called her at the house.

"Is your mom gone to her club meeting?"

"Yeah, she should be there all afternoon," Red answered.

"Good! I'm going to be there in ten minutes," Kenny told her, laughing over the phone. "I want you naked and waiting for me on my bed."

"Okay."

"Do you love getting screwed by me?" It

was a question he asked a lot.

"Yes, Kenny, of course."

"Say it," he told her. "Say it loud and like you mean it."

"Yes, I love getting screwed by you, Kenny."

He laughed. "I'll be there in five minutes."

She'd done what he asked. She'd stripped down completely. She'd combed out her ponytail, letting her hair drape down her back. She put on more makeup, lots of eye shadow and lip gloss. She posed herself on the bed, like the women in the magazines he'd shown her. She loved him and that's what girls who are in love do when guys ask.

Kenny had walked into the room ten minutes later, with five of his closest buddies.

A light tap on the bungalow's front door startled Red into the present. Through the thin beveled glass window at the top, she could see Cam's face.

She got up and let him in.

"What are you doing here so late?" she asked him.

"I always drive by on my way home," he admitted. "And when I saw the light on, I thought I'd see what you're up to."

"Nothing," she answered. "I just can't sleep."

Cam nodded. He reached out to hug her and reflexively she pulled away.

"What's wrong?"

"Oh, nothing," she assured him quickly. "I'm . . . I'm just tired, I guess."

He reached out to smooth a hair away from her face. "When I looked through the door at you sitting there, you reminded me of Daniel, all balled up and defensive. Are you the scared armadillo?"

Red huffed. "I have plenty to be scared about," she said. "My business, everything I've worked for, is about to go belly-up. And I've got a couple of innocent little kids that are dependent on me."

He nodded. "It's a tough time," Cam agreed. "But lots of people live like that all the time. If they can do it, we can do it."

It was on the tip of Red's tongue to pick up on the word *we*. These weren't his grandkids. It wasn't his business. And certainly the other stuff, the stuff she wouldn't talk about, none of that concerned him. He could just walk away. But she'd given him more than enough chances to do just that, and he hadn't. She wasn't sure she would have made it this far without him.

"Thanks for being here, Cam," she said.

He smiled at her. "Come sit down on the couch and let me hold you for a while."

She agreed. What she expected was to sit side by side with his arm around her. Instead, Cam sat sideways on the couch and put her in front of him, her back to his chest, so that he could wrap both his arms and his legs around her.

Red felt herself relaxing into the position. It felt very safe.

"Okay," Cam said. "Let's talk about stuff that doesn't scare us."

"What do you mean?"

"It's a game I made up for myself," he answered. "When I was a kid and got scared, I'd deliberately force myself to think about other stuff. Good stuff. Think of one of the happiest moments in your life and tell me about it."

Red mentally ran through a montage of moments that made her smile. But to her surprise all the ones that came to mind included Cam or the kids. That was crazy. She'd been perfectly happy before Cam came on the scene. And since the kids had been dumped on her, life had been nothing but trouble.

"I can't think of anything," she told him.

"Oh, come on, try harder," he said. "Tell me . . . tell me about the day your daughter was born."

Red shook her head. "I don't think you want to hear that. There was lots of sweating and screaming involved."

Cam chuckled. "Begin after the sweating-and-screaming part."

"Well, the nurses didn't want me to see her," Red said. "I was still thinking that I would give her up for adoption. And the nurses said that seeing her would make it harder, it would make it real."

"But you wanted to see her anyway," Cam said.

Red nodded. "We'd already been through so much together. I wanted to kiss her goodbye and tell her what a great life she was going to have with some new mommy and daddy who could really care for her."

"So what happened?" he asked.

Red shrugged. "I was such a klutz. I didn't even know how to hold her, the nurse had to help me. It felt so awkward and un-natural."

His arms tightened around her.

"Holding her was a very bad idea," Red said. "She was tiny and vulnerable and I had no business even pretending for a moment that I could be a mother to her. I tried to hand her back. But just when I told the nurse to take her, she was needed across the hall. She said she'd be right back and she just left the room with me holding the baby."

Red hesitated. She remembered it all so clearly, yet she hadn't thought about that moment in years.

"I looked down into her little face and it just scared me," Red said. "I didn't try to say goodbye or anything at all. The experience was just pure fear. She was my responsibility until the nurse got back and I was terrified that I might drop her or hurt her. So I guess I was holding her too tight and she began squirming in my arms. That made me hold her even tighter. But she managed to get one of her little arms free from the blanket and she held it up to me. At first I ignored it. I needed both hands just to hold her. Then I shifted a bit and held out a finger to her and she grasped it, really hanging on to me. That's when I noticed her hands."

"Her hands?"

"They were big hands," Red said. "I mean, of course they were tiny, baby hands, but the fingers were very long and very thin."

Red held up her own hands, which could have been described in exactly the same words.

"They're just like my dad's hands. That's when it hit me, I guess, that she wasn't just some terrible mistake that I had made. Some gigantic lapse in judgment that had humiliated me, embarrassed my mother and got me thrown out of my stepfather's house."

"Oh, Red," he whispered, pressing his cheek next to her own.

"I realized that my baby was part of me and part of my dad and that if I let her go, all of that would be gone forever."

"You couldn't do that," Cam said.

"I didn't do it," Red agreed. "That love I'd had with my dad, I just couldn't let it go. I decided to keep her and it was as much selfishness as anything else."

"But you've never regretted it."

Red laughed. "I regretted it a million times," she said. "Every time I screwed up or didn't live up or just saw the expression of unhappiness or disappointment on her face. I wished that I'd given her to some nice adoptive family, who could have probably managed her life a whole lot better."

"I really admire you, Red. You can keep a secret longer than any human I've ever encountered. And you can be as honest with yourself as you are with other people."

"Hey, when you're Bridge's mom, lying is

285

not tolerated."

"So you always told her the truth?" Cam asked.

"Most everything I've told her is the truth," Red hedged. "There are just a lot of things that I've managed not to tell her."

"Ah . . ." Cam nodded. "Same as you do with me."

"I've told you plenty of stuff I've never shared with anyone else," she admitted.

"And do you regret that?"

Red leaned back against him, resting her head against his shoulder she sighed heavily.

"Fact is, I can't believe how good it feels to just say things and not have to guard every word," she said.

"So we're making progress," Cam teased. "If we keep this up, in a decade or two, you might actually relinquish a real secret or two."

Red sat up just enough to glance back at him. "Hey, you talk like you're Mr. Transparency, but there's plenty of stuff you're holding back, too."

"The difference is that I will tell you anything that you ask," Cam said. "You just never ask."

"All right," Red said. "I've got a question for you."

"Shoot."

"Why did you get a vasectomy when you were eighteen years old?"

"Whoa! You've been keeping your ear to the ground on the gossip circuit in this town," he said. "Who told you that?"

"Tasha."

"Ah . . . lesson learned. Never entrust somebody with a secret at the same time that you're disappointing them."

"So it's true."

"It is true," he said. "I guess it's too much to hope that you're the first person she told rather than the one thousand and first."

"I don't know," Red said. "Does it matter?"

He shook his head. "I don't know," he said. "It's a lot like the secrets you've kept, not for myself but for someone else."

Red was surprised that he'd recognized this.

"I didn't want Aunt Phyl to find out," Cam explained. "I knew what I was doing, it was my decision and I think I did the right thing. But she's such a big believer in family, Daughters of the American Revolution, Daughters of the Republic of Texas, Alamo Heights Genealogy Society. All that is so important to her. But she never married or had children of her own. And I guess I didn't want her to find out that her family line ends with me."

"Why wouldn't you want to have a family?" Red asked. "Was it the music? I know a musician's life can be tough with a wife and kids. But to give up the option completely . . ."

"It had nothing to do with music," he answered.

"What, then?"

Cam's hesitation was so slight, Red thought she might have imagined it.

"My mom died of an hereditary disease," he said. "By the time I was in high school there was genetic testing to see if I carry the gene. So when I turned eighteen, I took the test and I do have the gene."

"What does that mean?"

"It means there is a fifty percent chance than any children I have would have the gene," Cam said. "And I decided there were enough children in the world with good genes, I didn't think we'd need any with my iffy ones."

Red turned in his arms so that she could look at him.

"And you are totally okay with that?"

"No, I wouldn't say I'm totally okay. And a lot of other people with this gene wouldn't have made my choice. But I still think it was the right decision for me. And I've learned to live my life pretty well just as it is."

Red nodded slowly, thoughtfully.

"Is that why you were attracted to me?" she asked. "With an older woman the whole baby thing just never comes up."

"Hey, that's not fair," he disagreed. "Remember, you having a daughter was a big secret. For all I knew you could have been seeking out some young stud for your desperately ticking biological clock."

"True," she admitted. "But it *is* a good reason to date older women."

"I don't date older women," he said. "You're actually my first, and to be totally truthful about it, it was your ass rather than your age that got my attention."

He reached between them to grasp the attractive feature in question.

"And if I'd known that first day that it was decorated with a gorgeous armadillo tattoo, I would have come roaring out of that booth and ripped your pants off with my teeth."

Red laughed. "Well, that's one way to attract more business to the bar."

"Speaking of attraction," Cam teased, "I've got some of that growing here in the front of my jeans."

"Oh," Red said. "I can fix that. I've got

just the thing. Would you like to step into the next room with me for a few minutes?"

"Ma'am, I'm shocked. This is Alamo Heights! Surely you are not inviting me into your bed."

"I believe it's actually your bed," she answered. "And I think we could call it an open invitation."

To: buildabetterbridge@citymail.com
November 19 11:09 p.m.
From: Livy156@ABrats.org
Subject: We went to a wedding

hi Mom we had a GREAT time today at the wedding of Cams friend. We don't see Cam so much these days because he is busy a lot but today we went to the wedding and he took Daniel and me with him. Red too.

Red and I both had new dresses that we bought. She let me pick out my own. It is very cool. Long sleeved and kind of square neck with tiny pleats. It is blue and has pink and yellow dots. I did such a good job in finding it that Red asked me to help her. She told me to find her something that YOU would wear and I did. Too funny!

The wedding was in the park. There was lots of room and it was near the river and there were other kids to play with and ducks to feed and everything.

The rings and kissing part of it was in the grass. The bride is real pretty and had a long white dress but it was sorta plain. When I get married I want a really spectacolar dress. O.K.?

We ate enchiladas and Cam played with a new band. Well, not really a new band but a lot of people from different bands that he plays with. The old band are breaking up so he is kind of doing try outs with other ones. So there were lots of musicians there. Cam played his fiddle and also the keyboard and the mandolin. I didn't even know he could play mandolin.

The most coolest thing was Daniel. Cam had him play with the band! Well he didn't play by himself. Cam did the fingering on the fiddle and held Daniels hand on the bow but it was like Daniel was playing himself and he was so proud. Every one clapped and Red and I just clapped and laughed and clapped and laughed.

Daniel is so happy here now. With the new school and Kelly and Cam and even Red. He is like a little kid I guess.

Guess who we saw at the wedding? The evil old lady that lives behind us. She is Cams aunt. Poor Cam she is so mean. She didn't speak to us but I saw her looking at us. I am glad I don't have mean relatives.

We are driving down to the Valley again tomorrow. Yuk, it is so far in the car. But we want to see Abuela. I will tell you how she is.

Love you forever and miss you. Don't worry about us. Daniel and I are fine.

Livy

21

With all the troubles in her world and worries she couldn't even speak about, Red was surprised at how much fun she had at Brian's wedding. She hadn't really wanted to go. There would be a lot of their college friends attending and she'd feel out of place. But Cam had just assumed that she would. She refused to confess that she thought the company might be out of her league.

Getting Olivia to help her dress in a conservative and comfortable disguise helped a lot. As did the champagne.

Red didn't normally drink. It was a conscious decision on her part. As a young woman without education or experience in the world, she had chosen the path for herself based on the lives of women she saw around her. And what was patently obvious was that women who drank or did drugs never seemed to get out of the life, they just got deeper and deeper in.

She had chosen to be clear-eyed and clear-headed. That had always worked for her. But this beautiful fall day at Brackenridge Park, the smudged edges of an alcohol buzz seemed perfect.

Both Olivia and Daniel were on their best behavior. Not due to anything she had said. Apparently the concept of good manners worn with good clothes was something Bridge had successfully instilled in them. And it probably helped that there were plenty of other kids to keep them busy. Brian's new bride had a large extended family, with lots of brothers and sisters bringing along plenty of nieces and nephews.

The patriarch of the clan and Brian's new father-in-law was a gangly, rough-talking man who refused to remove his ball cap, even for the prayer during the ceremony. He sat most of the afternoon on a chair beneath a shade tree, chewing tobacco and spitting into one of the white paper cups emblazoned with wedding bells.

Red attempted a friendly conversation with him. She'd already met his wife, who was genuinely cheerful and easy-going. The father of the bride, however, was not particularly friendly or even pleasant. Added to that, he seemed to be far from the sharpest knife in the drawer. After carrying the load

for more inane conversation than she would
have put up with from her bar's most
habitual drunks, Cam showed up for a rescue.

As they eased away, Cam shook his head
and whispered to her, "Remind me, next
time I'm complaining about anything, that
at least I'm not related to that guy."

Red laughed. "He's what we call in the
business all foam and no beer."

Cam looked very handsome, she thought,
in a Johnny Cash sort of way, black suit,
black hat and boots. He was among the
musician friends of Brian that took turns
filling up the tiny stage area of the pavilion
for a celebration jam session.

The music was great and when Cam
brought Daniel up to help him fiddle, the
entire reception was totally charmed.

For Red, the one fly in the afternoon ointment was the appearance of Aunt Phyl. Red
was initially surprised to see her and then
realized that she shouldn't have been. Cam
and Brian had been friends for years.
Brian's parents were from Terrell Hills
rather than Alamo Heights, but the two had
been in classes together since junior school.

She did not greet Red in any way and Red
made a point not to look directly at her.
She knew better than to bring her own

disagreements to somebody else's party.

The children also recognized her. Daniel hurried to Red's side.

"What's up?" she asked him.

"That woman is there," he whispered. "She's right over there."

"What woman?" Red feigned ignorance. "Oh, the one that Cam calls Aunt Phyl? Or did he say it was Ant Hill? Or Can't Swill? Pant Pill? No, I think it was Plant Kill?"

Daniel began giggling. Red put her arm around his neck and gave him a half noogie.

"You and me, bud, we is not a-scared a no one," she declared in a whisper.

He nodded agreement. Not another word about it was spoken, but Daniel continued to hang close for about fifteen minutes. Then apparently he became convinced that the threat from Cam's aunt was less dangerous than the appeal of feeding the ducks with the other kids.

The woman was perfectly groomed and fashionably dressed. But from what Red observed, she wasn't stuck up or overly fastidious about her acquaintances. She spoke to everyone, including all of the bride's very sweet family. And when Red spied her seated under the shade tree with the cranky tobacco spitter, Red allowed herself a very self-satisfied giggle.

The menu was Tex-Mex and all the kids, including Olivia and Daniel, were trying to eat their weight in enchiladas. Red found herself busy getting drinks, rescuing napkins and wiping up spills. She fell into these tasks rather naturally and quickly noticed that, for the most part, grandmas were in on this. The actual parents, giddy with the unaccustomed freedom of a grown-up party, were mostly oblivious to the near disasters occurring minute by minute.

Strangely, Red did not find this at all laborious. The kids were having fun. The food was plentiful and as long as they ate it instead of using it as artillery, it all seemed fine.

After, the kids were finished and off on more adventures, the grandmas cleaned the table and sat down together, huffing and chuckling with exhaustion. Most of the group was easily ten to fifteen years older than Red, but she felt a strange kinship that was wholly new.

A very old granny brought a basket of fresh, hot tortillas and set them in the middle of the table. It seemed like such a welcome idea that another retrieved a huge bowl of guacamole and a plate of jalapeños.

Red enjoyed her share, washing it down

with more champagne.

"You're raising your grandchildren?" one of the women asked.

Red nodded, her mouth full.

"I'm raising one of mine, too," the woman said. "I love him, but it wears me out. It's hard to chase a toddler when you're sixty-two."

A heavyset woman with thinning blond hair and a mass of freckles agreed.

"I keep three of my six grandkids all day," she said. "And I have two more coming before and after school. I'm exhausted."

The other women were nodding. "You think when you finally get your own kids grown, you're done," a woman with a bright-red birthmark on the side of her face said. "Sometimes it doesn't work out that way."

There was agreement on that statement, as well.

"Is your child unable to care for her kids?" the sixty-two-year-old asked Red.

"It's just temporary," Red answered. "My daughter is deployed to Afghanistan."

One of the bride's aunts laid her hand atop Red's. "Oh, you poor dear! You must be frightened to death."

"No, my daughter is a professional soldier," Red answered.

The woman nodded sagely. "That she may be, but she's your baby and she always will be."

Red might have disagreed with her, but a memory of toddler Bridge, looking so small and frightened as she waved a tearful good-bye from the doorway of the night-shift day care flashed in her mind. A lifetime of similar goodbyes and a blind trust in Providence to keep her safe had been the only way they could get by.

"Of course she's my baby," Red answered. "We grew up together."

The group of grandmas knew exactly what she meant.

As the evening ran on, the grown-ups got louder and the kids got more quiet. The colorful strings of lights around the pavilion made the area seem more intimate. Daniel found his way to the chair beside her, where he sat, willing his eyes to stay open as he began to yawn.

Cam came to the table and asked her to dance.

"We'd better be getting these kids home," Red told him. "And you'll have to drive. I've had too much of this." She held up her empty champagne glass for evidence.

"Okay, but not until I've had a dance," he said. "The musicians never get to dance.

It's a slow one and I'm so good at that. I hate to miss the opportunity."

He held out his hand and she took it. He led her out to the ten-foot square of wood flooring already crowded with couples. Cam pulled her close in his arms, but she resisted, putting a respectable distance between them.

"What?"

"Daniel and Olivia might be watching," she said. "And for sure your aunt Phyl is."

He chuckled. "Red, you are such a puritan at heart," he told her.

"Nobody would accuse me of that," she said.

"Because nobody knows you like I do."

"I wouldn't be so sure about that, cowboy," she teased.

"I am sure about it," he answered with complete seriousness.

She looked away, uneasy with the honesty in his eyes.

"Okay," he said. "If you're going to ruin my fantasy of feeling you up on the dance floor, then let's play a game."

Red grinned up at him. "Guys who suggest games are usually up to no good," she asserted.

"Guys are up to no good generally," he agreed. "But it doesn't mean you can't play with them."

"What's your game?"

"You tell me something that I don't know about you," he said. "And I'll tell you something that you don't know about me."

"Now, why would I do that?" Red asked. "I'm famously secretive as you remind me constantly."

"You'll tell me because you've had too much champagne and because I've already said that I know more than anybody about you and you've got to prove me wrong."

She looked up at him, stern and determined.

"I am not talking about Bridge's father or anything about my life before I came to San Antonio," she stated firmly. "I've never even talked to Bridge about that, so you can't expect that I will share that with you."

"Okay."

"And I'm not going to talk about any of the men that I've been with before you," she said. "That's just none of your business."

"Agreed."

"So what else could there be that you want to know?" The question was genuine and Red was surprised by his quick response.

"I want to know about how you got that

armadillo tattoo."

Cam momentarily allowed his hand to drift lower and caress the location.

Red deftly moved his hand back to her waist. He was grinning at her and she couldn't resist him.

"I got it right after I first started dancing," she said. "You are right about me, I am not totally a free spirit. Getting up in front of all those men wearing virtually nothing, that was hard for me. Embarrassing. Humiliating. It's an ugly business. Putting cash in the G-string, that's what most people think it's about. But there are all these jerks who want you to take their twenty with your thighs or let them stick it between your butt cheeks. I had one guy who always wanted me to pick up his money by sitting on it so it would stick to my crotch."

Cam's grasp on her tightened, but she didn't pull away.

"I just felt so naked, so exposed," Red said. "One of the older gals told me to get a tattoo. The thing with the tattoo is that nobody can make you take it off. So there's a part of you that remains all yours always."

Cam thought about that explanation and then nodded understanding.

"So why the armadillo?" he asked.

Red gave a little laugh. "I didn't know what to get," she said. "The other girls had hearts or flowers, some cartoon characters. One really nice gal had the poison symbol, you know the skull and crossbones. Yikes!"

Red shook her head, recalling all those long-ago people and the world that had been her own.

"I went to a local tattoo parlor, but I still didn't know what I wanted. I looked through his book and I didn't see anything that really appealed to me. So I said I had to think about it and walked out. Next door to the tat shop was a gardening place. I saw a father and his daughter there and he was picking out a child-size garden rake for her. The scene just stopped me because when I was a kid my dad bought me one just like it."

Red relaxed into the story and the memory. "My dad said I needed my own rake because I was worse than an armadillo for digging up the flower beds."

She smiled up at Cam. He was smiling, too.

"The more I thought about it," Red continued, "the more I thought it fit. The more I wanted it to fit. Armadillos are mostly night creatures. You might catch them out in the daylight, but they never seem happy about it. Whether you think they are cute or ugly is a matter of opinion. But like me, they certainly stand out as looking different." She grabbed a handful of her long red hair and held it out as evidence. "And they go about their business, not trying to hurt anybody."

"Not to mention that they have some pretty formidable armor to keep others from hurting them," Cam said.

"Yes," Red said. "They are pretty good at keeping others from hurting them."

Cam pulled her close and ran his hand down her back to clutch her right buttock.

"Now that I know more about it, I love it even more."

She laughed, more pleased with having told him the story than she was willing to admit.

"Now you," she said. "You have to tell me something about you that I don't know."

The song ended and they stopped to join the other dancers and those sitting at the tables in applauding the musicians. Brian had deserted his new bride to join in on the jam. And when they struck up one of his favorite tunes, he tried to wave Cam over.

Cam shook his head. Wrapping his arm around Red's waist he led her off the dance floor and out into the surrounding darkness of the park. It was cooler away from the crowd and the night air had a real November nip.

"Do you need my coat?" he asked.

"No, the cool breeze feels great," Red said. "Now, are you thinking you can just walk me out here in the dark and kiss me and I'll forget about you living up to your end of this bargain?"

He stopped abruptly and turned to her. He lifted her chin and planted the sweetest, gentlest kiss against her lips.

"Mmm, that was nice," she whispered.

"It was your idea," he pointed out.

"You still have to give up a secret," she said.

"I know," Cam answered. "And I want to. Actually, I have two that I want to tell you. My problem is, I can't decide which one I have to tell first."

"Tell me the best one," Red said.

"Okay," Cam answered. "This is the best one. Red, I don't think you know this, but I want to marry you."

She stood there, frozen in place. In the shadows of the trees, she couldn't see his face, but she knew the expression on it. Suddenly, she was cold and ran her hands along her folded arms for warmth.

"It's getting late," she said. "I need to get the kids home."

22

Sarah Carson called her the morning of the first cement pour. The line of cement trucks with their ever-tumbling loads were mating up with dump trucks filled with gravel. The workmen shouted above the din to hear one another. Inside Red's Hot Honky-Tonk Bar, nobody bothered to talk. The noise easily drowned out speech. Even the jukebox couldn't be heard.

Red did manage to pick up the phone and with a finger in the opposite ear, conduct a conversation.

"The Thanksgiving cupcakes will be a lot easier," Sarah assured her. "We only have to serve them to the kids in our class."

"But I guess we still have to get twenty kinds," Red replied. "I should have kept my schematic."

"Oh, it's much easier with the class," Sarah said. "We know what each child is supposed to eat and we just put the names right on the cupcakes with a toothpick flag."

"Ah."

"It's a little more planning, but a lot less chance for a mistake," Sarah said. "Of course, it was Tasha's idea. All the ideas that get implemented come from Tasha."

"I guess it's good to have someone with ideas."

"Yes, well, maybe so," Sarah said. "And I promise to be there with you this time."

Red wrote down the hour and date and agreed to be there on schedule.

"And Brad has the contract ready for you to look at," Sarah continued. "He really wants to talk to you about it, but he's having a horrible week. Is it possible for you to get away and meet him in his office?"

"Sure, I could do that," Red told her. "Truth is, I'd love to get away from all this construction chaos."

She wrote down Brad's office number and as soon as she hung up with Sarah, she called him.

She was very grateful that the receptionist found a place to squeeze her in early that afternoon. She really wanted Cam to go with her. He knew Brad and he knew about attorneys. She hesitated to ask him, though. Things between them had been not strained but touchy since Brian's wedding and his mention of the dreaded M word. They hadn't discussed it further, but Red suspected that he was just biding his time and she didn't want to hand that time to him on a platter.

Still, it would be so much better to have him beside her. To have a second pair of much more educated eyes to look at the contract and ask the questions.

As she turned those thoughts over in her mind, she realized that she was scared. Going to Brad's office was getting out of her comfort zone and she was just plain chicken.

Determined, she mentally stiffened her spine. If she could stand up to street toughs and mean drunks and bar room lotharios, she ought to feel right at home in a building full of lawyers.

She called Karl to come in early. As soon as he arrived, she donned a suit jacket to cover her assets, twisted her hair into a giant blob atop her head and stepped into the highest high heels she could find in the apartment closet. When a woman was ready to do battle, she needed to walk tall.

The law firm's office was in a high-rise bank building near Main Plaza. Red found the place easily and went inside, head held defensively high. To her relief, she did seem to blend in without much trouble. In fact, she thought to herself, the downstairs receptionist with her short, tight skirt and revealing V-neck décolletage looked less lawyer ready than Red herself.

Brad appeared delighted to see her, though he was all business. They sat down at a table in his office and he spread the pages out before her.

"What I've put together," he said, "is a counteroffer to the developers' baseline."

"Huh?"

"Merton, Wythe and Stone never expected you to sign that contract," Brad said.

"They didn't?"

"No," he answered. "I'm sure they hoped that you would, but they would not have expected you to take this deal."

Red swallowed, thinking how close she'd been just to signing it and getting it in the mail.

"So what I've done," Brad went on, "is to ask for everything you could possibly want and then some."

"Like what?"

Using an expensive pen as a pointer, Brad indicated and explained several clauses in the updated agreement.

"We've asked for a significant discount on a ten-year lease price," he said. "And we want the developer to pay for all repairs and upgrades your business will need to cope with the changes and inconvenience that the river construction has brought. I ball-parked the wall project for the patio at ten thousand dollars. I thought, ideally, you'd want a limestone that would be similar to that used in the river project. And naturally, you can't have a new limestone wall without veneering the old building to match. Once the business has been through all of this renovation, we'll require a minimum two years' notice to vacate."

Red sat there with her mouth open.

"Don't expect that we'll get any or all of this," Brad said. "Because we won't. What I'm pushing for is another counteroffer that will get us what we absolutely need to have, and that's a reasonable timetable to vacate."

"Oh," she said, trying to take it in. "So you think that no matter what, I'll eventually have to move."

Brad leaned back in his chair, appearing to choose his words carefully.

"It's likely," he said. "How much do you understand form-based zoning?"

"I've never even heard of it."

He went to a cabinet across the room and retrieved a file of legal-size papers that included a photocopied map of an area north of downtown.

"River North, the area between downtown and the Pearl Brewery area, is being re-zoned. The new zoning is not based on what is there now and how that area is being used, but was designed specifically to achieve a certain desired outcome."

Brad talked at some length about what the planners had in mind. He showed Red drawings that had been done. One in particular he held up, with his fingers over the legend.

"Where do you think this is?" he asked.

She looked at the tree-lined street of two-story brownstone houses and a colorful cable car.

"New Orleans?" she suggested, it being the only city outside of Texas that she'd ever visited.

Brad shrugged. "Most people say San Francisco," he told her. "But New Orleans is a good guess, too."

He took his fingers away from the map's corner. And she read the words with shock: *River North Redevelopment, Avenue B.*

"That's where my bar is!"

Brad nodded. "The city wants to take an underutilized downtown eyesore and create a walkable, mixed-use urban neighbor-hood."

"Mixed use?"

"That's retail and residential side by side."

"Okay, so my bar could be in between these houses."

Brad shrugged. "Businesses like yours are not usually considered appropriate for that zoning."

"Businesses like mine?" she repeated.

He nodded. "I'm sure, from the zoning standpoint, it would be said that you're too loud, you draw a rowdy crowd and you aren't the right fit with family homes."

"I'm just a neighborhood bar. Doesn't every neighborhood need a neighborhood bar?" Red asked.

Brad let out a long, concerned sigh. "They might have a neighborhood bar," he said. "But as your business exists right now, most people wouldn't think of it as a neighborhood bar. It's a honky-tonk and for all our love of Texas tradition, nobody wants to live next door to one."

"Oh."

"And this redevelopment is going very upscale," Brad continued. "Staying would mean seriously rethinking your business model. The people who are going to live on that block are going to be drinking a lot more martinis and mojitos than Shiner Bock."

Red remembered joking about having

teatime for the ladies who lunch at the Bright Shawl.

"The thing to remember is that this is still a long way off," Brad told her. "That's why I think the ten-year lease, while optimistic, is still within the realm of realistic. And maybe you'll be thinking about retiring by that time anyway."

Red had not really considered retiring at all, ever.

Brad went over every part of the paperwork they were sending to the developer. He was very careful in making sure that Red understood every word of what she was signing and what the next steps would be.

"I fully expect to have a small flurry of paperwork from every attorney they can contact," he said. "That's their next step, to try to intimidate us with how big they are compared to how small you are. We are not going to get distracted by that. Rezoning, redevelopment, that all takes time and in a famous-for-siestas city like San Antonio, it takes even more time than usual. They are going to want to be drawing income from you while they're waiting. And keeping a business, any business, on that street, keeps cops patrolling and vandals and squatters out. You're a good deal for them. And no matter what they say, you've got to remember that."

Red signed all the papers and thanked Brad for his help.

"Let's see what kind of agreement I can get you," he said. "Then you'll know whether you really need to thank me or not."

She headed back to the bar, feeling better about the short-term but more worried about the long. She glanced out at tacky, run-down and unappealing Avenue B and wondered aloud, "Why do things have to change?" Her life was good. She was happy. Everything had been going great. And now it all seemed to be going to hell in a hand-basket.

She parked her car and went through the gate to the back patio. Halfway across, Cam called out to her from the stairs.

"What's up?"

"Nothing," she answered.

He came down the steps, shaking his head. "Something," he said.

"What makes you think that? My amazing business jacket?"

"Your hair," Cam answered. "We've been through the polygamist wives and Mrs. Olsen meets Pippy Longstocking. Today you look like the governor of Alaska."

Red chuckled and began pulling the clips out.

"You have beautiful, long hair," he told her. "Don't let any of the hometown harpies scare you into hiding."

"I just had a meeting with Brad," she told him.

"Then I'll bet he was disappointed not to see you looking like your gorgeous self."

She smiled up at him and he planted a kiss on her forehead.

"So what did the man say?" he asked. "Should I start rounding up volunteers to defend this place like the Alamo?"

Red shook her head. "He thinks we'll get to stay here a while," she said. "He's hoping to get me ten years."

Cam nodded thoughtfully. "Ten years is good."

"Brad says that maybe by then I'll want to retire," Red offered with a laugh. "I guess he thinks I'm even older than I am. I really almost never think about retiring. Do you?"

Red watched as the smile disappeared from Cam's face and a puzzling, indecipherable expression took its place.

"No, I never look that far ahead."

23

The morning was cold and overcast as Red stepped into the kitchen. Olivia and Daniel were still yawning over bowls of instant oatmeal.

"What do you think, Olivia?" Red asked. "Today is the party in Daniel's classroom. Can I wear this? Do I look okay?"

Both children looked up.

Red was trying to follow Cam's advice. She had on dark slacks and a casual sweater. She'd pulled her hair away from her face with a clip, but the length of it still hung down her back, past her waist.

"It's okay," Olivia said after a moment of assessment. "You look fine."

"I think you look pretty," Daniel said.

Olivia shot her brother a look of incredulity.

"It's true!" the little boy defended. "Of all the grandmas that I've seen, she is way more the prettiest."

"Why, thank you, Daniel," Red said. "I think you're cute, too." She ruffled his hair and he giggled.

"Can we go down to see Abuela for Thanksgiving?" Olivia asked. "It won't seem like a holiday without family."

Daniel's smile waned a bit.

"I think it's *may* we go down to see Abuela," Red told her, avoiding the question.

Olivia bristled. "I don't think that somebody who didn't even finish high school should be correcting my grammar."

Red raised an eyebrow. "Then I won't, unless you make a mistake. As long as you're perfect, you won't hear a peep from uneducated me."

Olivia gave her a disgusted, unhappy look.

One step forward, two steps back, Red thought to herself.

Within a half hour, both children were clean-faced, appropriately dressed and donning jackets for the walk to school. Olivia's bout of surliness had disappeared completely as she clearly and competently did a mental checklist of what she and her brother should have in their backpacks.

"All right, we're ready," she told Red finally.

Red put on her own jacket and they

headed out into an autumn morning in Alamo Heights. With large numbers of live oak, mountain laurel and anaqua trees that never lose their leaves and the rugged mesquite, with leaves too small to make an impression, fall in San Antonio was almost a misnomer. But the November wind swept down the street, stirring up small whirls of red leaves from the elms and sweetgum and vibrant yellows from mulberry and sycamores. Red imagined herself, if only for a moment, like anyone else in the world, bundled up and moving in a purposeful direction.

Olivia hurried on ahead, eager to meet up with her friend Nayra before class. Red and Daniel set their own pace.

Daniel was too excited about the day to even notice his surroundings. Talking a mile a minute about the planned activities for this last school day before Thanksgiving, he bore almost no resemblance to the frightened little boy he'd been just a couple of months earlier. And his ability to speak English certainly hadn't suffered from lack of use.

"And I have the most lines of anybody and I memorized all of them by heart," he told Red proudly.

"Wow," she responded, appropriately impressed.

"And I have a great costume, too," he said. "But I can't tell you about it because it'll ruin the surprise."

Red nodded soberly. "Right, you don't want to ruin the surprise."

"It's really cool!" he assured her, clearly struggling not to reveal all.

Casually he reached up and grasped Red's hand as if it was the most natural thing in the world to do.

Red was startled at the touch, then inexplicably buoyed by the feel of the small palm that clutched her own. She tried to remember if she'd ever done this. Had she walked Bridge to school? Of course. Had she listened to her daughter's happy chatter? Surely she must have. But none of those moments came to mind, only the fears, the worry, the guilt. It was as if all the stress and struggle of those days had robbed them of any joy.

But it couldn't be just the stress and struggle that had been her thief. She had plenty of stress now and plenty of struggle, yet somehow it was different. *She* was different.

"You know, Daniel," she told him, "I'm really glad about how well you're doing in school. You come home with stars on your papers nearly every day."

"I like school," he told her. "Livy always told me it was awesome, and now I know she's right."

Red nodded. "Yes, Olivia is right about a lot of things."

"And Mrs. Reardon likes me," he added. "She likes me a lot. And she's really proud of how hard I work. She's going to tell Mom that when Mom gets home. She promised."

"And your mom is going to be really proud of you, too," Red assured him.

Daniel's chest pumped up immediately and he grinned ear to ear. "Thanks, Grandma," he said.

He began to skip and because she was still holding his hand, Red began to skip, as well.

By the time they got to the sidewalk in front of the school, they were both laughing.

In Daniel's classroom there was less hilarity and more chaos. There were more parents than kids and although the tables had been pushed to either side of the room and the chairs were lined up in neat rows, everybody was standing. Mrs. Reardon quickly got her students, including Daniel, to come behind a five-foot-high panel decorated with a forest scene. The artwork was clearly done by many little hands. There were acorns bigger than some of the trees and some sort of animal, maybe a horse or a rabbit, was hidden in the branches. But a big happy sun shone overhead and the ground was apparently covered with snow, though few of these Texas children would have ever seen it.

Sarah was suddenly beside her.

"Where's Elliot?" Red asked.

"Mother's Day Out," she answered. "Are you ready to head to the cupcake corner? I'm supposed to be there, but I've been waiting for you."

Red glanced around to see the spot in question, not ten feet away. Tasha was there.

Red gave Sarah a look. "You can't let her intimidate you," Red whispered.

"I know," Sarah answered. "But she's been doing it so long and so well."

They both laughed.

"Come on."

A few steps later, Red greeted the other member of the Cupcake Committee.

"It looks like you've got everything set up perfectly," Red told her.

"Well, no, it's not perfect," Tasha disagreed. "I wanted each of the children to have the character they play on the top of their cupcake. But Squanto and Priscilla Alden got switched somehow."

"I hate when that happens," Red said.

Tasha glanced up at her sharply, but when Red didn't even crack a smile she let it go.

"Sarah, I hope that you will at least *mention* how disappointed the children were with this mistake when you talk to the bakers."

"I will, absolutely I will," she assured her.

Tasha turned her attention back to Red. "So I guess this is a big day for Daniel," she said.

Red nodded. "He told me that he has the biggest role. I'm not sure if that's true or it's just big to him."

"Oh, it's the biggest role," Sarah assured her quickly. "The turkey is the narrator of the whole story. It takes a lot to memorize the entire story."

"He's a turkey?"

"Yes," Tasha answered, pointing to the bird-topped cupcake with the little toothpick bearing Daniel's name.

Red laughed. "Well, I guess the turkey would have the biggest role in the Thanksgiving story."

"He didn't tell you he was going to be the turkey?" Tasha asked. It sounded strangely like a criticism.

"He said it was a secret and he couldn't tell," Red explained.

"Of course, it's always a secret," Tasha replied. "But they always tell. Kids this age just can't keep a secret. I know mine can't."

"Daniel can," Red said proudly. "He must get that from me. I'm pretty sure that blabbing when you're supposed to keep your mouth shut has got to be an inherited trait."

Red was fortunate enough to see Tasha's jaw drop before, with a smattering of applause, Mrs. Reardon came out from behind the panel to welcome the guests and commence the performance.

Daniel was the first one out. He was wonderful. His turkey costume included a lot of fat plumage as well as a beak on his head and some long red wattles. His eyes were big, but he looked straight at the crowd as he recited the story of the first Thanksgiving. The other children came out and did their lines well, though some of the pilgrims were given coaching from Mrs. Reardon from behind the panel.

In less than ten minutes it was all over. The kids were bowing and everyone was cheering.

"They did so good!" Sarah exclaimed, though Mia was one of the few who'd unfortunately messed up her part.

"They were great," Red agreed. "It was just wonderful. I really wish my daughter had been able to see that."

"Oh gosh, Clarissa videoed the whole thing," Sarah pointed out. "Your daughter has e-mail, right?"

"Yeah, Olivia writes to her all the time."

"Then I'll get Clarissa to send it as a feed," Sarah said.

"Do you think she'd mind? I don't want to be a bother."

"My God, your daughter is defending the country, the least we can do is send her son's big moment to her."

Clarissa didn't mind at all. In fact, she seemed excited by the idea that her artistic production might have an international distribution. When Red didn't know Bridge's e-mail address, Clarissa volunteered to work out the details with Olivia.

Word quickly spread among the attendees. And as the first graders were eating their cupcakes, Mrs. Reardon made an announcement.

"I just want everyone to know that because all of my students did so well today, Tradd's mother, Mrs. Cook, is going to send a film of our program all the way to Afghanistan so that Daniel's mother, who couldn't be here with us, will get to see it."

There was a shriek of delight from the kids. Red locked eyes with Daniel. He was thrilled, too. Too thrilled. The expression of happiness that was on his face also had fear. Red knew immediately, as if she were feeling it herself, that he was scared he might cry in front of his friends.

Like a shot, Red was across the room and dragging him out the door.

"We've got to go tell his sister, Olivia," she announced loudly. "And show her Daniel's costume."

As they made it out the door, Red heard Mrs. Reardon suggesting to the children, "Let's see if we can find Afghanistan on our map."

Daniel was flat against the hallway wall. He was biting down on his lip, hard. Red dropped onto her knees in front of him.

"It's okay, punk," she told him. "It happens to me, too. We know we're not supposed to cry in front of people. And when we're angry or sad, we can keep from doing it. But sometimes, when we're really happy, it sneaks up on us."

Tears were rolling down his cheeks now.

"I tried not to even think about it," he said. "I didn't even want to think about her not being here. About her not seeing me. I did real good, didn't I?"

"You did great," Red said. "And you are

just going to make your mama's day. I know it."

Daniel threw his arms around Red's neck. He was still trying to choke back his emotion. "I miss her so much," he said.

"I miss her, too," Red told him and she realized it was true. "Every day there are things that happen with you and Olivia, and I want to tell her about them or ask her about them or just talk about when she was a little girl."

Daniel stepped back slightly and wiped his eyes with the back of his hand. "I want to tell her stuff every day," he admitted. "How many more sleeps before she's home again?"

Red shook her head. "I'm not sure," she said truthfully. "But fewer every day. She's supposed to be here by Christmas."

"She'll be like my Christmas present."

"She sure will," Red agreed. "Now, are you ready to go find your sister's classroom and show her what a turkey you are?"

Daniel giggled. "Don't call me a turkey," he said.

"Oh, I know," Red said. "You're not a turkey, you just play one for Thanksgiving."

To: buildabetterbridge@citymail.com
November 27 8:05 p.m.
From: Livy156@ABrats.org
Subject: Sad news

Mom something terrible has happened. Kellys husband has been hurt. We don't know much about it yet. He is in a field hospital like yours and they will move him as soon as he is ready. He is burnt so he will probably come here to San Antonio but we don't know.

I dont even know what to write. Could you call us Mom? I know it's the middle of the week but Thursday is Thanksgiving. I think you can call on a holiday can't you.

Livy

24

The Wednesday before Thanksgiving, Red was on her own at the bar. Karl had gone to the coast for a long fishing weekend and her one waitress called in sick.

Red wasn't that worried. The crowd would be small, she thought, and guys who were too lazy to step up to the bar could just learn to do without beer. That wasn't going to happen.

She hadn't expected much of a crowd. No band was scheduled to play that night. However, since moving the music stage inside, she'd allowed jamming when there was nobody on the playbill. Perhaps because it was the eve of a holiday or just a co-incidence, a half-dozen guys with guitars, basses, Dobros and harmonicas, even a con-junto accordian player, showed up.

The mishmash of players were, collec-tively, not that good, but they were certainly that loud. And they were having a fine time, just the thing to draw a crowd. By nine o'clock it was standing room only.

Red had her hands full. But business was always welcome.

What was not welcome was the news that came on the phone from Kelly. With the din of noise behind her, Red could hardly hear what the young woman was saying, but her near-terrified desperation came through loud and clear.

"Sit tight, I'll be there as soon as I can," Red promised as she hung up the phone.

She glanced around the room. The din was nearly deafening. If she walked over and pulled the plug on the microphone, it would probably still take an hour to clear the room.

"Watch the bar," she told Hector, who looked genuinely surprised at the request. "I've got to make a phone call, I'll be right back."

Red eased her way out the front door and onto the sidewalk. It was cold and she didn't have her jacket, but the chill running through her had nothing to do with the weather. She flipped open her cell phone and called the most familiar number on her speed dial.

"Hey, babe, what's up?" he answered.

"Where are you?"

"I-35 coming into Austin," he answered.

"I just passed the Niederwald exit. Why?"

"Shootfire! I was hoping you were closer," Red told him. "I need to get home to the kids right now and I've got a bar full of yodeling cowboys and a crowd of sweaters packed in shoulder to shoulder."

"What's happened?" Cam's concern was evident in his voice.

"It's Kelly," she answered. "Kelly's husband has been wounded."

"Oh shit," Cam said. "I'm getting off at the next exit."

"From what I could hear and I missed a lot of it, it was an IED and he took some shrapnel, but his injuries are mostly burns. Right now he's in a field hospital, but he'll be transported to Europe for surgery."

"Is that good or bad?" Cam asked. "Is he less injured, so they don't need to do surgery immediately? Or more injured, so they need to get him to a hospital with better facilities?"

"I don't know," Red said. "And Kelly doesn't, either. But the poor girl is frantic. She's desperate to get to the base, to get closer to the action and find out the details."

"Of course she is."

"I was hoping you'd be able to go over and relieve her until I get there, but you're not going to get there any quicker than me."

"Maybe Olivia and Daniel could be on their own for an hour," Cam said.

"Yeah, maybe," Red said. "If it was something else, then for sure. But this is too close. This is their biggest fear, that something could happen to their mother. And for them, Kelly's husband and their mom are in almost the same place. Remember Daniel after his *abuela* had her stroke? Somebody needs to be there."

"I'll find somebody," Cam assured her. "Go back, close up as quickly as you can and I'll find somebody."

"Who are you going to find?"

"I'll call Sarah and Brad or . . . Hell, Red, I know nearly everybody in Alamo Heights. If I can't get somebody to go sit with a couple of scared kids for an hour, then I'm not much good to you, am I?"

With that agreement, Red went back inside. Hector had given away several beers on the honor system. Red wasn't sure how much honor there would be, but she couldn't worry about that now.

She plunged into the crowd, squeezing her way toward the stage. An errant, unwelcome hand pinched her backside as she passed and she couldn't even be bothered to call the guy on it.

When she finally made it to the stage, one

of the musicians pulled her up beside him and gave her a big hug. With a weary smile and don't-mess-with-me body language, she took over the microphone.

"Excuse me! Excuse me!" the crowd quieted but the guitars still played.

"Hold it, guys. Hold it!"

One by one the musicians quit playing.

"I want to thank everyone for coming out tonight," Red said. "But we're going to need to close this up."

There were sounds of shocked disbelief followed by booing.

"I know, I know everyone is having a great time," she said. "But I've got a family emergency and I have to close the place down."

"I just got my beer," a bearded guy Red didn't recognize called out. She guessed that he'd be one of the honor purchases she'd have to collect.

"I know, I'm sorry, but this happens," she said. "Everybody needs to drink up and settle up. You guys on stage, I want to have you back here playing music real soon, but right now you've got to pack up."

There were innumerable questions and more than enough bellyaching. Red didn't want to get into the specifics and did not. Let them think whatever they're going to think, was her philosophy.

By the time she made it back to the till, a grouchy line of customers had formed. Red cast a quick glance at her watch. This was going to take some time. She sure hoped that Cam could come through for her.

She began summing up the tabs and taking the money as quickly as possible.

The worst grumbling came from the newer customers, but even the regulars weren't happy about suddenly having the entire rest of the evening without a plan in sight.

To every prying question asked, Red smiled as warmly as she could manage and replied, "It's a family emergency. I'm so sorry to put you out this way."

But collecting the money owed her wasn't the only thing that slowed her down. One of the musicians, a fellow in his forties, was completely out of it. The other guys packed up his gear, but he could hardly walk to the door.

"Man, I'm sorry," he repeated over and over.

He was clearly in no shape to drive.

"Who's with this guy?" she asked the few patrons left. "Any of you know him? Who can give him a ride?"

"I got a car," the cowboy told Red, managing with some difficulty to pull the keys out of his pocket.

"We're going to get you a ride," Red assured him. But no one stepped up to help.

She got on the phone and began calling for cabs.

"I'm so sorry," he said again. "I had a few beers and smoked some dope, but I was going to be here all night. I'll be sober by closing time."

"I'm going to send you home in a cab," she assured him. But that was easier said than done. Thanksgiving was not one of the holidays when tourists flocked to town. The cabbies that ran the route from airport to downtown hotels were always willing to swing by Red's place. But tonight they were all at home with their families. Red ended up begging a dispatcher at *Fiesta Cab.*

"Look, I'm going to have to leave here. If it were ten degrees warmer outside, I'd leave this guy on the sidewalk."

The woman finally agreed to send someone. And after another forty minutes and twenty thousand "I'm so sorrys," Red was finally able to pack the cowboy and his guitar into the backseat of a taxi.

As the car drove away, she offered a mental "hallelujah!", as well as a "good riddance to bad rubbish."

She locked up and got in her car. Still, when she turned onto the street near the house, she checked her watch again and saw that it had been two hours since she'd talked to Kelly. She hoped it wasn't the longest two hours in the woman's life.

When she pulled up to the house, she didn't see any cars at all. Kelly was gone. Maybe *she'd* decided that Olivia and Daniel could stay by themselves. Red parked the car in the driveway and hurried to the porch.

The sight that greeted her in the bungalow's living room was jaw-dropping. Seated in Cam's big comfortable chair was Aunt Phyl.

The woman didn't seem nearly as startled to see Red as Red was to see her. Instead, she immediately put a finger to her lips for silence and then pointed to the nearby travel crib. Sleeping inside was baby Kendra, with a blanket in her hand and a thumb in her mouth.

Aunt Phyl stealthily rose out of her chair and tiptoed toward the back of the house, motioning Red to follow.

Dumbfounded, she did.

"What are you doing here?" Red whispered as soon as they were safely in the kitchen. She could hear how accusatory her words sounded, but she couldn't stop herself.

"Cam called me," the woman answered defensively. "He couldn't get anyone else. He said the traffic is awful, but he'll be here as soon as he can."

Red nodded slowly, trying to take it in.

"Do the children know that you're here?"

"Yes," she answered. "They may still be awake, but they went to bed about an hour and a half ago. I think they're both in Olivia's bedroom."

Red didn't even know what to say about that. She imagined their faces, terrified to be left to the mercies of this mean witch.

"Are they all right? I'm sure they were scared to death of you."

Aunt Phyl at least had the good grace to blush. Her words, however, were pointed and huffy. "The children and I worked out a compromise," she told Red. "I have apologized to them for losing my temper and we're all going to get along because Kelly and Kendra need us to."

Red wondered if she was included in this compromise. "What's Kendra doing here?" she asked.

Aunt Phyl shrugged. "The child was sleeping. That poor young woman doesn't have any idea what the next few hours are going to bring. I thought that whatever it is, sitting up or pacing the floor or just staring into space and waiting, it would be harder with a cranky baby."

"Good thinking," Red said, wishing the idea had come from anyone but this woman in her kitchen.

"Kelly said there are several bags of frozen breast milk in the freezer. But Kendra normally sleeps through the night without a feeding," Aunt Phyl continued. "She did get a little fussy a few minutes ago. I changed her diaper and walked the floor a bit and she fell back to sleep. I don't know a lot about babies. The last one I held was Cam."

As if on cue, Red heard the front door open and close. A minute later, Cam was with them in the kitchen. He wrapped an arm around Red's waist and pulled her close enough for a kiss on her temple.

"Are you all right?" he asked.

She nodded.

He released her to go to his aunt. She tilted her head, offering a cheek, and he dutifully kissed it.

"Thank you for coming to help, Aunt Phyl," he said. "I know you two didn't exactly get off on the right foot, but we really appreciate your help."

Red noted the word *we.*

"That poor young woman," Aunt Phyl said. "My heart just went out to her. I was glad to be able to help."

"How were the kids?" Cam asked. "I know this must have frightened them on so many levels."

Aunt Phyl was thoughtful for a moment. "I believe having me in their living room proved to be a welcome distraction. The children were able, perhaps, to focus on me right here instead of all those out-of-control things far away."

Cam nodded. "There might be something to that. Either way, thanks. Do you want me to walk you home?"

She picked up her bag from the kitchen table and pulled out a flashlight. "I think I still remember the way," she said.

She walked to the back door, but as she touched the door handle, she hesitated.

"I'll be serving Thanksgiving dinner to-morrow afternoon, Campbell," she said. "Why don't you invite your lady friend and her family to join us?"

Cam smiled as if delighted by her words.

"May I call you in the morning to let you know for sure?" he asked.

"That would be fine." Aunt Phyl let herself out the back door.

Red and Cam watched the flashlight beam

as it moved across the backyard and through the alley gate.

Cam pulled Red's back against his chest and wrapped his arms around her.

"I know she isn't somebody you would have invited into your house," he said. "But I couldn't reach anyone else. She was always good to me and she was good to my mother. I knew she would be sympathetic and that, despite what happened in the backyard, under these circumstances she wouldn't be mean to Olivia and Daniel."

Red nodded. "She kept Kendra here. That was a really good idea. Kelly has really helped me by taking care of Olivia and Daniel. I should help her by taking care of Kendra."

"Yeah," he agreed. "That's good."

"I'd better go peek in on the kids," Red said.

"Wait," Cam said. He nuzzled his cheek against her temple and planted a tender kiss on her shoulder. "I was worried that this would make you more afraid for Bridge."

Red nodded. "I'm sure it's that way for the kids," she said. "But me . . . I've been afraid for Bridge all her life. I couldn't believe they let me leave the hospital with her. I had no money, no place to go, no place to live and no one to ask for help.

They gave me a car seat and a bag of diapers and put me on the curb. I had to leave the car seat 'cause I couldn't carry the baby and the car seat, too. I guess I've gotten used to thinking that somehow she'll make it. And she's always so smart, so determined. She really can take care of herself."

"I guess she gets that from you," Cam said.

"Me?" Red was incredulous. "No, I'm a mess. Bridge is really together."

Cam made a kind of humorless chuckle. "You were seventeen, broke and friendless with a baby. And now, thirty years later you've made a life for yourself, raised a bright, responsible daughter and own your own business. Most people wouldn't describe that as a mess, they'd describe it as a triumph."

"Most people don't know what all I had to do to get here."

He turned her in his arms so he could look her in the eye. "Red, do you really think that matters? Do you think there is anyone living on earth who can't look back at the past and feel ashamed? Nobody's lived a perfect life."

"I'm not ashamed of anything I had to do!" Red insisted with more vehemence than necessary. "Well, not ashamed exactly. I'm . . . I'm embarrassed. And I'm sorry that . . . that the life I provided for Bridge was what it was. It was the best I could do, but it was a lot less than she deserved."

He pulled her tightly into his arms. "It's a lot less than you deserved, too," he said. "That's why I so want to give you more, at least while I can."

25

Thanksgiving morning began early. Kendra awoke without her mom anywhere to be seen and let out a howl. Red hurried in to pick her up. The baby did not seem so consoled by the wild woman with the red hair, so Red went to the kitchen and heated water in the microwave to thaw out some breast milk.

Olivia and Daniel were in the room a minute later, sleep tousled and in mismatched pajamas.

"I forgot," Olivia said. "I heard Kendra crying and I wondered why she would be here. I forgot." The initial disbelief in her voice quickly morphed into guilt. "Kendra's dad is hurt, Kelly is scared and I forgot."

"You remember now," Red said. "That's what's important."

"But I forgot!"

"That used to happen to me," Cam said.

He was leaning on the hallway doorjamb,

already dressed in his jeans and shirt. Daniel ran over to him. Uncharacteristically, instead of high-fiving or fist bumping, Cam picked the boy up and held him. Daniel wrapped his arms around Cam's neck as if holding on for dear life.

"What do you mean, it used to happen to you?" Olivia asked.

"When my mom was sick," Cam answered. "She was really sick and for a very long time. We moved here to live with my grandmother. Still, some mornings when I'd wake up, like for a moment, I wouldn't remember. I'd think things were the way they had been before."

"Did you feel bad about it?" Olivia asked.

"Yeah, I felt terrible, terrible for a long time," he said. "Finally I talked to my mom about it. Then I felt better."

"What did she say?" Olivia asked.

"She told me those memory lapses were angel gifts."

"Angel gifts?"

"What's an angel gift?" Daniel asked.

Kendra's crying quieted to hiccups and sobs as Red handed her the bottle of milk.

Cam carried Daniel into the living room and seated himself on the couch with the child beside him. He patted the cushion on the other side and Olivia went to sit with them, too.

"My mom said that God and all the angels in heaven understood how hard it is for a little kid to have to deal with really grown-up things. Things like someone being sick or hurt, someone leaving or even someone dying. That sometimes it just had to be that way, but nobody up there liked it."

The children nodded, listening intently. Red was changing Kendra's diaper but listening, too.

"So sometimes God would let the angels come down and sprinkle some forgetful dust on the child. So that when she's just waking up or he's in the middle of a great game, the boy or girl could forget, just for a few moments, and be just a kid again."

"Cool," Daniel said.

Olivia wasn't so easily convinced. "I never heard of 'forgetful dust,' " she said. "It sounds more like *Peter Pan* than catechism class."

Cam shrugged. "Maybe you're right," he said. "That's just what my mom told me. She's in heaven now, so she probably knows better than she did then. But it did kind of make sense for me. I mean, what other explanation is there? That I was a bad person because I forgot? I don't think I'm a bad person. Do you think I'm a bad person?"

"No!" Daniel exclaimed.

"No, of course not," Olivia agreed. After another moment to consider, she liked the idea better. "It does kind of make sense. I've been playing before and thought about yelling something out to my mom before remembering that she's overseas. So this forgetting is kind of like that."

"Yeah," Cam agreed. "I think that it is."

Kendra, now clean and dry, got set down on the rug and crawled over to the sofa to be near Olivia and Daniel, who were more familiar to her than the adults. She tried unsuccessfully to pull herself up at Olivia's knee, so the girl picked up the baby.

Red went to wash her hands and face and whip her hair into a more controllable knot. When she returned to the living room, Kendra was snuggling closely to Olivia, perfectly content.

"Okay," Red said. "How about some breakfast?"

"I want pancakes," Cam announced.

"YES!" the chorus shouted in unison.

"Uh . . . well, yeah, I can probably make pancakes," Red said.

Cam looked at the kids. "I don't like the sound of that," he said. "Maybe *we* should make the pancakes."

"YEAH!"

As the horde descended on the kitchen, Red made herself useful by picking up, making beds and getting herself showered and dressed.

Daniel had just called out for her to "come and get it!" when the phone rang. It was Kelly. Red didn't ask any questions, but the young woman poured out what bits of news that she had and asked about her baby.

"Kendra's great," Red assured her. "We're getting ready to sit down to breakfast and I think she may get a piece of pancake to gnaw on with her cereal."

"My parents are flying in about ten o'clock," Kelly said. "And my in-laws will be here tomorrow. So, I'll come back and get her in a couple of hours."

"That's fine," Red said. "Sooner, later, whatever works for you. And keep me on your shortlist if you need someone to take care of her anytime."

"I don't know how you'll take care of her. I worry who you'll be able to get to take care of Daniel and Olivia."

"It will all work out," Red assured her. She was glad to hear Kelly sounding more like herself, more in control. Yesterday had really rattled her, but today she was back to being her calm and competent self.

"Don't spend a minute worrying about me or the kids," Red told her. "You need to concentrate on taking care of yourself and that fine husband of yours."

Red hung up and walked slowly into the kitchen.

They were all waiting for her and the room was quiet. Pancakes set on every plate, getting colder minute by minute.

"That was Kelly," she told them, to no one's surprise. "She sounds fine and she's going to be by in a few hours to pick up Kendra."

The kids continued to wait patiently, big brown eyes looking up at her.

"Her husband has been evacked to Germany," Red reported hopefully. "She actually talked to him for a minute, though he didn't say much because he doesn't feel real good. He was burned in an explosion. But the good news is that, as soon as he's ready to be moved, they are going to bring him here to San Antonio to treat him at the BAMC burn unit. So they'll all be together right here in town and we'll get to see them and maybe help them."

Olivia nodded solemnly.

"So Kendra's dad is okay and he gets to come home?" Daniel's question reflected a naiveté that Red was loath to dispel.

"Yes. He's hurt and it's going to take him a lot of time to get well, but he's coming home."

That was good enough for Daniel, who stuck a fork into his pancakes enthusiastically.

Olivia looked about to reprimand him, but gave a quick glance toward Red. Apparently taking her cue from her grandmother, the young girl, with the weight of the world back on her small shoulders, also dug into the pancakes.

The makeshift family cleaned up the kitchen together and the kids took turns in the shower.

"What are your plans today, beyond Kelly?" Cam asked. "I'm thinking the drive to the Valley to see Abuela is off."

Red nodded. "It'll be way too late to do that by the time Kelly gets here. And I really don't want to be out of town, in case we're needed."

Cam agreed.

"I can go to Central Market. They're probably open this morning and I can buy some Thanksgivingish something for us to eat," he said. "Or, if you think you're up to it, we can eat dinner with Aunt Phyl."

Red rolled her eyes. "I don't want to be

beholden to her," she said. "I don't want her cooking just for us."

"She always cooks," Cam said. "She fixes a big dinner every year and because we don't have any family anymore, she invites strays."

"Strays?"

"People who don't have anywhere else to go on Thanksgiving."

"Well, I guess we qualify," she said.

"But we don't have to go," Cam assured her. "I don't want to drag you over there if you're going to be uncomfortable."

Red sighed. "I'll ask the kids," she told him. "If they're willing, I am."

So that afternoon, after a very upbeat and optimistic reunion with Kelly, they all dressed in nice clothes to walk with Cam through the back gate between the two yards. Daniel was cowering a bit and held Red's hand. Olivia was defensive, chin up, so like Bridge.

It turned out that defenses were not needed. Aunt Phyl might be a mean old battle-ax, but she was also the perfect Alamo Heights hostess, delighted to see them, eager for conversation and flawlessly cordial. Despite her late night of baby-sitting and the stress of putting on a huge holiday dinner, Aunt Phyl was fabulously groomed and wearing a dress with the kind of understated elegance that is never found on the rack.

The house itself, though not terribly large, was intimidating. The entry hall boasted a wide staircase. To the left was the front room, open and welcoming with a fire in the stone fireplace. The furniture was mostly antique, upholstered in brocades. The only kid-friendly place to sit was a couch, which was, regrettably, white. The music room directly across the hall had floor-to-ceiling bookshelves, a couple of delicate, uncomfortable-looking chairs and a grand piano in the center.

Cam led them into the front room. To Red's relief, the children sat down cross-legged on the rug, leaving the white sofa available for someone else.

The assembled guests were an interesting bunch. There was a slightly smelly old man, the widower of a friend of a friend, who complained about something every time he opened his mouth. There were three older widows, as different as women can be. One was large, loud and flamboyant, and wearing a pink beret. Another quiet as a mouse, whose main interest seemed to be the activities of the children. The third sat alone, chain-smoking on the back deck. A young couple, new to the neighborhood, were of most interest to Olivia and Daniel. Their son, Magill, was seven. All three had seen each other at school, and were now grateful to have another kid for holiday acquaintance. Finally, the last to show up were two international students from the University of the Incarnate Word. This was their first-ever Thanksgiving and they were eager to participate in all the traditional customs.

The extralong dining-room table hinted at days when the family was much larger than it was now. It was covered by a delicate cream-colored cloth and set with sterling-silver and antique china.

When Red caught sight of it, her jaw dropped.

"It's pretty, huh," Cam said. "My great-great-grandmother was a buyer of all things beautiful. Almost everything in this house came down from her."

"What about Daniel and Olivia?" she whispered to Cam. "What if they drop something?"

Cam shrugged. "Don't worry about it, Red. These are plates. I've broken more than one. Besides, ultimately, Aunt Phyl and I will both be gone and every stick of furniture, every piece of crockery will end up at some big estate sale. It's just stuff. It really doesn't matter."

Red could only hope that his aunt Phyl felt exactly the same.

Fortunately, the dinner went without any breakage at all. The smoker came in from the cold. The grouchy, smelly man continued to grouse. The fawning would-be grandmother giggled with Olivia and the boys. And the woman in the pink beret fired questions at first one person and then another, until most everyone had revealed a few pertinent facts about themselves.

Red revealed the very minimum, but that seemed to be okay with the pink-beret lady, as she'd already figured out that Red was Cam's girlfriend.

"And I like her," the woman announced to Aunt Phyl, Cam and anyone else still listening. "She seems to have a good head on her shoulders."

"Uh . . . thank you," Red said.

"It's about time you brought a girlfriend around, Campbell," Pink Beret continued. "That girl from high school was the last one I remember. I was beginning to worry that you'd become one of those water-bed bachelors with a different woman every night."

"No, ma'am," Cam responded. "And I think water beds have kind of gone out of style, even for wild bachelors."

"There are children at this table," Grouchy

354

Smelly Man pointed out.

The conversation quickly turned to the students, who were from Paraguay and Thailand, respectively. Most of the rest of the dinner was spent discussing holiday feast days in their home cultures.

When the diners, stuffed and sleepy, left the table for the more comfortable chairs of the living room, Red stayed to help with cleanup.

"I can get this," Aunt Phyl told her.

"I can help," Red replied with certainty. It was enough to accept this woman's hospitality. She was not going to allow herself to be viewed as a mooch.

The neighbor offered to help, too, but she was almost immediately called away by her husband, who apparently needed her help in telling the story of their honeymoon trip to Costa Rica to the young man from Paraguay.

Clearing the table went along fine without conversation, but once the two women were working together in the kitchen, the silence was unpleasantly noticeable.

"These dishes are really pretty," Red finally said.

"Thank you," Aunt Phyl answered. "How was Kendra last night? Did she sleep well?"

The young army wife, her adorable baby

and wounded husband was a subject that they both had an interest in and no conflict about.

Red let her in on the latest developments.

"Well, we'll certainly have to keep that family in our prayers," Aunt Phyl declared.

The silence lingered again, but Red had almost filled the dishwasher and she was hoping that she could then, in good conscience, make a hasty retreat. But Aunt Phyl still had something to say. She removed the neatly pressed apron she had donned and began drying her hands on it.

"I . . . I was wrong about your grandchildren," the older woman said. "I suppose I've become unaccustomed to having their exuberance and energy around. I said some terrible things about them. And I was wrong. I apologize."

"Okay," Red said uneasily. She had the feeling that the apology wasn't the end of it.

"I watched them at the wedding and here and of course, I talked to them some last night," Aunt Phyl continued. "And despite what I said, they are nice, well-behaved children. You should be very proud."

"It's my daughter who should rightly be proud," Red pointed out. "Up until a few months ago, I had almost no contact with Olivia and Daniel. Their behavior is a credit to her, not me."

"Still, you must have at least raised her right," Aunt Phyl said.

"I did my best at the time," Red conceded.

"So there," Aunt Phyl said. "We're agreed that the children are lovely."

"Yes, we can agree to that. Thank you, Miss Early."

"You have to call me Phyllis or Phyl, everyone does."

"All right," she answered. "And then you'll have to call me Red. That's about all I answer to, except Grandma these days."

"Very well, Red," Phyl replied. "I'd be pleased to do that. But I'm going to be more honest with you now than you may want. I'm sure you are a person with fine qualities. Still, I don't think you're right for my nephew."

Red said nothing.

"I know what you're thinking," Phyl said.

Red doubted that completely.

"You're thinking that he is a grown man with experience in the world and a level head on his shoulders. I am merely his old-maid aunt. What could I possibly know about what's best for him?"

"No," Red told her. "That's not what I'm thinking at all. I'm thinking that this is another thing that you and I agree on. I am not the woman for Cam. I . . . I care for him too much to not want more for him than I have to offer."

If Phyl was pleased with this revelation, Red didn't stick around long enough to find out. She left the kitchen and made her way to the front room. However, most of the guests had moved to the music room where Cam and the three kids shared a crowded piano bench.

Grouchy Smelly remained in the front room alone and waved Red over to join him. She wanted to resist, but there was standing room only around the piano and she was ready to get off her feet.

With a wan smile, she took the chair at an angle to his own.

"I don't care for music," the man announced to her. "Never did. I don't see what people like about it. It makes me have to talk louder to be heard over the noise."

Red was tempted to suggest that shutting up might be a cure for that, but she didn't.

"Cam always plays something when he's here," Grouchy Smelly continued. "I can't seem to stop him, so I quit even trying. Sometimes, though, I ask him to play Woody Guthrie. I know he likes Guthrie and he's one musician that I can admire. Not for the music, it doesn't seem like much. But for being a man's man, a true American, not a Communist like his enemies used to say. Woody was always taking up for the little guy. That's what's stinking wrong with this no-account world. The good always die young. A fine fellow like Guthrie leaves this earth too soon, while the rest of the worthless guitar pickers in the world live on."

Red cleared her throat and decided to try to keep the guy on a subject he liked instead of let him go off on another rant.

"I don't know that much about Woody Guthrie," Red admitted. "Of course, I know 'This Land is Your Land' and 'Oklahoma Hills.' And 'Vigilante Man,' I like that one a lot."

Grouchy Smelly offered a hmm of agreement, so Red plunged on.

"I've heard performers I admire, like Willie Nelson and Ray Wylie Hubbard, talk about his influence on their music."

"And Cam, of course."

"Yes, Cam, too."

"Woody, I guess, had more influence on Cam than most. Changed the whole direction of his career. That boy had serious opportunity in classical music. He could be playing at the philharmonic. That's surely what Phyllis wanted for him, but Woody Guthrie lured him away."

Red remembered that he'd said as much to her, but she hadn't questioned him and Cam had not elaborated.

"Well, I'm glad he decided to play honky-tonk," Red told the man with a light laugh. "I never would have run into him if he'd been playing at the dad-blamed symphony."

Grouchy Smelly chuckled lightly, apparently appreciating her deprecating humor.

"And I'm sure he would have been sorry to miss out on a looker like you," the man said. "Woody sure was lucky for him. But unlike most, Cam didn't get interested in Woody for his music."

"He didn't?"

"Heck no, Cam got interested cause of his disease."

Red was puzzled. "His disease?"

"Yeah, Woody died of Huntington's chorea — I think they just call it Huntington's now," the man said. "He's probably the most famous person to ever have it. It's the same disease Cam's mother had."

"I didn't realize that."

"Yeah, damn shame." The man nodded gravely and sighed. "Damn shame for the both of them."

To: buildabetterbridge@citymail.com
November 28 10:17 p.m.
From: Livy156@ABrats.org
Subject: Thanksgiving

Mom wow it was so great to talk to you. We just got off the phone and I have to go to bed but I had to write and say I love you one more time. It was so great to hear your voice. I had a good time at Cam's aunts house. That was weird because she has not always been nice to me and Daniel but lately she is. The food was really swell except for the stuffing it had like oarsters in it. TOO GROSS. The pumpkin pie was real good. You have to know that's true cause Daniel ate two pieces.

We played with a kid from our school that we didn't know and we sang songs with Cam. It was cool. But the best part of Thanksgiving was to come home and hear the phone ring and find out that it was you.

We miss you so much Mom. I know you miss us too and that we just gotta be brave. I can do that. And Daniel to. But it was good for Daniel to talk to you. He is still a kid and all but I think he is going to be O.K. He tells himself that now that Kendras dad is coming home that everything is fine. I know better, but I am not telling him.

I am so glad you got the video feed of Daniel as the turkey. It means a lot to him for you to get to see him. And you don't need to thank me about it cause all I did was give Mrs. Cook your email. It must of been Red who got her to record it.

She is not so bad as I first thought. Bad but not SO bad. You know. I miss you and love you. I am so sleepy I have to say good nite. Take care of yourself don't worry about us.

Livy

26

On Friday and Saturday, Red had no option but to take the kids with her to the bar. Cam had missed a recording session in Austin and was catching up over the weekend. And although Kelly had suggested that maybe Olivia and Daniel could stay with her, Red thanked her and turned her down. Her tiny apartment on base was already bulging with her parents, as well as her in-laws, and she had enough on her mind without two extra kids, even if they were Olivia and Daniel.

The kids were stuck upstairs in the apartment for ten hours both days, and even with their stalwart determination to do what needed to be done to help, it was tough. The trip to the Valley on Sunday included a litany of complaints and an open rebellion at the very thought of having to be picked up after school and hanging out all evening in the apartment the next day.

"I promise to work something out as quickly as I can," Red told them.

Her first task on Monday morning was to contact the Hearts Apart organization. She crossed her fingers that they would come up with someone as wonderful as Kelly on very short notice.

The response was not all that optimistic. "This time of year is very busy for everyone," she was told. "I will do what I can, but most of our clients who want to work are already working."

Discouraged, Red called Sarah to see if she had a babysitter she could recommend.

"I use my mother mostly," she admitted. "I've had a college girl, a friend of the family, a couple of times. But I doubt she could stay late on school nights."

"Yeah," Red agreed. "I really need someone older and more mature."

"I'll ask around," Sarah assured her. "Lots of people have nannies who know other nannies. Surely we can come up with somebody."

"Thanks, I appreciate it."

"No problem," Sarah answered. "And if you want to leave the kids here with me until you get something settled, that would be fine."

Red thanked her and left the possibility

open. But what she wanted was for the kids to be in the house they'd begun to consider a home. They had been bounced around enough already. They'd have to move again when Bridge came home. That was soon enough for more upheaval.

She contacted a couple of agencies and was waiting for calls when the postman came by. Gabe was very married, but he took every chance he got to flirt with Red. She flirted back, but they both knew it was all just in fun.

He set her stack of mail atop the bar.

"Can I get your autograph, gorgeous?" he asked. "I've got one I need you to sign for."

"You make me feel like a movie star," she answered as she both signed and printed her name on the official-looking green forms.

"A movie star, huh?" he said.

"Yeah," she replied. "About half-hungover."

They both laughed and he handed her a big, thick envelope. The name on the front certainly caught her eye. It was addressed to Ms. Emmaline Rose Cullens. She had been E. R. "Red" Cullens for so long, the sight of her old name was jarring. She glanced at the return address and saw it was an unfamiliar law firm in Dallas.

Brad had warned her that her landlord would undoubtedly barrage her with paperwork from threatening attorneys on their behalf. She didn't even bother to open it. She just stuck it in her purse to pass on to Brad.

After the third, unimpressive callback, Red was ready to give up. It was almost time for school to dismiss. She had no choice but to go and get the kids and bring them back to the apartment.

Then the phone rang one more time. It was Aunt Phyl.

"Now, I told you that if you needed something, you should call me," she said without preamble and sounding annoyed.

"Well . . . uh . . ."

"I just heard that you are frantically trying to find someone to stay with the children. I am right here on the far side of your backyard fence and you didn't even think to mention it to me."

"Uh . . . well, Phyllis, I know you're busy —"

"Busy at what? My club meetings and charity boards are all during the day. And I am not about to waste my evenings making inane conversation while drinking gin and tonic at the Argyle."

"I don't want to impose."

366

"Nonsense," Aunt Phyl answered. "I know the children and they will be safe with me. Call the school and tell them that I will be picking them up."

"I'll call," Red told her.

"Good, and don't worry another moment about it," she said. "I'll talk to you when you get home."

Red hung up the phone and then stood there staring at it. Problem solved. She felt as if things shouldn't be so easy. Was it just that she'd become so accustomed to them being hard?

But the world was still full of hard things. Kelly's husband was flown into BAMC on Wednesday.

"It's not nearly as bad as it could be," Kelly told Red. "He'll have a lot of scarring on his face and neck and arm. But he's not really disfigured. He's going to need skin grafts, of course. The arm is the worst. He'll probably lose some use of it. And then there is the pain. It is just inhuman how much he suffers."

Red could hear the suffering in Kelly's own voice. But she chose to follow Kelly's lead and see this very bitter glass as half-full.

On Thursday morning, only minutes after the children went to school, the phone rang.

It was Sarah.

"We've got to get started on the kids' Christmas party," she said.

"Good grief!" Red complained. "They just had a party last week."

"Every holiday needs a party," Sarah answered. "I try to think of it as teaching them the importance of social occasions. What are you doing right now? Can you go shopping with me?"

Red had a million things to do, but she allowed herself to be drawn into a search for the perfect Christmas decorations.

"As usual, it's all really touchy," Sarah told her later in the car. "We're celebrating Winter Festival so that non-Christians don't feel excluded."

"Okay," Red said. "So no Baby Jesus in the manger."

"Worse than that," Sarah said. "No Christmas trees, no Santa Claus, no reindeer. Even Frosty the Snowman gets people nervous."

Red laughed, and Elliot, in his car seat behind her, giggled, as well.

"Have you thought about your Christmas shopping yet?"

"No," Red told her. "I don't really do much of a celebration."

"But what about the kids?" Sarah asked.

"Kids have to have Christmas."

"My daughter should be home," Red told her. "Her tour is up and she thought she would be home by Christmas."

"Doesn't that make the holiday bigger?"

"I think the kids will want to just be with her," Red said. "And I don't think she'll want to be with me."

"Will the kids be moving out of the school district next semester?" Sarah asked.

"I suppose so," Red told her. "I don't know. It's not up to me."

"Oh, I hope not," Sarah said. "That would be such a shame. They are so settled here."

Red couldn't help but agree with that. Daniel was so happy. And Olivia would really miss seeing Nayra every day.

"It's my daughter's decision," Red said, wishing for perhaps the first time in her life that she had more influence in that. "Bridge will do what's best for the kids. She's a very good mom."

"Of course she is," Sarah said. "She's probably just like you."

That statement was so wholly incorrect that Red actually hooted at the suggestion.

"Bridge and I couldn't be more different," Red insisted. "If you ever meet her, you'll see."

"Not if," Sarah said. "*When* I meet her. I

like you and adore the kids. You're part of life in our community. Didn't Cam warn you, nobody gets out of Alamo Heights without strings attached."

Inside the megastore, they wheeled Elliot's stroller through the rows and rows of holiday decorations. Red had no opinion on most of it. Sarah finally went for a red-and-white theme, with red tinsel and redbirds in the snow.

"Our kids love the idea of snow," Sarah said. "They haven't been around it enough to know how cold and miserable it can be."

At the checkout stand, Red insisted on paying.

"I can't let you do that!"

"Oh, yes you can," Red said. "You've been paying for everything up to now. Your cupcake tab alone would probably pay for Elliot's college education. Not to mention how grateful I am for all the work that Brad's done on the contract."

Red suddenly remembered something and began digging in her purse.

"Wait, here it is." She pulled out the fat letter from the Dallas lawyer that had been stuck in her purse for four days. "I meant to send this to Brad. Could you give it to him?"

"Sure."

When Red got home from their shopping

trip, she had to rush to get ready. By the time she got down to Eight Street and Avenue B, it was past time for the bar to open.

To her surprise, it already was.

She walked right through the front door to find Cam already behind the counter. The place was still empty, but anyone showing up could have gotten a beer.

"You opened up."

He shrugged. "Just trying to show you what a good help I could be."

"I'm convinced," Red said. "With the kids, with the bar, with keeping my sanity, you're a wonder on all accounts."

She added to this vote of confidence a quick kiss before stashing her purse on the shelf beneath the cash drawer and unlocking the floor safe.

"Why aren't you in Austin?" she asked.

"All finished."

"Wow, great, congratulations," Red told him. "Did you get a job offer?"

"Yeah," he answered. "But I turned it down."

"Why would you do that? With Brian working his full-time job, the band is going nowhere."

Cam nodded. "Yeah, it's pretty much over."

"And the young kid you were working with, you said you liked him. You said he's an up-and-comer."

He agreed. "The kid has every chance of doing something big. He's got lots of talent and he's not afraid to surround himself with talented people. His sound is unique. He's physically appealing and has both the ambition to push himself forward and the determination to see it through. I think he's got a real shot. And I told him that."

Red put her hands on her hips and shook her head. "I don't get it, Cam. If he makes it big and you're playing in his band, then you're making it big, too."

Cam shrugged. "I'm not that interested in making it big."

Red gave a chuckle of disbelief. "I didn't know honky-tonk fiddlers were allergic to success."

"I'm not allergic to success," he said. "But the band is leaving on tour in three weeks. They'll be traveling all over the country. They're playing two hundred dates next year. I'm not interested in doing that."

"Why not?"

"Because I'm happier staying here," he answered.

Red was methodically separating the change into the cash drawer, but it was hard to concentrate with her thoughts going a mile a minute.

"I just hope that you're not staying here for me," she said. She knew her words sounded harsh, but she was afraid they needed to be.

"No," he answered. "I'm staying here for me."

He stepped closer and put his arm across the cash register, effectively halting her work.

"You must have heard from Aunt Phyl and her friends how I gave up a promising future in classical violin. Didn't you ever wonder why I didn't pursue that?"

"Because you liked Woody Guthrie better."

Cam gave a slight chuckle. "Woody and I have a bond, that's for sure," he said. "But that's not exactly why I've done things the way I did."

"Then why?"

"Because I wanted the time more than the music," he answered. "Do you understand what that means?"

"No, not really."

"Classical music is more like an apprenticeship. You play for years and years behind musicians that are better than you. It's a lot of time, a lot of hard work, a lot of waiting." He removed his arm from in front of the till and folded both across his chest. "Honky-tonk fiddle, no waiting. You just get up and start playing. Maybe you can only play in open jams or with fly-by-night bands, but you get to play, the music is fun and you're in control of your life. Your time is all up to you."

"I think that's what the grasshopper said when he was frittering away the whole summer."

"Maybe so," Cam agreed. "But life is too short to waste any of it waiting to live."

Red thought that he might have a point, but for some reason, she didn't want to give it to him. "You're very fortunate that you have the opportunity to make that choice."

"Everybody gets to make that choice in one way or another," he said. "I work, I don't owe money to anybody, I don't mooch off anyone. I make a living. It's not a fortune, but I'm careful. I own myself. I don't have a time clock or a boss, or even a tour with two hundred gigs scheduled."

He wrapped his arms around her waist and pulled her toward him. "I have a woman I care a helluva lot about and if I choose to be with her instead of hanging out with a bunch of boring, lug-head guitar players, that makes me brilliant, not lazy. Besides, the poor, struggling-musician thing, the chicks think that's really hot."

Red laughed. "I think I'm getting too old to be put in the 'chick' category."

"Yeah, that's what makes you so much more of a challenge. And I love a challenge," he said, and made a growling noise. "What do you think my chances are of luring you into sex on this bar in broad daylight with the door unlocked?"

"Not likely," Red told him.

The phone began ringing.

"Ah . . . and the woman is saved by the bell."

27

The phone call was from Brad, who said he had news that he didn't want to wait to share. He agreed to stop by the bar on his way home. Red spent the afternoon trying not to think about what the landlord might have offered. But every time she glanced around at the crowded interior that now functioned as her whole place, she both hoped and tried not to be too hopeful. She didn't want to be disappointed.

But the grin on Brad's normally stoic face was enough to dispel even the most stubborn fears.

"We certainly didn't get everything we wanted," he assured her quickly. "But I feel really good about what we did get."

The pronoun "we" caught her momentarily off guard and then she realized that, of course, it had been "we." Without Brad, she would have signed that other terrible contract. And without Cam, she wouldn't have ever called Brad. And without the kids, she would have never gotten to know Sarah.

With that thought in mind, she got Brad seated in the back booth.

"Could you wait here a minute while I find Cam?" she said.

She hurried out the back door and up the stairs. She found him in the middle of the apartment, working on the computer, surrounded by sheets of music and instruments.

"Sorry to interrupt," she said. "Brad's downstairs and I thought you'd want to hear what he has to say."

Cam didn't even hesitate. They hurried back down the steps. As they walked toward the back door, Cam clasped her hand. Normally she would have pulled away, but at that moment, she welcomed his touch.

Inside, they made their way to the back booth. Brad politely stood up as Red took her seat, and he and Cam greeted each other with a handshake.

Once they were all seated and with the briefest of preliminaries, Red asked the question.

"So, what's it all say?"

She indicated the paperwork that Brad had spread across the table. A number of paragraphs within the document had little red and yellow sticky arrows pointing to them, and there were notes attached in several places.

"Well, maybe I should get the bad news out of the way first," he said. "They are not putting any money in the building beyond routine maintenance. They will be tearing the building down eventually, so they are not going to sink money into upgrading it."

Red sighed and nodded.

"Better news is that they will help defray the cost of what they're calling 'security fencing' and they've offered seven hundred dollars for that, payable on receipt of the contract."

"You can't get much of a fence for seven hundred dollars," Red pointed out.

"I think they came up with that figure as half the cost of a chain-link barrier," Brad said. "But you are not limited to using the money for that. If you want to put up a better, more attractive option, you can do so, but they'll still only kick in seven hundred dollars."

"Okay."

"But the best news, and I almost wish I could have a drumroll for this," Brad said, grinning broadly, "is that they have agreed to extend the lease for ten years at the current rate. Within that time frame you can break the lease with sixty days' notice. They can break the lease, as well, but must give you a full year to vacate the property."

"So I can stay here ten years?"

"Maybe," Brad said. "You can stay here as long as this building is here. And they've got to give you a year's notice before they tear it down."

"That's great, Brad," Cam said.

He sounded completely pleased. Red wasn't so sure.

"But what if they decided to tear it down fourteen months from now?" she pointed out. "If I sign this, they can come back in here after the first of the year and say I've got twelve months to get out."

"Yes," Brad agreed. "They could do that. But it's not likely that they will. If they were planning to tear the place down that soon, they wouldn't bother signing an agreement with you. They'd just send a notice of eviction. Even two years out, they'd probably just stall you rather than bother with a lease."

"Okay, so it's not one or two years from now," she said. "But it could be three years or four years."

"Sure," Brad agreed. His expression had sobered considerably. "But that gives you three or four years to figure out what you're going to do. That's a lot of time to put together an alternative plan."

Red sighed. "It's too bad that I don't *want* an alternative plan," she said. "I just want to stay here."

"Oh," Brad said, looking completely deflated. "I don't think I can get that for you. But I can . . . I can continue to negotiate. No lease is truly unbreakable, but I can ask for a high penalty. I might be able to get that for five years. I think it's very unlikely that I'd get that for ten. And they would probably expect you to pay a premium for that."

"But do you think this is a better deal?" Cam asked, tapping his finger on the paperwork.

"Yes, it is," Brad said. "From my perspective, what they've offered here is not overly generous, but if they'd given much more, I would have been suspicious that there was something going on that we don't know about. What it seems like is that the decision about the building is a done deal. Because of its age, its condition and because it doesn't fit in with the style of the new development, it's just gone. Allowing you to stay here until actual redevelopment starts is what I went after. I thought you understood that."

"I did," Red told him. "And I do. I guess I just hoped somehow that they would come back, with 'oh, it's too much trouble, just keep that old building.' "

"Red, this is a good deal," Cam said.

"I know," she agreed and forced herself to smile at Brad. "It's a great deal, Brad, and I appreciate it. I just . . . well, I just wish things were different."

"I'm sorry," he said.

"Where do I sign?"

Brad, in his thorough, lawyerly way, wanted to go through each specific aspect of the contract. That took another half hour, at least, and the bar was getting noisier and more crowded by the minute. Finally she put her signature on it and Cam brought over drinks for a toast of celebration — beers for him and Brad and an iced-tea highball for Red.

She made a point of thanking and thanking and thanking. She realized that he'd thought he'd pulled a real coup, only to be met with her unrealistic disappointment. Intellectually, she knew he was right. Emotionally, however, she couldn't quite make herself happy about it.

As Brad carefully returned the contract into the manila envelope it came in, Red was reminded of the other letter she'd gotten this week, which she'd given to Sarah to pass along to Brad. She started to mention it, but Cam spoke first.

"You've got to get a babysitter some night and bring Sarah down here with you," he said.

"Absolutely," Red agreed. "I'm a big believer in giving the good people of Alamo Heights an opportunity to knock a few back and kick up a row."

Brad chuckled. "I don't know," he said. "Sarah is sort of a white-wine-and-string-quartet sort of person."

"Really?" Red said. "I imagined her as a get-drunk-and-listen-to-honky-tonk kind of gal."

Brad left just as the band was tuning up and Red forgot to ask about the letter.

The evening got busy and Red was glad. She didn't want to think about the papers she'd signed. She didn't want to think about the future. By the time the last cowboy had hit the trail and the front door was locked down for the night, her keep-the-customer-happy smile had become overwhelmed by her sense of disappointment.

As she tallied the receipts, Cam came and sat across from her at the bar.

Red spoke without looking up. "It was nice of you to stick around all night, Cam.

But if you're thinking to lure me upstairs for a midnight quickie, I'd like to remind you that your elderly aunt is waiting up for me. She knows what time I close the bar and that you're living upstairs. And she is not at all keen on me humping and bumping her adored nephew."

"I agree, the less time Aunt Phyl has to speculate about the carnal nature of our relationship the better," he said. "Though that wouldn't stop me if I thought I could get your pants off. But I really just wanted to talk to you."

"Speak," she encouraged, still counting the money.

He hesitated only a half minute. "I know you were bummed about the deal Brad brought to you," Cam said. "I wanted to talk it out with you, see if I can help you feel better about it."

Red heaved a big sigh and glanced up to meet his gaze. "I'm feeling about as good about it as I'm going to be," she said.

"I think it's an excellent agreement, Red. It gives you time and flexibility and options."

"I know that."

"But I don't see you smiling," he said.

"I've got nothing to smile about," Red told him. "Don't you get it? I want this place here, where it is and like it is. And now I have this disaster sitting out there on the horizon. It doesn't matter what I do around here now, how the business grows or doesn't grow. Either way, this bar is headed for the wrecking ball sooner or later and there is nothing I can do to stop it."

Red was looking straight at Cam. He stared at her for a long moment, then sort of shivered as if physically shaking off her words. She could read nothing in his expression. The very blankness of it angered her, somehow. She shook her head and waved at him, dismissive.

"Forget it," she snarled. "There's no way you can understand the way I feel. This place is my life. I've put all my hopes and dreams into it. And then a piece of paper arrives that says 'Too bad! We're going to make it disappear.' No rhyme, no reason, no justice, it's going to be destroyed and there is not a damn thing I can do about it. There's no way that somebody like you could get their mind around that."

There was an instant of tension between them that almost crackled with electricity. Cam slapped his hand against the bar with such force that Red startled.

"You think not?" he asked her. "You think that I haven't had dreams that were destroyed, hopes and plans that were ripped from me? You are so wrong, you don't even know how wrong you are."

There was nothing that put Red in a fighting mood faster than a man raising his voice.

"Oh, really," Red answered sarcastically. "Tell me, then, I'm all curious. What have you ever wanted that you didn't get? You live this free-as-a-bird life. Your parents left you a roof over your head. You don't work any harder than you want to. You always have a sex buddy, and you'll never have to support a family. No strings, no ties. How hard is that?"

"No ties? I'm the one who asked you to marry me. You're the one who won't even talk about it."

"Yeah, you would pick an older woman, busy with her own business and not very demanding on your time or attention."

"Right," Cam answered, matching her sarcasm with his own. "I want to make a life with you because you're so easy and uncomplicated."

Red had no snappy comeback to that.

"I didn't stay down here to have a fight with you," Cam said, getting up from the bar stool. "I know the uncertainty of it all is scary for you. I thought I could help. Guess not."

He walked across the room and out the back door. She watched him go, regretting having lashed out. She wasn't mad at him, she was mad at the whole world. He was just the closest target in that group.

Red finished counting the money and locked it in the safe. She grabbed her purse from beneath the till, checked the security bar across the front door and turned out the lights. Once out on the patio, she secured everything and set the alarm.

The lights were still on in the apartment. She gazed up at them for a long moment and then silently admonished herself. *Walk to your car. Get in. Go home.*

But instead, she climbed the stairs and walked into the apartment without bothering to knock. Cam was sitting on the bed. He'd heard her on the steps and was looking in her direction.

"I love having sex after a fight," she told him.

"We need to talk," Cam replied.

Red pulled her shirt off over her head and threw it on the floor.

"Cam, you know me well enough by now to understand that this is the only way I can say how I feel about you."

28

Dawn was not yet on the horizon, but it was a lot closer than it should have been as Red pulled into the driveway. She cut the engine in the street and coasted to a halt, hoping stealth was on her side.

There had been no call from Aunt Phyl saying *Where in the devil are you?*, so Red held out hope that the older lady was snoozing contentedly in front of old reruns of *Matlock*, unaware that she was almost four hours late.

Red tiptoed up on the porch and put her key in the lock as quietly as possible.

She needn't have bothered. The living room was empty. Lights were on in the kitchen and the aroma of fresh-brewed coffee permeated the air.

So much for not having to explain herself.

Red walked into the kitchen, reminding herself of the working-mother's motto — better to lose your self-respect than lose your best babysitter.

"Phyllis, I am so sorry," were the first words out of Red's mouth.

Aunt Phyl looked up from her reading. "The morning paper got here before you did," she said. "Get yourself some coffee and I'll share." She pulled out the front section and scooted it toward the chair opposite her.

Red went over to the counter and poured herself a cup before sitting down.

"I won't do this again," Red said. "I never asked Kelly to stay all night, and I shouldn't have expected you to do it. I have no excuse. I got in an argument with Cam and I stuck around until we sorted it out and then . . . and then I fell asleep."

Aunt Phyl sipped her coffee.

"Please don't quit on me," Red pleaded. "I know I deserve it. But I really need you. And I won't do this again. It's only one month until my daughter is home. I really hate to make the kids take on another new person."

"Your daughter is coming home in a month?" she asked.

"Yes, she told us that she'd be home by Christmas," Red said. "And both the kids and I are really counting on that."

"So the children will go home with her?"

"Yes. . . . Well, they'll go somewhere with her. She doesn't really have a home at this point. Just some household goods in a storage unit. But she'll find a place and she and the kids will move there. And Cam will move back here and I . . . I'll go back to my apartment over the bar."

Aunt Phyl was nodding.

"Please, Phyllis," Red said. "It's just a few more weeks. Please forgive me and stay. The kids need you."

Red suffered a long, anxious silence.

"I told you I would be here," Aunt Phyl answered finally. "A late night now and again won't kill me."

A sigh of relief whistled though Red's lips. "Thank you, Phyl," she said. "I'll . . . I'll make it up to you somehow."

Aunt Phyl raised an eyebrow at that. "When a lady receives a favor," she said, "rather than trying to cancel it out, she should take it as an incentive. If you truly didn't deserve it, then you should work harder to be certain that you merit it the next time."

"Wise words," Red said.

"They're not mine, actually, but my mother's," Aunt Phyl said. "It's strange how carelessly we listen to our mothers, yet the important things they teach us, we never

389

seem to forget."

"You're very lucky," Red said. "Not all mothers are wise. I certainly wasn't."

Aunt Phyl nodded as if considering her statement. "I'm not sure women are able to make that judgment about themselves," she said. "What about your mother?"

"My mother? Good God, she was worse than me," Red said. "Different, very different, but I think worse."

"I'm sorry."

Red shrugged. "No, it's okay. I did better than she did and Bridge is doing better than me," she said. "By the time Olivia is raising children, maybe our family will be passing down wise words just like yours."

Aunt Phyl gave a small smile. "It's my mother who had the wise words. Me, not so much. Maybe I might have done better if I'd had children myself. But that just didn't happen."

Red nodded.

"So perhaps I couldn't be a true parent to Campbell, but I am very protective of him."

"Of course you are," Red said.

"Not simply because I love him, which of course I do," Aunt Phyl continued. "But also because Campbell has needed protection."

She raised her head, looking Red directly

in the eye. There was no overlay of polite convention or feigned friendliness. The woman was being open and honest and telling it as she saw it.

"A bright, handsome, interesting young man from a good family can capture the attention of a lot of women," Phyllis said. "Normally such a fellow would still be shallow and selfish in his youth, and that would offer him some protection, but Campbell has never been like that. Even as a teenager, he was full of fun, like any other boy, but there was a maturity there, a need to nurture that just made him different."

Red didn't find anything to dispute in his aunt's description. "I guess that's just the kind of guy he is," she said.

Aunt Phyl shook her head. "That is the kind of guy his life made him into," she said. "How much has Campbell told you about his mother's illness and her death?"

"A bit," Red answered. "He obviously loved her very much."

"Death is never easy on a child and he saw far too much of it," Phyl said. "He was still coming to grips with the loss of his mother when his father died. And he was barely out of high school when he lost his grandmother. It's been just he and I in this family for a long time now."

391

"So naturally that makes the bond between the two of you stronger," Red said.

"Yes, it does," Phyllis agreed. "Death tears families up and also brings them together. But if it were just death, maybe I wouldn't worry so much. His father was killed in a car crash. It was shocking and dramatic. His grandmother, old before her time, died in her sleep, peaceful at last. But it was his mother's death from Huntington's disease that was so hideous, insidious. It was soul killing."

"Soul killing?"

"Maybe not for her so much," Phyllis said. "For the last few years, she hardly knew who she was, let alone what was going on. But it was horrifying for those who loved her and had to watch."

A heavy silence filled the room.

"My brother couldn't do it," Phyl told her. "Once she began to lose her faculties, he sent her home to live with her mother and he rarely saw her again."

"That's awful," Red said.

Phyl nodded. "It was, but that's the way it was. The beautiful, witty, artistic woman he married turned into a twisting, jerking creature, drifting into dementia. It was so horrible and so sad, I still get angry and weepy about it. I cannot imagine how

Campbell, who was by her side every day to the very end, ever had the courage to go on with his life."

"But he did," Red whispered.

"Yes, he did," Aunt Phyl agreed. "And I wished for him that someday he could find someone who would make him happy, someone he could make a family with, and that he'd be able to leave all that sadness behind him."

Red nodded. "Of course you'd want that for him," she said. "I even want that for him."

"And you and I have exactly the right person in mind," Phyl said. "Someone young and sophisticated and cultured, who can give him children and help him establish a place for himself in the community. A nice young woman like Tasha, perhaps."

Red made no comment.

"That's how it should be for him. We both know that. But you see, Red, the thing is, Campbell has his heart set on someone else. A woman very different from one I would have chosen for him."

The older woman looked across the table at her meaningfully.

"I want you to know I haven't encouraged him in that at all."

Slowly, Aunt Phyl nodded. "Well, perhaps

it is time that you should. I really think for once, Campbell deserves to get what he really wants."

To: buildabetterbridge@citymail.com
December 1 5:19 p.m.
From: Livy156@ABrats.org
Subject: It is December

Hiya lovely Mom do u know what? It is December and I think it is my favorite month. Cause it is the month when you come home. I am SO happy. They turned on the Christmas lights on Broadway Street and it makes me so happy to see them. Red and green with big reeths. And at school we are decorating. Other kids r happy 2. They are happy cause they are thinking about presents and candy and Santa Claus. But I am different. I am not thinking about Santa Claus I am thinking about my mom. Every twingle light every Christmas carol every HO! HO! HO! says you are coming home real soon.

Nayras mom said I can go shopping with them on Sunday afternoon. If I do then I miss seeing Abuela cause seeing her takes the whole day. Daddy should not a moved her so far away from us. Cam says I am so lucky to have 2 things in one day I really want to do. Red says that maybe it would be good for Daniel to get some alone time with Abuela. But it is up to me. So I don't know. I guess I probably could go another time with Red. But it would

395

be SO fun with Nayra.

Daniel is good. He is happy and he is doing better on the violin. He likes to practice more now cause Aunt Phil listens and praysis him a lot. She is kinda weird old lady but she likes us now. She praysis me to but it means more to Daniel. She did bring a box of old make-up and jewelry for me. Nayra and I got all glam. The next day she brought hats. Not like caps but like ladys hats. My fav is a flat red one with a feather and has this red net stuff that hangs in front of your face. Aunt Phil says I can keep it but I can't wear it to school.

I got to go she has dinner fixed. I luv U Mom. Don't worry about us. Daniel and I are fine. When u get home I got a ka-zillian kisses I been saving for U.

Livy

29

It was too early on Sunday morning when the phone started ringing. Red assumed it would be Olivia, who was at Nayra's house on a sleepover, but it wasn't.

"Hey, Red, it's me."

Red was surprised at the sudden whoosh of pleasure that poured through her. The sound of her daughter's voice had, not so long ago, filled her with waves of guilt. Now it just reminded her how much she missed her.

"Bridge, you sound great."

"I'm fine," her daughter agreed. "Sorry to call so early."

Red hastily glanced at the clock. "It's time for me to get up, anyway," Red answered. "We're traveling back and forth to the valley today, so we'll need to get up and get on the road."

"How's Abuela doing?"

"Honestly, Bridge, she's still pretty bad

off and it's like she's kind of stuck," Red said. "I don't see a whole lot of improvement since she got to that place. And I am going to tell that to Mike myself, if the sorry sack of shit ever calls to talk to his kids."

"Don't waste your breath," Bridge told her. "When I get home, I'll try to see what I can do about finding a better place for Abuela. I don't think Mike cares where she is, as long as it's no inconvenience to him."

"You're probably right."

"How are the kids?"

"They're okay," Red answered. "Olivia's having a sleepover at Nayra's and then a big day of Christmas shopping. Daniel's really excited to go see Abuela without his big sister in charge."

"I'll bet."

"And Cam is driving down with us," Red said. "Daniel really likes that. Those two will probably make stupid jokes and have belching contests the whole way. I guess it's a guy thing."

"The kids like him a lot," Bridge said. "It sounds like you picked a really good guy."

"Yeah, he is, but you know me. My hookups with men have a real short shelf life. I'll likely be dumping him for some mean-tempered loser as soon as I get a chance."

"Well, don't," Bridge stated unequivocally.

"You are in complete charge of your life and you can choose to be happy if you put your mind to it."

Red smiled into the phone.

"Oh, darling," Red told her. "I don't know where you got your view of the world, but it's one of the things I most admire about you."

"Thanks," she answered quietly.

There was a long, almost too intimate moment of silence and Red hurried to fill the gap.

"Daniel's already had breakfast and is in the shower. Let me go holler at him. I know he wants to talk to you."

"Wait," Bridge said. "First I need to talk to you. We've had a bit of bad news here."

"What kind of bad news?"

"Not the worst kind," Bridge assured her. "Just a hiccup really. I may not be able to get out of here by Christmas."

"They haven't extended your tour?"

"No, nothing like that," Bridge assured her. "It's just a logistical snafu. I may be a few days later than I thought. I'm still aiming for Christmas Eve, but it's looking from here that I might not get moving as soon as I thought. I don't know how the kids are going to take that. I know they have their hopes up. It could be three or four days, maybe even a week after Christmas."

"Then we'll wait," Red told her daughter. "Christmas this year is not a date on the calendar, it's when you get home."

"I don't know how well that will go over," Bridge said.

"It will be fine," Red assured her. "You've raised some very good, very thoughtful kids. I'll make sure that more waiting just adds to the anticipation."

There was a long hesitation on the other end of the line.

"I appreciate that, Red," Bridge said finally. "You've been really good about this."

"I'm happy to get a chance to help," Red replied honestly. "It's little enough to do for the person who saved my life."

"Saved your life?" Bridge's tone was incredulous.

"Yeah, Bridge, I think you probably saved my life," Red said.

"I don't know what you mean."

"And I don't know if I can even explain it," Red answered. "I guess . . . well, I guess I had more than my share of chances to get lost down some dark roads. But then I had you and you needed me to try harder. If I hadn't had you, someone I loved and who needed me, I might never have had the guts to make the best I could out of where I

400

found myself."

Red paused for a moment, wondering if she'd said too much.

"You know why I gave you your name?" she asked.

"Because the first place we lived was under a bridge," her daughter replied.

"That's true, but it's more than that. You were my way to get from a bad life to a better one. So . . . so I owe you."

"Taking care of my kids, I think that makes the past as paid in full," she answered.

When Daniel got on the line, his conversation with his mother went well. He didn't quite know what to make of the new timeline, where the arrival of Christmas was based on Mom and not December 25. But by the time Cam showed up and they got on the road, he was going along with the change of plan.

The trip down was very much how Red had described it to her daughter — boys being boys. Two and a half hours of knock-knocking and rude noises.

They stopped for lunch on the road at Chentes in Alice. Cam and Daniel played a game where Cam would direct Daniel's attention elsewhere and then grab the taco off his plate. Daniel would make a big complaint and then, a few seconds later, clumsily attempt to do the same to Cam. Cam would look away as he was supposed to. Daniel would grab the taco. Then Cam would make a complaint. The taco traded hands three or four times before Red decided to step in.

"It's really not very sanitary to keep passing food around like that," she scolded and then glanced past Cam. "Is that a fire truck?"

Both guys turned to look. Red grabbed the taco and by the time they glanced back, she'd taken a giant bite out of it.

"Guess it's mine now," she said.

The protests were only silenced by the arrival of flan for everyone.

After lunch they drove straight south to McAllen and the nursing home where Abuela, as well as her sister, Tia Celia, shared a semiprivate room. Both ladies were delighted by the arrival of Daniel. Tia Celia seemed to think he was one of her grandchildren and kept talking to the boy as he tried to communicate with his *abuela.*

Red waited at the doorway, not wanting to crowd into the small room but unwilling to just leave Daniel completely on his own. The little boy followed the example his sister had set for him and maintained the usual style of their visits. He sat next to his old *abuela* and held her hand. Skipping back and forth between English and Spanish, he told her everything he'd been doing. When his news about games and school and home began to wind down, he struggled to come up with new things to say. Red gave him much credit for valor and didn't even fault him when he sunk to the level of first-grade jokes.

"What did the tortilla chip say to the cracker? I am not cho cheese."

The old woman made no attempt to talk. Even smiling the half smile she had left seemed more of a strain than a joy. But shining from those brown eyes, huge against her hollowed cheeks, was a feast of pleasure at having the boy by her side.

When it was time to leave, Daniel kissed his grandmother on the forehead. *"Te amo, Abuela,"* he told her.

The bright smile he'd given the old woman turned into a trembling lip by the time he reached the hallway. Red squeezed his young shoulder to offer what comfort she could.

"Abuela is different on the outside," she told him. "But inside, Daniel, she's exactly the same as she always was. And she still loves you so much."

Daniel nodded.

In the nursing home's main living room, they joined Cam, who was listening intently to an elderly man on the couch beside him.

Daniel broke away from Red and ran to Cam. He opened his arms and the child propelled himself into Cam's chest. Red watched as Cam enfolded the boy in his arms and hugged him tightly.

"Hey, guy," Cam said as he loosened his grip. "Let me introduce you here. This is Herelio." He indicated the man beside him. "Herelio, this is Daniel."

The boy regained his composure and offered his hand to the elderly man. Instead, the man patted Daniel on the arm and spoke rapidly to him in Spanish.

Daniel answered him in a polite and deferential tone.

Cam rose to his feet, there were goodbyes and handshakes all around. Then they headed to the car.

"I didn't think you spoke enough Spanish to carry on a conversation," Red said to Cam.

He shrugged. "He's an old man with stories to tell," Cam answered. "I didn't understand hardly any of it, but all I was required to say was 'sí' — yes — and 'verdad?' — is that the truth. Herelio could take it from there."

Outside, Daniel quietly climbed into the backseat of the van and strapped himself in. Red, who had done the driving on the way down, was relegated to the passenger seat. When Cam turned the wrong direction out of the parking lot, she questioned him.

"We're not headed straight home today," he said. "Daniel and I have some important business to take care of here."

Red glanced at the boy in the backseat. His expression was as curious as her own.

The important business turned out to be an amusement park where the three of them spent two hours racing go-carts and splashing around in bumper boats.

By the time they headed up the road toward San Antonio, Daniel was exhausted but had regained his smile.

They stopped for burgers at the Dairy Queen in Falfurrias. Red took the opportunity to call Nayra's parents to find out how the shopping trip went and to let them know when they'd be by to pick up Olivia. She talked to Olivia for a couple of minutes. Olivia was having a great time and the two girls were already plotting for the future.

"Nayra has to stay a weekend with us now," Olivia insisted.

"We'll see," Red hedged, suspecting that the girl's very protective parents were already less than overjoyed by Red's late-shift work schedule and nontypical family situation.

As she hung up, Red thought about what might happen to her granddaughter's new friendship once Bridge came home.

Once they were back on the road, she mentioned her concerns to Cam.

"Well, she can certainly stay at my house with the kids until she figures out what to do," he said. "You and I will just have to start bunking together at the apartment." He feigned a leering eyebrow. "That'll give you a lot of opportunity to make it up to me for the loss of my house."

She laughed lightly and shook her head. "Be careful what you wish for, cowboy, it might turn out to be more than you can handle."

"I'll take my chances," he promised.

"Why do you call Cam a cowboy?" Daniel asked from the backseat.

"I call all my guy friends *cowboy*," Red answered. "That way I don't have to remember their names."

"I thought you were asleep," Cam said.

"No, I'm just resting my eyes," he assured them.

The little boy's eyes continued to rest and a few minutes later, his head leaned over at an angle and his mouth dropped open slightly.

"It's nice of you to offer your house, Cam," Red said. "But Bridge is so independent. She's not going to want to accept anything from you or me or anyone. She'll have to find a place that she can afford to rent."

"I'll talk to Aunt Phyl," he said. "Her posse of the blue-haired and well-heeled owns property all over town. Maybe she can come up with some appropriate place to suggest to Bridge. I mean, it makes sense. It's a good neighborhood and it's close to Fort Sam. So, it's really a question of finding something that Bridge could afford where the kids wouldn't have to make another change of school."

"That would be great," Red said.

She leaned her head back in her seat, watching the lights on the dark road ahead.

"I hope . . ." She hesitated.

"What?"

"I hope I still get to see the kids after Bridge gets home," she said. "She's never really seemed to want me around much. And that didn't bother me. I didn't know them. But now I do. I don't want to go back to seeing them once or twice a year."

Cam nodded. "I know exactly how you

feel," he said. "I'm crazy about those kids. And right now I'm the most visible male figure in their lives. But I don't have any standing at all. I hate to think about Daniel or Olivia needing me and I might never even know it."

Red thought about that for a long moment.

"So, what we'll have to do is stay friends," she told him. "Even after we're not together anymore."

Cam snorted. "How many of your old sex buddies are you friends with, Red?" he asked rhetorically and then answered the question himself. "None. When you dump us, well, just stick a fork in it, 'cause it's done."

Red knew he was right. Her breakups had always involved plenty of angry screaming and animus. They'd included a variety of thrown objects, irrational threats and occasional bloodletting.

"I . . . We'll have to do it differently," she said. "I'm old enough to behave like a grown-up. And I think you are, too."

"I'd like us to behave like grown-ups," he said. "Do you even know how grown-ups like us behave when they are best friends, cherished lovers and great in bed together?" Cam didn't wait for her to answer. "They agree to make a life together. They go down to city hall and sign a paper that says, 'it's *us* now, not just *me*,' and they stand up in church and say, 'For better for worse, in sickness and in health. Only death can tear us apart.' "

"Don't start this now," Red said.

"Looks to me like the perfect time," he answered. "You can't run away. You can't even start a fight because you'd wake up Daniel. I can't imagine a better chance to get you to talk to me about something so important."

"Cam, I can't marry you," she said flatly.

"Because you don't love me?" he asked. "Answer honestly now, we owe each other the truth."

She sighed. "I do love you. I admit that. But I'm not very good at loving people."

"That's not what I see, Red. I see you loving your daughter enough to change your life for her. Loving these kids with all the natural openness we'd expect of any grandmother. And loving me, even against your better judgment to do so."

"Cam, you don't know all that I've been, things that I've done."

"No, and I don't care," he answered. "I'm not going to be scared off by your history with other men. I'm not those other men.

And this is not then, it's now. I believe in living for now."

Red shook her head and sighed. "Cam, you are a terrific guy. You'd make a wonderful husband. But I know your type. It's a great type but it's not the right type for me."

"My type? When have you ever had a clue about who I am?" he asked. "You thought I was a wastrel musician. Then you thought I was a trust-fund kid. Now you just think I'm lazy and lack ambition."

"I don't think you're lazy," Red corrected. "I just think . . . Cam, I understand that you want to save me. That's not a bad thing. A lot of men like to be the hero that rescues the woman who's made a mess of her life. But I can't be the kind of woman who gets saved."

"Save you? You think I want to save you?" Cam shook his head and chuckled lightly. "Red, you're the one I'm counting on to save me."

"I don't know what you're talking about."

"Do you remember at Brian's wedding that I told you there were two things I wanted to tell you?"

"Yeah, vaguely. Once you said the M word, I wasn't ready to hear anything else."

"I had two things that you needed to hear and I didn't know which one should go first.

Frankly, I picked the wrong one. I thought that explaining first that I want to marry you made sense because the other is something I really don't share with just anybody. It's not the kind of thing I'd tell a woman who was only my girlfriend."

"Okay," Red replied uneasily.

"Tasha told you that I got a vasectomy when I was eighteen, right? And I told you it was because I carry a gene for my mother's disease."

"Right," Red agreed.

"It's not just my mother's disease," Cam explained. "It's more like my family's disease. My disease."

Red took a startled breath.

"My mother died from Huntington's," he continued. "So did my grandfather, or at least we think so. Back then, doctors knew so little that he was never really diagnosed. Huntington's is an inherited disorder caused by a defect in a gene that allows brain cells to die. It's a pretty awful disease and it has no cure."

Red's brow furrowed.

"It's a late-onset disease," Cam continued. "Most usually, it doesn't show up until people are forty or fifty years old. By then, people with the disease already have a family. If you have the gene and you have a child, the baby has a fifty percent chance of getting the gene, as well."

"And you have this gene," Red said.

"Yeah," he answered. "In 1987 they came up with a genetic test that could tell you if you're a carrier. As soon as I was old enough to sign for myself at the doctor's office, I had the test done. When it came back positive, I decided to have the vasectomy."

"Because you needed to make sure that you didn't pass it on to anyone else," she said.

"Not exactly," he answered. "It was more than that. It was taking control of what I could control. Because there was so much that I could not."

Red sat beside him in the dim light of the van's interior and tried to straighten up her world that had so unexpectedly tilted.

"So you carry this gene," she said. "But you're not sick."

"I'm not sick today," he said. "That's what I try to stay with in my life. You accused me of being the grasshopper who fiddles away all summer instead of being sober and working hard like the ants. I've always had a different take on that story. They put it out as if the grasshopper doesn't survive because he didn't do what the ants did. But for me, the grasshopper knew that nature did not

412

mean for him to survive the winter. It was his fate to die with the first hard freeze. So why shouldn't he choose to fiddle as long as he could still hold the bow?"

The moment was neither silent nor still as the traffic picked up. Red was completely speechless. She could hardly get her thoughts into coherent framework, let alone utter a statement.

"Every day that I wake up fine is not something that I'd take for granted," Cam said. "They have treatment for symptoms and there's research being done, a lot of promise with stem-cell therapies. People have hope on the horizon. But right now, the straight deal is that if I don't get hit by a bus or shot by a jealous husband, I'm probably going to die of this disease. I'm probably going to die fairly young and it's not going to be a very easy death or one I'd ask a lesser woman than you to watch. You're a survivor, Red. You make the best of the worst blows the world can dish out. That's the kind of woman I need by my side. And I'm a very lucky man to have found that in somebody that I also love."

30

Red was very groggy the next morning, drinking coffee at the bar. She hadn't gotten much sleep. After picking up Olivia and getting the kids washed up and tucked into their own beds, she'd found Cam still waiting in the living room. He looked as nervous as she'd ever seen him. She hadn't said anything and she didn't know what to say.

He gave her a little peck on the cheek as if he didn't trust himself to actually kiss her.

"I'm not going to push you on this," he said. "I know you'll give me an answer when you have one. You've got the whole story on me now. You know where I'm coming from and what I want from you. Take your time and think about it. Think about us in terms of us. Don't bring up the past or worry about the future. Try to think about how good we are together now and how much that could bring to both our lives."

"I . . . uh —"

"Think!" he commanded. "Just think. I'll see you tomorrow."

Tomorrow was now here, but having lain awake most of the night, she was hardly in a mood to appreciate it.

When Cam came breezing in a few minutes later, he appeared to be his usual happy, rested, enthusiastic self.

"You're here early," he said to Red as she poured him a cup of coffee.

"I called a contractor last week after I signed the lease agreement," she said. "He's supposed to meet me here this morning about getting the patio fenced and up to code."

He nodded. "It's good to get that started," Cam said. "The worst months for the patio were always January and February. If you could get it ready for a big reopening around the first of March, that would be great."

Red nodded.

"What are you looking so sharp about this morning?" she asked him.

"I'm subbing for a friend who's supposed to play in a Christmas chamber concert," Cam answered. "He's got the flu and I've got the gig. Rehearsal starts in a half hour."

"That sounds good."

"Well, we hope I will," he joked. "I'll see if

I can get tickets. It might be something the kids would enjoy."

They drank their coffee together, as companionably as ever. Red marveled at how easily they could act as if everything was the same, when inside she felt such an intensity of upheaval.

The contractor showed up right on time. Cam only had time to shake hands with the man and offer Red a hasty wish of luck.

Outside on the patio, Red tried to restate what she'd already told the contractor on the phone. The man wasn't interested in a lot more talk. He was a get-down-to-business kind of guy, which Red really appreciated.

He walked around the patio for more than a half hour, taking measurements, checking angles and inspecting what was there.

At first Red shadowed him, expecting questions. But the man did what he did silently and without comment. So eventually she wandered to one of the patio tables and took a seat. It was colder sitting than walking around, but her jacket was warm and the chill on her face kept her alert.

She needed to think about the future of the bar. But the memory of Cam's voice kept crowding in. And along with that, damning reminders of things she had said to him. How she'd whined about the uncertain fate of the bar. She winced as she recalled her words.

How did a person live like that? she wondered. How did Cam muster the courage to get up every morning, not knowing what was going to happen?

As that thought wound its way through her brain, it caught her up short and she almost laughed. Did she wake up every morning *knowing* what was going to happen? Did anyone ever really know what the future was going to bring? Not at all.

Red realized that she'd spent so many years trying to avoid the most dangerous of life's roads that she'd lost sight of the truth about driving. Nobody gets out of this world alive.

Cam was completely right. The river that used to calm her hectic life was to be an amusement ride for tourists. The business that she poured all her time and energy into would someday be gone. And she and everyone she ever knew or loved would someday be nothing more than dust.

But that day wasn't today. Today, the sun was shining, her grandchildren were in school learning, the bar was scheduled to open on time and the guy she loved was still in love with her.

It was almost selfish to expect anything more.

The contractor sat down across from her at the table. He spent several minutes writing things down, comparing notes and making calculations before he finally spoke.

"I'd want to make some more calculations before I put it all in writing," he said. "But I can give you a pretty close estimate of what you're looking at here."

Red and the contractor talked for several minutes. They walked around the patio together. Finally, they shook hands and agreed to speak again later.

She walked him back through the bar and unlocked the front door to let him out. Checking her watch, she decided it was close enough and proceeded to getting the lights on and the place completely open for business.

The phone rang. It was Sarah, wanting to hash out the rest of Winter Festival in Daniel's class. Red wrote down where she was supposed to be and when. Then mostly she just half listened as Sarah gave her details about the particulars that Tasha had insisted upon, as well as Sarah's personal opinion of those choices.

"Shootfire!" Sarah said suddenly in the middle of chatter about a planned craft project on making penguins from paper plates.

Red laughed. "You're hanging around with me too much, Sarah," she said. "Now you're beginning to sound like me."

"I forgot your letter."

"My letter?"

"Remember the letter you gave me the day we went shopping? I was supposed to give it to Brad, but I just found it here still in my purse."

"Oh, don't worry about it," Red said. "Brad told me I might be hearing from other lawyers. That's probably one of them. We've already signed the deal. It's done. I don't know what else could be said about it."

"Well, whatever," Sarah said. "Still, I'm taking it out of my purse right now and setting it on the table in the front hall. This is where Brad puts his keys when he walks in the door. He'll be sure to see it."

"Great. Thanks," Red said.

Around three-thirty, just after she made her usual after-school call to make sure that the kids were home and Aunt Phyl was in charge, Cam returned from his rehearsal.

"How was practice?" she asked him.

He grinned at her. "I think I've earned myself a beer," he answered.

"That good, huh?"

He sat down across the bar from her.

"How did the meeting with the contractor go?"

"We'll see what the man says," she told him. "He's going to get back to me with the hard-and-fast dollar details. I like his ideas and he seems knowledgeable enough about the construction and the city codes."

Cam nodded. "So it's really just a question of whether you can afford it."

"I have to afford it," she said simply. "It's reinvesting in the business. If I want to have a business, I've got to put money back into it."

"Do you have enough money?"

"Maybe," Red answered. "It depends upon how much the contractor needs up front."

"You know I'll lend you anything and everything that I've got saved. Or I'll go with you to try to get a loan. I'll bet we could get Brad to go with us, too. I'm sure he does that kind of thing all the time."

"I'd rather not go into debt at all," Red admitted. "It'll be really tight around here, but if I can pull the funds out of operating expenses, it would put me in a better place in the long run . . . or the longer run."

Cam gave her a nod of understanding.

Red leaned forward on the bar, getting close enough that her words were almost intimate. "I guess I'm beginning to get used to the idea of a living with an uncertain future."

"I think James Dean said it best. 'Dream like you'll live forever and live like you'll die today.'"

"Good advice," Red said thoughtfully.

"It's always worked for me," he said.

They just stayed where they were for a long introspective moment. Then, controlling the edge of her lip that was so tempted to grin, Red asked, "James Dean? Now is that the guy who makes sausages or the *Rebel Without a Cause* guy?"

Cam gave her a long-suffering look, then leaned closer. "For a comment like that, woman, I ought to swat that armadillo until he's blushing red."

And then he kissed her. He really kissed her.

Red heard the regulars hooting and applauding, but she didn't pay any attention.

To: buildabetterbridge@citymail.com
December 14 3:30 p.m.
From: Livy156@ABrats.org
Subject:

Mom I am SO excited about u coming home. Nayra and I went shopping and I bought us something that you are gonna like SO much. But I am not gonna tell u what it is so that you will be surprised. Course u r gonna be surprised anyway cause Daniel and I are a lot grown up while u were gone. And when u hear us play violin your gonna freak!

Red told us that u may not be here at Christmas but that it will be Christmas when you're here. So I am trying to be ok with that. Daniel asks every day how many more days. That is annoying but I don't get up in his face about it cause I understand how hard it is to wait.

I remember last time u came home and we were SO excited then to. And then you came and it was our regular life. But then you had to go back again. Daniel doesn't really remember that. I guess he was to little. Course he knows u were gone but he doesn't think it was then like it is now. I have not told him that it is that way and that when you get home and we are regular again it will only be a while until you are gone again. I think that is just too much for a 1st grader. Maybe by when u leave next he will be in 3rd or something. And I will be older to so u wont have to worry so much about us when your gone. And now we know Red and she is not so bad at all so it will be ok. It is like Cam told me not to waste good time today by worrying about tomorrow.

So I wont. I will just be happy tomorrow and the next day and next and next and then you might be here. YEA! I luv u Mom and when u get home we are not going to worry about you any more.

Livy

31

Olivia and Daniel were in the final throes of going-to-school chaos when Cam showed up, interrupting the last-minute search for homework and jackets and whatever. He immediately pitched in, proving he could both have a serious discussion on the relative merits of Batman versus Hulk while locating a picture book on insect larvae. He found the latter beneath the couch cushions.

Finally the two Lujan children were on their way to school. Red and Cam stood together on the porch and watched them to the end of the street and onto the school grounds.

"So why are you stopping by so early?" Red asked.

"Just hoping for a cup of coffee with a good-looking grandma," he answered. "And I need to dig my tux out of the back closet and see if it's ready to go or if I have to drop it by the cleaners."

"You have a tux?"

"I'm a musician," he answered. "That's like asking a cowboy if he's got a saddle."

"Hey, cowboy, have you got a saddle?"

He grinned and raised a suggestive eyebrow. "I prefer riding bareback, ma'am," he told her.

"That's right, I remember that," she said. "But it's been such a long time, I can hardly recall."

This flirtation might have headed to its logical conclusion had the phone not begun to ring.

She went inside and he followed her. She answered the phone, while he went past her and into the kitchen. By the time he brought her back a cup of coffee, she'd finished her conversation.

"That was Brad," she said. "He's on his way over here. He's got something to tell me that he didn't want to say over the phone."

"Is there a problem with the lease?"

Red shook her head. "He said it wasn't about the lease, but he wouldn't say what it was. Maybe he's decided that he doesn't want me around Sarah and his kids. I'm probably a bad influence on her."

"Oh, please, that's ridiculous," Cam said. "It can't be that."

"Well, whatever, stall him," Red said. "I've got to get a shower and put on some makeup."

Red raced through her morning ablutions, but she could already hear the two men talking in the living room before she was quite presentable.

When she finally joined them, Brad was sitting on the edge of Cam's favorite chair, nervously sipping a cup of coffee. Cam was seated across from him on the couch. Both men rose politely to their feet as she walked in.

Red stifled a grin at their Alamo Heights manners, vowing just to enjoy it.

"So what's up?" she asked Brad as she took her seat.

He pulled the thick envelope that she'd received by certified mail a week earlier.

"I just opened this today," he told her. "It was not meant for me. It's not about the building. I'm . . . I'm so sorry . . . I . . ."

"What is it?"

Brad hesitated. "I'm sure not the one to break this kind of news, but . . . I'm so sorry, Red. Your mother has passed."

"Passed what?"

"She's . . . uh . . . she's passed away," he clarified. "She died almost eight months ago. The family has been unable to contact you. They just recently heard that you were here in San Antonio."

Red stared at Brad. She heard what he was saying. She even understood it. Her mother, Patsy Grayson, was no longer around for Red to despise and fear and serve as an example of how not to mother. She tried to drag up some feeling of grief, some feeling of loss. But she didn't have any.

She looked up at Brad. His expression was stricken. He probably had a wonderful mom, Red thought. He would never comprehend her own ambivalence.

"Thank you, Brad, for bringing me this news," she said. "Of course, it is a tremendous loss. But my mother and I were not close. In fact, I haven't seen her in thirty years." She glanced over at Cam. "I guess it's too late to send flowers."

Red rose to her feet. "Thank you for bringing me this news," she repeated.

"Ah . . . there's more," Brad said. "That was, that was just the cover letter."

"Oh." Red sat back down.

"Your mother named you as a beneficiary to her estate," he said. "The lawyer wants to meet with you to go over the details. What he's indicated here is that the property was distributed to other family members, but that there is a sizable bequest of cash for you."

"What?" Red was not sure she was hearing this.

"She has left you some money," Brad rephrased as simply as he could. "It's fifty thousand dollars."

Red continued to look at him unbelieving. "My mother left me fifty thousand dollars?"

"Yes."

Suddenly, the fog in Red's brain cleared and she was in as much control and as much certainty as she'd ever been in her life.

"I don't want it," she said.

Brad nodded sympathetically. "You're in shock," he said. "You've just lost your mother."

"I lost my mother a very long time ago. I don't want any money from her."

Brad was at a loss for words. He turned to Cam for help.

"I don't think you have to make a decision about this today," he said.

"I've already made the decision," she told Cam. "I don't want anything from her, dead or alive. I don't want a dime."

"It's not like money has people's names on it," Brad offered. "It's just money. It was in a bank or investments that have to be turned into cash to pay the bequest."

"I don't want it."

"Okay," Cam said. "If you don't want it, you don't want it." He turned to Brad. "So do we just ignore the letter or what?"

Brad's jaw dropped open.

"Uh . . . well, uh . . . we can't just leave it open. We'll need to respond so that they can close up the estate. You can refuse it," he said. "There's a provision in state law that allows you to refuse an inheritance. I don't know much about it. People don't usually do it."

"It's what I want to do," Red said. "I want to refuse it."

"What happens then?" Cam asked.

"I'm not really sure," Brad said. "It depends upon how the will was written. It might just go back into the whole of the estate to be redivided or it might pass to another beneficiary. I'll have to talk to this attorney to find out what the provisions are."

"Kenny should just have it," Red said.

"Kenny?"

"My . . . my stepbrother," she answered. "All that money was my stepfather's. I'm sure that his father would have expected it all to go to him."

"Well, I'll call and inquire later this morning," Brad said. "If you think about it more and want to revise your thinking, I'll be sure to give us a little breathing room before we completely reject it."

"Completely reject it," Red said. "I don't want it."

Brad rose to leave. Red and Cam did, too. The men shook hands and Brad gave Red an anemic hug.

"I am so sorry for your loss," he said. "Call me later," he told Cam.

Once he was gone, Red stood in the middle of the living room for a long moment, befuddled as to what she ought to be doing.

"Here, put on your coat," Cam said, handing it to her.

"What?"

"We're going for a walk."

She didn't argue. Somehow she didn't have the will to do so. Passively, she followed him out the front door and down the porch. Red put her hands in her pockets. Cam threaded his arm through hers and they began walking.

Red hardly glanced around as they went up one street and down another, weaving their way through the neighborhood that had become so familiar to her in such a short time.

Cam didn't try to talk to her. She was grateful for that. There wasn't anything to say. She felt strangely disconnected. It wasn't as if her mother's death truly meant any change to Red's reality. But the wall that she'd held up so formidably between that life and her current one had transformed inexplicably from one she'd thought was made of solid bricks and mortar to a mere illusion on thin paper.

When they got to Patterson Avenue they turned left onto the wide boulevard that once brought local commuters and city visitors by trolley car all the way from Broadway to the Argyle.

They continued walking, Cam as if he knew where they were headed, and Red as if she didn't care. It was a downhill trek, easy to make progress without a lot of effort. As they neared the last big curve in the street, with the giant high-rise condo and the University of the Incarnate Word in view, Cam abruptly turned again. This road — narrow, dark and shaded even in winter — was a steep incline.

"Where are we going?" Red asked for the first time.

"Someplace quiet," he answered and urged her onward.

Fortunately, it was not far. They walked

431

into an entrance that revealed mostly empty parking spaces, a couple of buildings with a courtyard and fountain. Beyond that was a wide expanse of open land on a gently manicured slope.

"What is this place?"

"It's the grounds of the Episcopal Diocese."

"Are you an Episcopalian?"

"Uh, more or less," he answered. "It doesn't matter. They don't mind people quietly walking here."

He clasped her hand and they strolled along a gray stone walkway that curved through the grounds punctuated by benches offering a seat with a view. Without hesitation, he turned onto a less formal path of gravel and dried leaves. Reddish-brown, it edged away from the parklike beauty to twist and turn among the trees. Then Cam abandoned that path, as well, for what was nothing more than a foot track through the brush.

"Are you sure we can go there?" she asked.

"I'm sure," he answered.

The way was far too narrow to walk two abreast, so Red followed him, trying not to trip over roots or encounter any snakes.

The place was quiet, amazingly quiet for the middle of a neighborhood. But as they moved along the trail, she became aware of the sound of trickling water ahead. As they got closer, Red could glimpse though the trees and underbrush a swift-moving little stream tumbling over ancient stones.

Cam edged down the side of a hollowed-out hill and stopped to turn back and offer his hand. Red accepted the help as she made her way closer to the water. He motioned to Red to take a seat on a huge gray limestone boulder that was a perfect vantage point to the site. Just a few feet away and slightly above them, water was bubbling out of the bluff they'd just descended.

Cam eased himself close beside her, wrapping an arm around her waist to hug her more tightly against him. Red didn't usually go for that kind of thing, but today she found it surprisingly comforting. The sun had momentarily escaped from behind the clouds and lit up the area of stones and water and tree trunks.

They sat together silently for a while as the tension in Red began to ease. She hadn't known it was there until it started to go away.

She wondered about this place. Had it been Cam's secret hideout as a boy? The place he'd come to be alone when life at home had been too hard to bear? She knew, without asking, that it must have been and she was honored that he was sharing it with her.

"It's nice here," she told him. "With nobody around."

He smiled and nodded. "But we're lucky to be here alone," he assured her. "This is a very busy place, you know."

"Busy?" She thought of the less-traveled track they'd just been on. "I don't think so."

"Absolutely," he answered. "Or at least it has been over time. They say humans have been coming down here, occupying this area, the Olmos Basin, for eleven thousand years."

"Eleven thousand? That's a joke, right. You don't mean eleven thousand."

"No joke." He gestured with his other arm. "All of this is a protected archeological site. They've found projectiles and pottery and even ancient graves dating back as far as 9000 B.C."

"I didn't think there was anything in Texas back that far," Red said.

"Surprising, huh," he said. "This area has been occupied since the end of the last Ice Age," Cam said. "It's almost too hard to get your mind around. Before the Pyramids were built, people were sitting right here where we're sitting, watching this small flow of water splash across those rocks."

Red was thoughtful.

"So there was an Indian town here?"

"It was more like a camp, I think," Cam said. "It was a perfect area for hunter-gatherers because it has available water and abundant game. And in a valley like this, there is some protection from the elements."

"That's interesting," she said.

"It is. When the Spanish came and agriculture took over as the mode of life, this was no longer really the place to be. Tilling the soil requires flatter ground. So the indigenous people built farms elsewhere. But as late as the 1920s, there were still bands of Native Americans that camped here in the basin during the summer."

"I can understand why," Red said. "It seems so . . . I don't know, peaceful, I guess."

Cam nodded. "It is peaceful."

"And it's so far away from all the noise and traffic and busyness of the city."

"Seems that way, huh," he agreed. "But that just proves that things are often not at all what they seem. This little stream is the very heart, the lifeblood of this whole city."

"What do you mean?" she asked him.

"This stream is actually one of the springs

that form the headwaters of the San Antonio River," Cam told her. "Most people think of the Blue Hole as the official start of the river. We're five hundred yards north of there, so for me, this is the true beginning."

Red studied the source of the water. It seemed to be seeping straight out of the large limestone boulders that made up the ten-foot bluff.

"So everything that's downstream," Cam continued, "the river itself and the seventh-largest city in the country, which has thrived on its banks for three hundred years, came into being from that gush of water pushing out around those rocks."

"Wow."

"Not a very auspicious beginning for something that ultimately enables so much."

"No," Red agreed. "You'd never believe that all that could begin from something so small."

They sat together in silence as the water continued to push out from around the boulders, swirling, puddling, falling and racing forward.

"Do you think I'm crazy for not accepting the money?" she asked him. It was changing the subject, but maybe it wasn't.

Cam turned slightly to face her and then put his forehead up against hers, as if doing a sci-fi mind meld.

"If you're crazy, I want to be crazy, too," he answered.

"That money, that could do us a lot of good," she pointed out.

"*Us* are going to be fine," he teased. "Especially if we're going to be *us.*"

She smiled at him, but her thoughts were still serious. "If I took the money, I could fix up the place without worrying about paying for it. I'd have something in the bank if and when we are forced out of our building. Or I could even use it as a down payment for a new building that I would own myself."

"All true," Cam agreed.

"It's like Brad said, money is just money. It's not like my mother will ever know that I refused to take it. That I threw it back in her face."

"No, she won't know," Cam agreed. "But you will. And if you think this is what you need to do, then I trust you."

Red looked up at him. His was a young face, but it was strong, it was lived in.

"You're not even going to ask me to explain?"

He shook his head. "I know you would tell me if you could," he said.

"Thank you," she said.

Red sighed heavily. It felt so good to lean against him. Such a relief after so many years of being forced to stand on her own. There was a long, sweet moment between them as the truth emerged in her consciousness. They were in this together. She no longer needed the walls that she'd built between them.

"My mother just walked away from us and never looked back," she told him. "I don't claim to know what all went on between her and my dad. I don't think anybody can ever really see inside their parents' marriage. But it was obvious to me, even as a kid, that my mom really disliked her life."

Red pulled the hair away from her face and tossed it behind her shoulders.

"My dad was a farmer and farmers always struggle," she said. "I guess they really struggle when they're married to women who like lots of things. And my mom did like lots of things. So Dad took a second job. But that was still not enough. Mom decided she needed to work, too. I don't remember thinking much about it at the time. She wasn't home anymore when I got off the school bus. But I just took care of my chores and the world went on."

Red's brow furrowed thoughtfully. "Looking back, I'd say the day she went to work at Grayson Automotive, she was already on her way out the door."

She glanced over at Cam. He was listening, clear-eyed and intent.

"Harv Grayson was actually a pretty good guy," Red told him. "He'd been married twenty-five years to his childhood sweetheart. They'd established themselves at the very top rung of what passed for a social ladder in Piney Woods. He had a successful business and she was big in church and charity groups. They'd raised a son who was smart and had as much potential as his father."

She gave a humorless smile. "They might have fit right in, here in Alamo Heights," she said. "But within one year, my mom blew all of that to kingdom come. Harv dumped his wife, forgot about his kid. He was totally ensnared by my mother and wanted to give her anything she wanted. And being the woman she was, well, she wanted it all."

Cam nodded, understanding.

"None of this touched me, none of it was really important," Red continued. "I had my daddy and we were a happy family. Truth is, I think we were happier than before she left. No more fighting, no more drama. Daddy and I did what we needed to do and didn't worry about wanting a lot more."

Red wiped her hands on the thighs of her jeans.

"If things had just gone on. If nothing had happened, my life would not have changed. I would have finished high school and Daddy would have walked me down the aisle to marry some local guy and I'd never have left Piney Woods." She heaved a sigh. "But when my father died, well, everybody just assumed that my mother would take me in."

"Of course," Cam agreed.

"I think she would have been willing to foist me off on some distant aunt somewhere, if she could find one," Red said. "But Harv really felt sorry for me. He could never see my mother as she was. He thought that she would want me with her. And she didn't want to look like she didn't."

"But she didn't."

"Right," Red said. "My mother didn't think much of me. For her, I was too much like my dad, I guess. And her greatest fear was that I would ruin her butt-in-a-jam-jar life."

"Narcissism, that's what shrinks call that," Cam said. "I think it's more or less incompatible with motherhood."

Red shrugged. "Maybe that was her excuse."

"So what happened?" he asked.

"Well," she said. "We all know that when you screw someone, payback is hell."

Cam agreed.

"All the time Mom was living high and mighty on Harv's money and cavorting around town in her Cadillac, the friends of Harv's first wife were anxious to bring her down. And there I was, her daughter, naive and countrified, such an easy target."

"Ummh," Cam sympathized shaking his head.

"I was ostracized at school, laughed at, talked about," Red said. "It was kid stuff, though I do think they were probably encouraged by their parents. Still, I could have managed that."

"But something worse turned up," Cam said.

Red nodded. She heaved a heavy sigh. This story was not one that she'd ever told aloud. She had to momentarily collect her thoughts as she focused on the racing water in the stream in front of her.

"Harv's son, Kenny, came home from college that summer, as he always did, to work at his father's dealership. He was an athlete, good-looking, charming and he seemed so grown up. No grown-up man had ever paid any attention to me. But Kenny did."

Red recalled perfectly how calf-eyed she'd been.

"He talked to me," she explained. "He listened to all my teenage-girl craziness. He took me for romantic drives around the lake. He gave me my first kiss. And I fell in love with him. It was easy. I needed somebody to love me."

Red was picking nervously at her fingernails. She hadn't even realized it until Cam took her hand in his own.

"Kenny didn't love me," she said, unwilling to meet Cam's eye. "I don't think he even hated me. I was nothing to him. I was a means to an end. He wanted to get back at my mother. To shame her, humiliate her the way his mother had been humiliated. He failed at that. The humiliation was all mine."

"What happened?" Cam asked.

"He seduced me. It wasn't any great accomplishment on his part. I mean, how hard would it have been? I was sixteen and desperately in love. I would have done anything he asked. So he pretty much asked for everything. And for the rest of the summer, I gave him whatever he wanted."

She did look at Cam then. Searching his

face for repulsion or judgment. She didn't find either.

"He started phoning me every time we weren't together," Red said. "He'd talk dirty to me on the phone. I would giggle and repeat things he wanted me to say. He told me it was just a naughty game. What I didn't know, of course, was that he was recording it all to play back to his friends. One afternoon he invited his buddies to meet me, naked. I was so shocked and so scared. I was so betrayed! They took photos of me trying to cover myself up while the other guys laughed and posed for the camera like it was some gang bang or orgy."

"Oh my God," Cam said.

"I always tell myself that I was lucky that I wasn't gang-raped."

"I am so sorry," he told her.

"Within days those pictures were passed around all over town," Red told him. "As far as anyone was concerned the boys were just being boys, but I was a certified slut. No, worse than a slut. They talked about me and Kenny, using terms like depravity, incest and perversion. After half a year of the whole town constantly reminding me that I was not a Grayson, suddenly Kenny and I were brother and sister."

She glanced over at Cam. He was still with

her. Red didn't know what he was thinking, but he hadn't walked away.

"My mother was so furious, she was out of control," Red continued. "She didn't for a second think that it might not be all my fault. She hit me and kicked me and called me horrible names, names I'd never even heard of. Harv was horrified, too. But he was at least as upset with Kenny as he was with me. He knew why Kenny did it and I think he felt sorry for me, but it didn't matter."

Red sat up straighter and brushed off her jeans as if she could whisk it all away.

"My mom threw me out. She literally locked me out of the front door with the clothes on my back and ordered me off the premises. I just stood on the front lawn, not having a clue of what to do or where to go. I kept thinking, 'She's my mom, moms can't do this, she has to take me back in, she has to let me stay here.' But it just got later and later. Finally the lights in the house went out. I slept that night on the lawn furniture.

"In the morning Harv came out and woke me up. He'd thrown my clothes in a suitcase and told me to get in the car. We drove to the courthouse in Crockett. Harv had called in a favor from a local judge. The man had me sign a bunch of forms and by lunchtime

I had manumission papers declaring me as an adult. Then Harv bought me a sack with a burger and fries and dropped me off at the bus station. He gave me everything in his wallet. Two hundred and thirty-five dollars."

Red knew she sounded matter-of-fact but, strangely, she felt that way.

"I came to San Antonio because that's where the next bus was headed."

"And you never talked to your mother again?" Cam asked.

"I called her about two months later," Red answered. "When I finally realized I was pregnant. I was so stupid, I didn't even know how to tell. When I found out, the first thing I did was call my mom. I remember it as if it just happened. The operator said, 'I've got a long-distance collect call from Emmaline Cullens. Will you accept the charges?' And my mother, as clearly and firmly as if she weren't lying through her teeth, answered, 'I don't know anyone by that name.'"

Red blew out a big puff of air. A long moment passed between them, only the sound of the water filled the silence.

"So I decided I didn't know anyone by that name, either," she said. "My daddy always called me Red. I've been Red ever since."

Cam twisted a thick lock of her hair around his fist. "I like it," he told her. "It's a no-nonsense name for a woman who put nonsense behind her."

"So, maybe now you can understand how I feel about the money," Red said to him. "Back when I really needed her, when she really could have helped me, she chose not to. Now, when I'm more than able to stand up for myself, she's trying to have a do-over or get rid of her guilt by paying me off. She's not going to need the money anymore, so why not use it to buy back the daughter that she kicked to the curb like a bag of garbage. Well, I don't come so cheap these days."

Cam wrapped his arms tightly around her as tears ran down her face and her body shook with sobs of grief and anger. He just held her there on that boulder, rocking her back and forth like a baby in his arms, allowing the last of her bitterness to spill out as the water from deep beneath the ground seeped out of the spring, swirling past them and into the world beyond.

As it went, Red began to feel cleansed. The shame and anger she'd clung to so tightly for years had been released and she began to feel better, lighter, hopeful.

When all the tears were dry and the comfort of his arms had become second nature, Cam finally let her go and rose to his feet. "Let's walk on down to Broadway and see if we can't find something to eat. I'm hungry."

"Me, too," Red said, surprising herself. "It's so strange. I've kept this inside so long. I thought if I ever let it out, it would just destroy me, destroy everything around me. But now I've said it. I've said it all to you. And the sun is still shining, the water is still running and all my body knows is that I missed breakfast and it's time for lunch."

He helped her back up the bank and she followed him along the track. When they were once again on the gravel path, Red took his hand.

"I just realized that my mother and I had something very much in common," she said.

"What's that?"

"Both of us got a phone call from our daughter that offered us a second chance to maybe get things right," Red answered. "I guess I'm just lucky that I had to take the call."

32

The week before Christmas was busy, more so than any Red could ever remember. Typically she would buy a few presents, put up some colored lights and tinsel in the bar and spend the day sleeping in. That was not going to cut it this year.

The party in Daniel's class went well. She'd become so accustomed to helping out that she now knew all the kids and they all knew her. Her years of working at the bar, translated into appropriate first-grade language, had made her approachable to the kids and apparently unreproachable among their parents.

With school out and the kids home all day, Aunt Phyl discovered so much that had to be done. Cam put a sweet-smelling fir tree in front of the living-room windows and retrieved the ornaments he'd grown up with from a few boxes in the attic.

Aunt Phyl supervised as Olivia and Daniel turned ordinary green limbs and needles into something magical, glittering and festive. They did such a good job, she insisted, that they must redo her tree, as well. For twenty years, at least, Aunt Phyl had contracted the services of an interior decorator to "dress her home for the season." This year had been no exception. But she went home and stripped the beautifully appointed and elegantly styled tree down to the lights. The next day, she had Olivia and Daniel redecorate it with homemade ornaments, Christmas cookies and strings of popcorn and cranberries.

"It was the most joy I've ever had out of a tree," the woman admitted to Red.

The evening of Cam's chamber concert, Red took the night off. She and the kids put on their best clothes and their nicest manners and went with Aunt Phyl to the event on the campus of Trinity University.

They had excellent tickets with a perfect view of Cam, who was seated on the front row among the violins. Red thought him amazingly handsome in his black tux. She was not at all familiar with classical music, but she had no reverse snobbery about it. Music was music and any live production had the potential to touch the heart. The concert did that admirably and she was surprised at how many of the holiday-themed pieces sounded familiar to her. But what truly stunned her was Cam's performance. She had watched him as the casual, happy-go-lucky fiddle player enjoying himself on the stage many times. But this music made him very intense. He was frowning through the entire performance. This music strived for a perfection that would have leached all the joy out of a honky-tonk crowd.

After the concert, Aunt Phyl took them to the country club for dessert. Cam met them there. Over chocolate Christmas pie with candy canes, Olivia and Daniel asked Cam questions.

"What's it like to be in the middle of all those instruments at the same time?"

"If you make a mistake, does the person next to you know it?"

"Why do they need that guy with the stick? He doesn't even play anything."

Cam took every question seriously and answered as best he could, even including some important practical lessons comparing teamwork and harmony with individual achievement. The children seemed to relish discussion about a world that was all new to them.

Aunt Phyl spotted an old friend and, to

Red's surprise, wanted to introduce Olivia and Daniel. From across the room, Red observed the two former "menaces and criminals" politely conversing with the table of older folks as Phyl looked on with pride.

"She probably should be introducing you, too," Cam said.

Red shook her head. "I don't want to meet anybody," she answered. "I'm happy with the tacky but dependable friends I've already got."

Cam chuckled.

"What did you think of the concert?"

"I liked it," she told him. "Beautiful music. And you were, by far, the most handsome guy on stage. But I'm glad you don't do that anymore."

"Why?"

"Because it doesn't seem to make you happy," she said.

"And you are concerned with my happiness?"

"It's become one of my top priorities."

Cam raised an eyebrow. "Well, you already know what I want very much."

Red shrugged.

"You need a hint?" he asked. "What has ribbons and bells, involves some vows and some toasting, goes on for a couple of hours and lasts a lifetime?" He hesitated. "It also rhymes with bedding."

"You want to go sledding?" she teased. "You'd better take that up with Santa Claus."

Laughing off his persistent question was the only thing to do during this time, when her own concerns took a backseat to the imminent arrival of her daughter and all the relief and upheaval that was sure to bring.

On his lunch hour, Brad brought by the papers to officially refuse her inheritance. Cam was by her side as Brad revealed details he'd gleaned from the Dallas law firm.

"Kenneth Grayson is executor of the will," he told Red, which was no surprise. "The will was actually changed shortly after the death of her husband, Harvey, a few years ago. Patsy Grayson added the two subsequent bequests without her stepson's knowledge."

Although the bar was empty, Brad lowered his voice as if passing on a juicy piece of gossip. "Grayson said he had no idea where you might be. He didn't think it was 'worth it' to track you down and was willing to just leave the money in limbo. But a few weeks ago he found out from an unexpected source that you were here in San Antonio.

After unsuccessfully trying to contact you himself, he turned the information over to his law firm."

"I'm sure Kenny will be delighted to hear that I've refused it," Red said.

"From what I gathered from his attorney, Kenneth Grayson is perfectly satisfied with the disposition as it is," Brad said. "He inherited all the property and the remaining shares of the business. Besides, the money you're refusing goes to the other beneficiary. It will just be added to her share."

"Who's the other beneficiary?" Red asked.

"Oh, it's your daughter," Brad answered. "Bridge Cullens Lujan."

Red was shocked into silence.

"Does Bridge know about this?" Cam asked.

"Not yet," Brad answered. "The attorney asked me about her whereabouts and I told him that she'd been overseas with the army, but that she was due home soon. I didn't give them her address, because I wasn't sure if she'd be staying at your house. They can locate her through military channels."

Red was still speechless.

"I hope you're not thinking to refuse her inheritance on her behalf," Brad said. "Because you won't be allowed to do that. The money was left to her by name. It's hers to do with as she sees fit. And with yours added to it, well, it's certainly a considerable amount."

"No, no," Red assured him, finally finding her voice. "I would never presume to tell Bridge what to do. Besides, that money could help her buy a house or pay for the kids to go to college. I'm just . . . just blown away that my mother even knew that Bridge existed."

Red gratefully signed all the papers that allowed her to throw the cash back in her mother's face, as well as make it possible for her daughter and grandchildren to benefit from it. She couldn't have been more pleased.

"It's worked out perfectly," she told Cam after Brad left. "There's only one unpleasant fly in the ointment."

"What is that?" he asked.

"I have never told Bridge anything about her father," Red said. "She didn't know about my family or my history. I've kept all that from her. Now it will all have to come out."

"Are you sure?"

"I can't let her find out from someone else," Red answered. "Once she gets this money and finds out that she had family in Piney Woods, she's going to be curious. And she won't be able to show up there without someone saying something, even if they don't know for sure."

"What does Bridge already know?" Cam asked. "You can't tell me that she never asked about her father."

"I just refused to talk about it. Finally, she accused me of being with so many guys I didn't know," Red answered. "Seeing the kind of life I've led, it was pretty easy for her to think that. So I just let her."

"It's always good to know the truth," Cam said. "Building a lie between you has probably always kept the two of you apart."

"I just don't want to hurt her," Red said. "She's already had to live through enough of my mistakes."

"You're the one who's always telling me how tough she is," Cam pointed out. "You've got to have a little faith."

As the holiday grew nearer, the anxiety about when Bridge would get home seemed to grow and grow. It affected everyone.

Red was torn between the eagerness to see her daughter and the genuine distress that Olivia and Daniel would revert to being strangers once more.

Cam began moving Red's things back into the upstairs apartment.

"These first couple of weeks, Bridge is going to want to be alone with the kids," he said. "She's going to need rest and they're going to need privacy. And they'll get neither if you're still there."

Aunt Phyl had taken up the task of finding an acceptable house for Bridge's family to live in as her goal in life, dickering over the phone to old friends in the real-estate business for hours on end.

The kids themselves were jittery as june bugs. Olivia began to have trouble sleeping through the night. And every day Daniel asked, "Is Mommy coming home tomorrow?"

She called on Christmas Eve to say she was in Kuwait.

"I'm going to be a few days late," she warned them. "But I've discussed this with Santa Claus and he says you guys still have to be good through Christmas until I get there."

"You're joking with me," Daniel said. "You didn't talk to Santa Claus. He's at the North Pole, not with you."

"No, of course he's not here," Bridge told her son. "This is no place for a busy guy like him. We exchanged e-mails."

Everyone felt better after the call and the kids agreed with Red that Christmas Eve would be postponed until their mother got home. And Christmas day would go on as planned.

Their plans were more in the spirit of Christmas anyway. Kelly had invited them to visit the hospital to see her husband and Kendra.

Aunt Phyl took the kids to her house, where cookie baking took up most of the morning. A few minutes after noon, they loaded up the car with cookies and presents and everybody.

They met up with Kelly at the hospital's family room outside the burn unit, ward 4E. Her mother-in-law was still there, helping. Aunt Phyl immediately picked up Kendra, as if the two were long-lost buddies.

Children were not allowed inside the intensive care unit. Instead, they visited with Kelly and the baby and handed out cookies all around the room.

Some of the patients from the unit were well enough to sit with their families. Their injuries were visible and often disfiguring. Red worried that Olivia and Daniel might be shocked or scared. But the children had been at the hospital many times when their mother worked there. They were not unaccustomed to the sight of wounded soldiers. And the atmosphere was not one of hushed reverence or tearful bravery. It was festive. It was Christmas and everyone in the family room appeared grateful to be surrounded by people who loved them.

Kelly wanted Red and Cam to meet her husband. After they washed their hands, they were buzzed into the ward. They followed Kelly to an alcovelike room within the ward and met her husband, Sean, for the first time.

He was quiet, seemingly shy with strangers. Red didn't know what to say to him. Should she tell him how sorry she was about his injuries? Should she ask about what had happened? As she mentally dithered about which direction was more polite, she heard herself matter-of-factly inquiring about the strange bandages that he was swathed in.

Sean seemed immediately more comfortable with relaying factual information.

"This is called Coban," he answered. "It's like a pressure dressing. Once you start physical or occupational therapy, they put it on you to keep the swelling down." He shot a quick smile toward his wife. "This is my big Christmas present. I just got it yesterday. I've been wearing Silverlon. It's a kind of wrap that looks like what a ballplayer might get for an athletic injury. But it's got silver in it that leaches out to kill bacteria."

Kelly added, "The Coban is like unmistakable evidence that he's moved from just recovering to rehabilitating."

"Congratulations," Red said.

"Thanks."

Red talked to Kelly as Cam and Sean shared what Red thought of as guy talk about sports teams and dove hunting. Neither sounded particularly involved with any of it, but they kept at it until they got to a subject they were both interested in — music.

Sean had been into rock, but he was interested in honky-tonk and Cam knew enough about both to discuss bands and trends.

"So do you play at all?" Cam asked him.

Sean hesitated. "I used to," he said. "I used to play guitar." With a kind of fatalistic half grin at his burned arm, he added, "I don't know if I'll be able to do it now. I've lost some use of my hand. My elbow is pretty stiff and the ends of most of my fingers are gone."

Cam nodded. "Could you hold a pick?"

"A pick?"

"I've heard about guys who switched hands," Cam said.

Sean raised an eyebrow in surprise. "I

hadn't thought about that," he said. "I don't know if a guy could ever get any good left-handed."

"Did you ever hear of Django Reinhardt?"

"No."

"He's one of the great jazz guitarists of the thirties and forties," Cam told him. "He was badly burned and lost two of his fingers when he was eighteen. They said he'd never play again, but he taught himself a new technique despite his injuries. If you had a left-handed guitar, you wouldn't have the dexterity issue."

"That's true," Sean said thoughtfully.

"Music is all in the brain anyway," Cam said. "And the brain is very good at compensating."

The two continued to discuss the possibility. As they did, the quiet, shy young man opened up to being the bright, funny, interesting fellow that his wife had wanted them to meet.

"I think we'd better go," Red said a few minutes later. "We don't want to wear you out."

"At least not on our first visit," Cam added.

"I'll walk you out," Kelly said, before adding to Sean, "I promise to be right back and carrying Christmas cookies."

Once they returned to the family room, there were hugs and high fives and Christmas greetings all around.

Kelly opened the present that Olivia and Daniel had bought for Kendra with their own money. It was a very soft little lamb that the little girl immediately began chewing on.

"Thanks so much for coming," Kelly said to Red. "It means a lot to me."

"You and Sean mean a lot to us, too," Red told her.

As they walked across the parking lot, Cam snaked an arm around her waist.

"They seem to be doing okay," he said.

"Yeah," Red agreed. "But it's still so scary. How much is he going to recover? How is he going to work? What are they going to do?"

"Hey, don't start looking down that road too far. You'll scare yourself," he told her. "Remember, we're learning to live happily with uncertainty."

Red nodded.

Later that night as she tucked Daniel into bed, she understood how hard it was for humans to do that.

"Mom is coming home tomorrow," Daniel stated firmly.

"Maybe tomorrow," Red told him.

"Maybe the day after."

"No, tomorrow."

"Okay," Red agreed with a kiss on his forehead. "I'm going to hope so, too."

To: buildabetterbridge@citymail.com
December 25 6:21 p.m.
From: Livy156@ABrats.org
Subject: Almost home

Mom I am hoping that by the time you read this you will be sitting here beside me. I don't think I can stand more waiting. We are still not having Christmas until you get here. But it looks like Christmas in my house and Aunt Phils house too. I guess everything you ordered for us on the internet must be here. Red won't let us open the packages until you are here, so they are still in the shipping boxs. Very funny! Forget red and green. Brown is now my favorite Christmas color.

We went to the hospital today to see Kendras dad. He is burnt on his chest and neck and his arm. We didnt get to see him but there were other burnt men there. They look bad but I remember how you told us to look past the outside. Their insides look real good. Before we went I reminded Daniel too and he was cool.

I have tried to remember everything you told me. I have tried to do my duty and be a good soldier at home while you are a good soldier away. I have done my best Mom. But now I

463

really want you to be home. Please be home tomorrow. I know you can't make the army moved faster and I am sorry that I whine but I miss you too much.

C U tomorrow! I hope. I hope. I hope. And I luv u as ever forever.

Livy

33

Red's daughter made it home the day after Christmas, but just barely. A few minutes after three in the afternoon, Bridge called to say she was stateside. Her commercial airline flight from the coast would arrive at the airport late. It might be the last flight of the day.

The place was rather quiet, except for the noisy exuberance of a small band of red, white and blue well-wishers. Everybody held signs and flags. Red would not have thought to bring anything, but Olivia, who had vivid memories of being through this before, told her what they needed. She and Olivia carried flags with streamers. And Daniel, with Olivia's help and some crayons, fashioned his own sign that read Welcome Home, Mom.

These were the families of the soldiers from the same medical unit as Bridge. They had been through the same long stretch of separation and they were feeling the same sense of adulation at a small victory in a big dangerous world.

Babies squalled. Young wives checked their lipstick a dozen times. Children like Olivia and Daniel peered down the long ramp in expectation.

When the first person dressed in desert camouflage was spotted, a whoop of joy went through the crowd. There was cheering and applause and shrieks of recognition.

Red searched the faces. *Is that her? No. Is that her? No.* Would she even recognize her daughter? Would she even know her if she saw her?

Suddenly Daniel broke away from the group and went running up the ramp. Red called him back and then caught sight of him enveloped in the hug of arms in uniform.

"Mom!" She heard Olivia beside her, jumping up and down. She was desperate to get to her mother, but determined to follow the *no admittance beyond this line* rule.

Bridge half carried, half dragged Daniel to the end of the ramp, where she dropped down to her knees to clasp both her children close.

Red stood back slightly, not wanting to intrude. This was Bridge's family. She deserved to have time to just enjoy them.

When she rose to her feet and acknowledged her mother, Red gave her a hug. It was quick, it wasn't much, but she hadn't hugged her daughter in way too long. Bridge seemed startled but not displeased.

With the rest of the loud, hugging, kissing, laughing crowd, they made their way to the baggage claim and picked up Bridge's duffel before heading to the parking garage.

Daniel and Olivia were both talking so fast, it was as if they were trying to get in every word they'd wanted to tell her in all the time that she was gone.

At last, close up, in the passenger seat beside her, Red cast quick glances at her daughter. Had those lines been on her face before? Maybe she was just tired. She was toned and tan, her red curls were smoothed back and tucked into a very neat and circumspect bun. She wasn't wearing much makeup, but she never did, allowing her freckles to be a part of her beauty, not a detriment to it.

As Red maneuvered through the airport traffic and onto the city streets that would get them home, the kids hardly took a breath. They were so excited. Daniel was rocking in his seat as if he could barely be tethered to the city around him. With a big smile, Bridge seemed to be drinking in their simultaneously jabbering voices as if it was an elixir of youth. She was laughing and listening and looked happier than Red could remember seeing her.

At the bungalow in Alamo Heights, Red pulled in to the driveway. She saw Bridge's eyebrows go up.

"Cute," she said. "Not exactly your style."

"It was Cam's grandmother's," Red told her. "He calls it his lace-doily crib."

"Wait till you see my room," Olivia gushed from the backseat. "I've got a bed with fairies painted on it. Cam's mom painted those fairies when she was my age. It is *so* totally cool, Mom, you'll love it."

"My room is where Cam's buddies stay," Daniel piped in. "That's why I sleep there, 'cause it's for guys."

The children piled out of the car and rushed to the porch. Red and Bridge walked to the back to get her duffel. Once the hatch was shut, Red held out the keys to her daughter.

"This one is the house," she said.

"You're not coming in?"

"Not unless you need me to," Red said. "And I don't think you'll need me. You should get some time with your kids."

"Okay. Thanks."

"I would like to come over tomorrow, since that's going to be Christmas for us," Red said. "If that wouldn't be intruding."

"No, it will be fine."

"And Cam's aunt, who's been taking care of the kids in the evenings, is fixing a holiday dinner tomorrow. You're not obligated to go. I'm not sure you'd want to spend your first day back with strangers."

Bridge raised an eyebrow. "People who take care of my children are not strangers," she said. "So we'll see you tomorrow."

Red waved goodbye to the kids and walked out to the CRX parked at the curb. The minute she drove away from the house, she began crying.

She would miss the kids. She would miss the strange new life in affluent suburbia. She would miss the little house. But she wasn't crying about any of that. Her tears were for the daughter, who turned out so well, now home and safe at last.

34

The official Christmas Day of the family began with Red's ringtone trinkling out the first few stanzas of "It Wasn't God Who Made Honky-Tonk Angels." Red buried her head farther in the pillow, determined to ignore it. Cam rolled over, spooning against her back, and reached beyond her to pick up the phone. He clicked the Talk button and then pressed the device against her face.

"Say hello," he suggested.

"Hello," Red moaned.

"Grandma! Grandma! You won't believe what I got, I got a scooter and it folds up and it's got a bell and Mom says I can ride it on the sidewalk and maybe to school but that's a 'we'll see' but I think I can and I got video games and Livy got her own computer. Her very own computer . . . and . . . and —"

"My turn," Red heard Olivia say, before a little muffled fumbling.

"My mom buys the coolest presents, wait till you see," Olivia told her. "When are you coming over? Mom said you were coming over."

Red had managed to pull herself into a seated position. "Uh . . . I don't know. . . . What time is it?" she asked.

Olivia hollered, "Mom! What time is it?" assaulting Red's eardrum.

A couple of seconds later, her daughter was on the phone.

"I'm sorry to call so early, Red," Bridge said. "It's only eight in the morning. But the kids just couldn't wait to tell you what they got."

"No, it's fine," Red said.

"As soon as you're up and dressed, come on over. The kids miss you and they want you to see all the plunder."

"Cam, too," Red heard Olivia say to her mother. "Invite Cam, too."

"Absolutely," Bridge said. "Bring Cam with you, too."

After she hung up, Red turned to assess the attractive naked man beside her.

"How did you know that call would be from the kids?"

He grinned at her. "Who else would be calling a tired old grandma on Christmas morning?" he answered.

"Who you calling old and tired?"

Cam laughed, grabbed her at the waist and flipped her over on her stomach and took a nip out of her right buttock.

"Ouch! What are you doing?"

"I just think it's time I took a bite out of your butt," he said. "I'm a man who likes nothing better than a hefty serving of aged armadillo for breakfast."

Red twisted beneath him until she was on her back.

"You no-account chicken sh—"

He shushed her insult with his lips on her own. By the time he'd finished kissing her, she was no longer interested in a conversation.

Consequently it was a couple of hours later before they showed up at the bungalow. After introductions, the inventory of gifts and the fashion show of new clothes, Cam and the kids began playing tennis on the new video-game system.

Red and Bridge ended up in the kitchen.

"This is a nice place," Bridge told her, indicating the bungalow. "It's very homey, in a nice neighborhood. It was a good place for the kids to be while I was gone."

Red nodded. "Cam says you can stay here as long as it takes for you to get settled," she said. "Aunt Phyl is looking for something else around here. She knows everybody in town and I think she'd like to help you find a place here so the kids won't have to switch schools."

"I don't know," Bridge said. "It would be great. But I'm thinking that with the prices in this neighborhood, we'd have to move into an apartment. And my kids really need a yard these days."

Red couldn't help but agree with that.

"Well, you're coming into a bit of money and that might help."

"Say what?"

"My mother passed away several months ago," Red said evenly. "She's left you some money."

"I thought you said that your parents were dead."

"My father was dead," Red answered. "My mother was dead to me."

Bridge just stood there, leaning against the kitchen counter, her expression full of questions.

"I didn't even know that she knew about you," Red said. "I haven't talked to her since I left Piney Woods at sixteen. But apparently she did, because she listed you by name on her will."

"Piney Woods? Is this Patsy Grayson?"

Red nearly choked.

"You know her?"

"No, I don't," Bridge answered. "But she's called me several times over the years. She first contacted me when I was in high school. But she didn't say she was your mother. She said she knew who my father was. She said that he was some rich muckety-muck in this podunk town and that if I confronted him, he would pay for my college."

"What did you say?"

"I told her I had my own plans and I wasn't interested," Bridge answered. "She sounded to me like somebody with her own agenda. The last thing I needed was to be dragged into something like that."

It was hard for Red to take in, that her mother had tracked her daughter down.

"Well, she's left you some money," Red said. "And it is yours, so you should take it."

Bridge nodded. There was a long silence between them before she asked the question that was on her mind. "Is the rich muckety-muck my dad?"

Red took a deep breath and answered as honestly as she could.

"Technically, yes," she replied. "But I like to think of him as more of a sperm donor."

Bridge chuckled lightly. "I've got an ex

that's kind of like that," she said. "Don't worry, Red. I have no intention of trying to drag some DNA stranger into my life. If you decided that he didn't deserve to be a part of our family, I trust that you had sufficient reason."

Red was surprised by this admission.

"Thank you," she replied simply.

"I'm the one who needs to say that, Red," Bridge responded, her voice softer and more serious. "I want to thank you for taking in the kids. I know you had to do it, but to be completely honest, I had my doubts about whether it would work. Maybe I'm remembering it wrong, but when I think about my childhood, all I remember is that you were always at work or asleep."

Red swallowed her guilt and nodded. "I don't think you're remembering it wrong," she admitted. "The reason I never take any bows about how well you've turned out is because I see your success as coming *in spite* of how you were raised, not because of it."

Bridge chuckled. "You know, just a few years ago I would have agreed with you," she said. "But now I think you're wrong. You did what you had to do to raise me. I can't even imagine what Olivia and Daniel are going to ultimately think of a mother who deliberately brings them into the world and then spends whole years on the other side of the globe from them."

"Don't take that guilt trip," Red admonished. "What you do is important. Yes, it's a sacrifice for you and one for the kids, as well. But you should be nothing but proud of doing your duty. And your children will be, too. They'll grow up to be better people living in what is hopefully a better world. Don't for one moment allow yourself to imagine differently."

Bridge grinned at her. "That's one thing I do remember about my childhood," she said. "If I was even hinting at a chance to screw up, you always read me the riot act about making good choices. So, okay, Red. I'll choose to give myself a break. But you have to give yourself one, too."

Around noon, the entire group traversed the alley gate to Aunt Phyl's house. The kids ran ahead and charged through the patio doors without even a hint of knocking. The adults followed, immediately swept up in the delicious aromas of the season. Phyl and Bridge hit it off immediately, possibly because they were both tremendous fans of Olivia and Daniel.

The meal was excellent and the children were boisterous, but not out of control.

Afterward, the family moved to the living room.

"I don't know if you've noticed, but there are several gifts still under my Christmas tree," the older woman announced.

The children pounced on that suggestion.

Olivia was instructed to find the name on the gifts and hand them out. And then everyone watched while that present was opened.

Cam got a pair of flannel pajamas. Red managed to hide a smile, since she knew from living in his house that he had an entire drawerful of very similar pj's and that he preferred sleeping naked.

Bridge was given a gift card to a department store.

"Since I hadn't met you, I had no idea what you might want," Aunt Phyl confessed.

Red got a pink cashmere sweater, which was beautiful and chic and modest, as well. It looked like something that Tasha would have loved to wear.

Daniel got real cowboy boots, which he didn't have and which he immediately put on.

And Olivia got a pair of earrings.

"They're not new," Aunt Phyl told her. "They were mine when I was a young girl. They're garnets and will look lovely with your complexion."

Everyone was very pleased. Aunt Phyl opened her own presents and oohed and ahhed over what she received.

"Oh, but there is one still under the tree," Phyl said, pointing out the tiny red-and-green box to Olivia.

Olivia glanced at it. "Yep, it's for Cam," she said, handing it over.

Cam quickly unwrapped the small box. From beneath a swathe of white tissue, he retrieved a key.

"What's this?" Cam asked.

"It's part of my big Christmas surprise," Aunt Phyl said. "You know that new high-rise that just went up?" she said. "Well I bought a two-bedroom condo on the sixth floor. With a view of both downtown and Alamo Heights."

"You're moving?" Red asked.

"What about your house?" Cam said. "You've always loved this house. Are you selling it?"

"Oh, I could never sell the house," Aunt Phyl said. "I'm doing with it what I always intended." She indicated the key, still in his hand. "I'm giving it to you, Cam. It is the Early family home. The last of the Earlys should certainly be the person to live in it."

"I already have a house," Cam pointed out.

"Yes, I know you love the bungalow, but here you'd have more room to have musicians over and set up a studio, like you've always wanted. The bungalow is just not right for that." She turned and smiled at Bridge. "What it needs is a nice young family to live there."

To: nayra22@AHTexan.net
March 2 9:08 p.m.
From: Livy156@ABrats.org
Subject: Awesome Sunday!

Nayra — OMG u wil not believe it! U know I had to go to the reopening of the patio at my grammas place today. It was a private party so Daniel and I could go. And it was REALLY cool with lots of people and a band and dancing. There were kids that I'd met before. A few from school. Mia Carson from Daniels class was there with her parents and Mrs. Ramirez's grandkids who I knew from her restuarant. It was pretty neat. Everyone knew Daniel and me. They were mostly friends of Red and Cam and people who come to the bar all the time.

Karl, he is the bartander fixed me an actual drink! It was called a Shirley something and it had a merrychino cherry and an umbrella in it. I felt totally like a teen or something.

So I am thinking that this is it. Nice afternoon party and my mom actually dances with a couple of guys. It's cool, but ordinary. And then Cam gets up on stage and he thanks everybody and all and then he says he's got a surprise that he hopes everyone is up for. And he picks up his fiddle and he starts playing and it is like dum-dum-da-dum dum-dum-da-dum, u know like here comes the bride and here comes Red down the apartment stairs. She is in like a long dress with flowers in her hair and carrying a bowkay. And she gets me and Daniel and Mom and Aunt Phyl and we all go up on the stage and they have a wedding. It was insane!

Everybody was cheering and shouting. I could not believe it! I asked Cam afterward if now I call him Grandpa. He said he would be honored. But I think he will always be just Cam to me.

The weirdest thing they added one extra vows to their vows. They did the regular ones better/worse and sickness/health and anyway the extra vow was something like I promise to always dream like I will live forever and live like I will die today.

Pretty cool.

Livy

QUESTIONS FOR DISCUSSION

1. Embracing uncertainty is a little unusual in what is basically a love story. Would a "happily-ever-after" ending be more or less satisfying to you as a reader?

2. Like Bridge, sometimes we are asked to do things that are in conflict with the responsibilities of taking care of our family. How do we forgive ourselves for that?

3. Red got a second chance at being a mother, but did she really blow the first chance or was that only her impression?

4. Gentrifying neighborhoods happens everywhere. How does your community balance needed change with preservation?

5. Olivia and Daniel handled their mother's absence in very different ways. Do you think birth order or expectations play the

bigger part in these differences?

6. Red imagined that if her father had not died, her life would have been very different. How common is it for our life direction to be drastically changed by events out of our control?

7. Events out of their control was the reality for most characters in this story, from Red, Cam and Bridge, to the children, even Aunt Phyl and Kelly, Sean and Kendra. Is control of our own lives actually just a myth?

8. As soon as he turned eighteen, Cam sought answers to his genetic makeup. With the stakes so high, would you want to know? Why or why not?

9. When Cam asked Red to face the future with him, he knew how much he was asking. Should he have asked? And would you take this on? Would you want your daughter, mother, sister to take it on?

10. Is being designated the "bad grandmother" a criticism or a badge of honor?

ABOUT THE AUTHOR

Librarian **Pamela Morsi** once asked herself what she would do if she ever won the lottery. She decided, given the chance, that she would spend her time writing fiction. Now, years later, she is still waiting to win the lottery, but RED'S HOT HONKY-TONK BAR is her twenty-first published novel. Pam lives in San Antonio, Texas, with her husband and daughter.